I sat on the edge of a 17th ce[...] [...]l-
ter flowing from the genitals o[...] [...]t
my face in the still waters at tl[...] n
old man. When did that happe[...] [...])-
pened? In those few seconds, [...] I
wondered if it was the pursuit of love that sustained me and not
the attainment of the love I pursued. What I had missed in pursuit
of a love I wasn't even sure would or could be returned. *Will she
see this wrinkled, rusted-out, old body and turn away in disgust,
or will she see me, the ageless me inside that has on some incomprehensible level always loved her? Will she recognize me as the
brown man she brought back to life?*

Doubt brought on by fear is a mean son-of-a-bitch. It whipped
my ass in that square on the first day she caught my eye. Only
forty-five minutes remained before the last train that would get
me home to Chris in time. The person I wanted more than any
other in the world was before me, and I couldn't move. I couldn't
even bring myself to call her name. I couldn't grab the brass ring
that eluded me for so long, that stood unobstructed only a few feet
away.

I took the long train ride home and returned to the fountain
for twelve straight days. Every one of those chilly mornings, I left
our flat, having made up my mind that I would reclaim my true
love that day. These were mornings following close on the tail
of sleepless nights spent wallowing in self-pity and shame. Then
every afternoon, just when she came into view, I'd decide not to
complicate her life by reentering it. Her rides seemed so simple
and pleasurable, her days organized and predictable. No just man,
I convinced myself, could take that from her.

On day thirteen, my world seemed to collapse in on itself. I
arrived at the square with Chris in tow and every shred of courage
left in my body stuffed tightly into my puffed out chest. *This is the
day I will make myself known to Marie*, I repeated to myself all
the way to Rouen. I decided to sit on the bench outside the post office this time, too near to run away and too close to hide. I decided
to sit directly in her line of vision, thinking that if she felt even an
ounce of what I did for her, we wouldn't need to exchange words.
She peddled around the bakery and onto the main road near city
hall. She was still beautiful.

Red Tail Heart

The Life and Love of a Tuskegee Airman

by

Kenneth W. Williams

Wild Child Publishing.com
Culver City, California

Editor: Marci Baun

ISBN: 978-1-936222-78-0--eBook
978-1-936222-98-8--print

If you are interested in purchasing more works of this nature, please stop by www.wildchildpublishing.com.

Wild Child Publishing.com
P.O. Box 4897
Culver City, CA 90231-4897

Printed in The United States of America

Chapter One

In my end is my beginning.

T.S. Eliot

The universe and crazy have conspired since the day I was born to deny me my unalienable right to be bad. It is not that I desire to do evil, but I do on occasion, want to be simply immoral in a benign, consenting adult sort of way. My insides boiled at times with the desire to give in completely to lust, greed and debauchery, but some people are meant to be villains and others, like me, are bound to the straight and narrow.

So I decided to wait for moral certitude to reign true before I made the move on Ariel Charlotte Stonington. I had good reasons to wait; first and foremost, I didn't love her, nor did I think I could love her. I felt only "the lust of the flesh" as my grandma would say. Second, she was still married to Bradford Simon, and screwing a married woman was still morally questionable if not outright unacceptable in 1990's America. The universe and crazy certainly wouldn't abide such behavior from me. I might have been willing to test their tolerance for the first two constraints, but not the third: I was her divorce lawyer and sleeping with a client was still the short train ride to disbarment that I wasn't willing to take.

Ariel and I had a momentarily pleasurable, if empty, carnal history. We disrobed jurisprudence and each other as law school classmates. To say we were "lovers" would prescribe more merit to the relationship than it deserved. To be blunt, we hooked up for sex whenever the urge hit us, or the circumstances permitted. Our relationship eased the stress of law school and satisfied our natural curiosities. But neither of us was adventurous enough to even suggest that it evolve into more.

Ariel grew up in the wealthy Connecticut suburb of Ridgefield north of New York City. I rose from the gritty north end of Hartford. She was born into braces, nose jobs, trust funds and day schools, and I into permanent overbites, afros, payday loans and white flight. The intellectual harshness of law school and our mutual discretion drew us together, but neither was enough to bridge the chasm stretching between our worlds. So we went our separate ways after graduation and tried very hard to live the lives expected of us.

Ariel married Bradford Simon right out of law school. I, along with several of our classmates, was invited to their Maui wedding. I had no doubt that my invitation was a manifestation of Ariel's second thoughts about Bradford. But I didn't want to tempt convention or fate, so I politely declined to attend and sent a $1,500.00 crystal punch service as a wedding gift.

Ten years later, a honey blonde, hazel-eyed, Ariel Stonington-Simon walked unannounced into my office and asked me to represent her in a divorce. I wanted her again within seconds after laying eyes on her. The desire came upon me as strongly as it had in our first afternoon together in my cramped law school dorm room. It took all my decorum to remain professional and appear appropriately sympathetic to her case. She was older and certainly no longer the fresh-faced twenty-something I knew in law school, but she had matured beautifully as time and money had been good to her. She wore a high-end designer dress, classic white pearls and two-inch heels. She still had the kind of body for which those clothes were intended. She exuded strength and vulnerability, both of which drew me to her in all the wrong ways.

Neither of our conventional lives had lived up to the hype. I was still unconditionally single and her marriage waited only for a state sponsored order of execution to end it. Divorce and loneliness primed us for the unconventional.

Ariel told me a week before her divorce was final that she never opened my gift. She drove around with it in the trunk of every car she'd owned since her wedding. I wasn't sure why. She opened it for the first time in my office to be appraised and accounted for as the last of her marital assets.

"I should take that back now that the marriage is off," I said.

"A crystal punch service, a little pricy wasn't it for a young lawyer with student loans to pay," she said.

"You'd be surprised the deal you can get from a brother named Mellon Head on the corner of Albany and Vine after 11:00 p.m."

"I halfway hoped that you'd pop out of this box one day, Chris, and say what makes us different didn't matter...," she responded before drifting off in thought.

"I admit to being a grade A coward, Ariel. Maybe you and I can reintroduce ourselves when this is all over. I could meet you somewhere halfway between Hartford and Ridgefield," I suggested.

Chapter Two

I went to the Garden of Love
And saw what I had never seen
And I saw it was filled with graves,
And tombstones where flowers should be;

William Blake

It was the first Monday in December 1996, six months to the day after she walked into my office and the final judgment day in her divorce proceeding. Sure, I took her case, and, yes, I successfully battled the urge to be more to Ariel than her lawyer. But I cannot claim to be too noble; you see, I pushed her divorce through the system in record time. This was the day that our attorney-client relationship would officially end. I'd be free from the possible retribution of the universe and crazy, as I believed that neither frowned on fornication between two free and consenting adults. *It will be a big payday for me in more than one way*, I thought.

Scott Witling, the double-breasted suit wearing *Hartford Courant* newspaper reporter sitting in the back of the courtroom, described the Simon proceedings in several stories as the velvet divorce. It was his way of saying that there was no drama, dirt or nasty accusations flying back and forth to sustain his gossip hungry readers. He would have skipped the reading of the final judgment, but he thought there still may be some front-page value in reporting how the court divided the multi-million marital estate.

"I'm fucking glad this one is almost over, Counselor. This one's boring as hell! Now, sixty year old, Technologies United's President, Jason Walters, and his 34 year old, European heiress wife know how to throw a newsworthy divorce. Rich motherfuckers mixing it up in court like trailer trash is what my readers want. Are you representing one of them?" he asked, looking for confirmation for what he already suspected. Sure the wife had spoken to me, but he was getting no confirmation from me.

As for the Simon divorce, it *had* gone unusually smoothly. Both parties were independently wealthy, reasonably discreet, by all appearances level-headed, and there were no sticky children to muck up the works. When the accountants finished crunching the numbers, Ariel's net worth exceeded Bradford's by a mere $1,400, mostly the value of that hot crystal punch service I gave her. She would get the house and grounds in Ridgefield, and he'd get the bungalow on the Cape and the flat in Manhattan. All in all, it was an equitable, almost exactly equal split of the martial assets as far as *I* was concerned.

What *I thought*, though, wasn't important as I soon discovered. I remembered at the end of judgment day why Ariel told me she wanted the divorce. Divorce lawyers don't usually concern themselves with the whys in a no-fault proceeding, so I hadn't given it a second thought.

"My marriage is a god-damned Olympic class decathlon. We compete for the favor of friends, the admiration of strangers, and, above all, the acquisition of wealth. I think the bastard even tracks my orgasms. I hate to think about who he's measuring me against. After ten exhausting years, I realized that I don't want a never-ending competition. I need more than that...I need real love," she said.

Real love? What's that? I thought at the time.

The Honorable Richard Ballard, a seventy-eight year old semi-retired judge, sat on the bench with his clerk to his right and the court reporter three steps below him to the left. This particular judge gave me hell every time I appeared before him. If I were a minute late, he'd call me to the bench and dress me down in front of opposing counsel with a jabbing finger and whisper yell. But he made me a better lawyer and he always called the case by the book. That was good enough for me. I'd take a crusty competent jurist any day over a kindly stupid judge with no clue about the law. Wesley Crane, Bradford's lawyer, sat at the defense table with the *Courant* reporter in the gallery a few rows behind him. The elderly bailiff sat in the jury box working a crossword puzzle.

"Counsel Crane, we are now ten minutes late starting this proceeding. Where is your client?" the judge asked.

"I don't know your honor, he is aware of the starting time of the hearing," Crane responded.

"Well you go out and call him, sir. Yours is not the only matter on the docket today," the judge ordered.

Crane got up and walked toward the door. Before he took five steps, the bailiff's walkie-talkie sounded a piercing alarm followed by a red alert.

"SP 7...J. W. Booth in the lobby. Move to secure areas" an authoritative voice ordered. I learned later that J. W. Booth was code for a shooter like the one that assassinated President Lincoln.

Bradford Simon burst through the door before the warning could repeat, turned and helped the door close behind him.

"There's a crazy man shooting people out there. Two deputies are down," Bradford stated calmly over the screams streaming in from the corridor. Bradford's cashmere coat lay loosely across his arm, and though he walked briskly, he didn't appear frightened or even flustered by the commotion outside. He reacted to the violence just the way safety officials tell you to act in an emergency; he kept his head about him and moved briskly to a safe location. In those first uncertain seconds, I admired Bradford's coolness under pressure.

"Everyone, get up and move quickly to my chambers," Judge Ballard ordered.

Bradford moved up the aisle with long smooth strides, and he made it to the bench before the elderly Judge Ballard could descend the three stairs separating him from our level. Bradford stopped at the base of the bar, pulled a gold plated Beretta from under the coat draped over his left arm, took aim and pulled the trigger, shooting Judge Ballard in the forehead at point blank range. He pointed the gun next at the clerk and court reporter. With calmness and precision, he unloaded one bullet into each of them before any of us could process what was happening.

The puzzle-master bailiff reacted first of those left standing. He reached for his walkie-talkie to call for help. Bradford's next bullet passed through the walkie-talkie shattering it in his hand and directly into the bailiff's soft upper pallet. The bailiff fell back into Juror Number 6's seat and slumped over lifeless.

Four shots into Bradford's courtroom killing spree, I had my first thought. *At least the* Courant *reporter will get away.* He was the closest to the ten-foot tall, five-inch thick, oak double doors at the back of the courtroom. Bradford's bullets wouldn't penetrate those doors even if he stood a foot away. Scott must have had the same thought at the same time. He ran for the doors only to find the handles bound together with handcuffs. Bradford turned his attention to Scott and aimed the sights of his golden Beretta from the front of the courtroom to the back. He planted a bullet in the reporter's back from thirty-five feet away. The bullet's velocity slammed Scott against the heavy doors before he crumpled to the floor.

Attorney Crane realized the futility of running. He raised his hands and began to reason with Bradford.

"Bradford, you don't want to do this. Stop it now before it's..." Crane said.

"You fucking loser, LOSER!" Bradford shouted and pulled the trigger for the eighth time that morning, connecting with deadly accuracy. Attorney Crane fell back over the railing separating the gallery.

Bradford looked at me. He stretched the gold plated Beretta in my direction. He turned it sideways slowly like a gangbanger especially for me. He turned his body sideways also and stood flat-footed six or seven feet away. From the gleam in his eye and slight smile on his face, he relished the idea of killing me. He knew my history with Ariel.

The gun pointing in my direction seemed only inches away. I thought about nothing else but that gun. I achieved absolute clarity as all other thoughts ceased to exist. I saw the etchings in the gold plating, the curvature of the sights, and the manicured finger poised to pull the slightly tarnished trigger. I discovered that the knowledge of eminent death compresses space as well as time. I stood straight, upright, facing him more petrified than in defiance. Ariel hid behind me looking over my shoulder. My hands where spread to my sides and back in a futile attempt to protect her. *How many bullets could I absorb and where before I collapsed leaving her exposed*, I thought. It was an instinctive reaction since I was convinced that I would be dead in the nanosecond it took a bullet to travel six feet. Bradford and Ariel would be alone in life then.

Bradford paused before firing and seemed indecisive for the first time since entering the courtroom 30 seconds earlier. His head rocked rhythmically from side to side, and his pupils looked up to the ceiling and as if he was counting in his head. I realized that he was counting when he finished using three of the fingers of his free left hand. He focused on me, raised his open left palm to the ceiling, and shrugged his shoulders. It was like he was apologizing to me for some slight. I braced heart, head and gut for the next bullet's impact.

Bradford shot. I heard the sound and felt the wind when the bullet passed my ear and lodged into Ariel's forehead just over my right shoulder. Her warm blood splattered on my face and back.

Bradford then put the gun in his mouth and pulled the trigger ending his own life.

Eleven people crossed the path of Bradford Simon's destructive rampage, but he had only ten bullets. Bradford never liked losing, and by his twisted logic, Ariel won their divorce by $1,400.00. My hot punch service put her over the top. Ariel was dead, Bradford was the villain, and again, the universe and crazy forbade me to be bad.

* * * *

Recovering divorce lawyers like me don't know shit about good marriages. We can write dissertations on the signs and characteristics of a failed marriage. We never encounter the good ones, though, and if we do, we're far too tainted to recognize them. Divorce work filled my bank accounts with good legal tender of the United States, but it did nothing to shore up my dissolving mental parity. We persuade ourselves that we provide a much-needed service by resolving brutally bad civil relations equitably and saving innocents from the atrocities of full-blown marital conflict. The higher moral goal was what was important, not the legal scorched earth policy that got us there.

"There must be more to love and marriage than money, used furniture, and hurt egos," I mused out loud trying to convince myself. My legal briefs, still stained with Ariel's blood, sealed the deal. I needed to get out. I needed to know that marital bliss was possible.

One death will cause you to reassess your life, but emerging from the carnage of seven friends, acquaintances, and colleagues drenched in their blood caused me to throw my old life away and start this shit all over again. I held my emotional breath in anguished anticipation of the next tragedy.

I needed to begin again.

I am thirty-six, never married, childless and not close to the altar. *Never married,* those words have peculiar meaning these days since many of my contemporaries were well into second marriages and working diligently toward a third. My pastoral love life generated memorable excitement. I grazed, chewed cud every now and then, but I never had enough substance to satisfy. My relationships never generated enough intensity and desire for me to commit my life to a woman even for the length of the average first marriage these days. Sometimes, I was ashamed of my unattached state; while at other times, I reveled in it and pitied the unhappy masses trapped in terminally bad marriages. But at that time, I needed to know that we could do better. With death so close on my heels, even a bad marriage might have redeeming value.

Chapter Three

What did I know, what did I know
Of love's austere and lonely offices.

Robert Hayden

Finding Uncle Roy

I returned to the office forty-seven days after Bradford Simon's killing spree. Dr. Taigbenu juiced me up on legal uppers
and tethered me to sanity with seven hours of intensive weekly
therapy. Too immersed in a drug-induced lethargy to sit upright
at my desk, I flopped down on the leather sofa in my office and
drifted off to sleep. As I slept, thoughts of my elderly expatriate
uncle blew through my mind like the swift summer breezes rolling
across the treeless Oklahoma prairies that gave him life. The impression of him was so strong that I could smell the faint and familiar scent of slightly spoiled milk that often trailed in his wake.
I associated Uncle Roy with the smell of sour milk like one associ-
ates peanut butter with jelly.

My feelings about my uncle had changed over the years from
abject fear to sympathy and, finally, unbridled admiration. Uncle Roy suffered thirty odd years of grinding human solitude and
emerged from his dead, dry chrysalis triumphantly into the world
the rest of us long occupied badly. In his metamorphic rebirth,
Uncle Roy spread his glorious wings, declared his presence to
the world, and squeezed every ounce out of life thereafter. After
a forty-year false start, he enjoyed love and marriage on a grand
scale. I resolved then that I needed to go to Uncle Roy for solace
and rejuvenation.

Hazel, my secretary, buzzed my desk intercom thirty minutes
into my second nap. "Chris, you have a call on line nine," she said.

"Take a message. I need this nap more than a new case right
now."

"It's a lawyer from France...it's about your uncle Roy."

"What about him? The lucky som-bitch...he ruined love for all
of us. He's cruising on the high side of life without a care in the
world," I retorted sarcastically.

"Chris, pick up, please. This is serious!"

The hurried sternness in Hazel's voice changed my feigned disinterest into genuine concern for my beloved great uncle. This time maybe it wasn't about his business in America or the state of Grandma's health; maybe it was about him. I moved to my desk, picked up the receiver, and depressed line nine.

"Hello, this is Chris. Yes, he's my great uncle...I speak French, if it's easier for you. ...No, not now! ...When did he pass? ...Was it some kind of accident? ...Just his time, huh? ...No, I'll be there tomorrow or Friday at the latest. Give my secretary the details, please."

I transferred the call back to Hazel and hung up the phone. My little remaining strength seemed to flow out of my legs and run down a drain of despair. I buried my face in my hands and massaged my now aching forehead.

"I'm not ready for more death. Not Uncle Roy. Lord not now," I pleaded under my breath.

Uncle Roy guided me through an important phase of my life, and I needed him alive especially now. Every word he spoke to me held meaning that I struggle to comprehend to this day.

"You can't go now. I really need you," I begged.

My heart ached before I knew it. Not that ill-defined heart we attribute to love, but the flesh and blood heart pumping inside of me ached. The ache curled up into a ball and worked its way up my esophagus. It burst through the drug-induced fog bathing my mind and came forth in clear, salty tears and halting sobs. I could not stop once fully engaged in crying. *"It is a man's duty not to cry in difficult situations. It is his manly obligation,"* I tried to convince myself. *"A man is not supposed to let it all out; he must suck it up and keep a stiff upper lip."* Still the tears flowed freely, my lips quivered uncontrollably, and my mournful moan broke the silence.

I knew then that I loved Uncle Roy deeply, though I'd never told him so. I loved him with the same depth and passion I held for Mom, Dad, and Grandma. I already missed him, and for several hours alone, I recalled with fondness my memories of the times we shared together.

Chapter Four

What happens to a dream deferred?
Langston Hughes

I sucked it up and snapped into full-blown lawyer mode when enough time passed to get over the suddenness of the loss. I persuaded myself that my time to mourn fully would come later. For now, I made plans to get to France. I barked orders at Hazel.

"Hazel, call Air France and arrange a flight for me to Paris tomorrow, one passenger, business class, Concorde. Find out if they have a special bereavement fare and get it if they do. I'll need a driver waiting at the airport. Charge it to the AMEX and Uncle Roy's new estate file which you're going to open today. Get my mother on the phone and put her through on line seven. Clear my calendar for another month. You're in charge starting exactly four hours from now. Don't do anything to get me disbarred, and remember if I am disbarred, you're fired."

Line seven blinked red and beeped.

"Mom? Yeah, this is Chris. Mom, I got a call from France this morning...it's Uncle Roy, he passed. ...No, the lawyer said natural causes. You know, he was up in his 80s. I'm trying to book a flight to Paris for tomorrow."

"Lawd, Lawd, this is gonna kill Mama," my mother said referring to Grandma.

"If you and Dad want to come, call Hazel, and she will get your tickets. Don't worry about paying for them, and I'll leave some cash with Hazel for you all. Okay, love yah."

"How you doin', son? I know how close you two were and you got a lot on yah mind these days," Mama said before I could hang up.

"I'm gonna miss 'im, Mama, but I'll be all right," I responded.

I hung up quickly. I refused to hear my mother cry, especially over a real matter of life and death that my money and legal prowess could not fix. I wanted to tell her that the last few weeks have been the worst of my life. I wanted her to know that my practice disgusted me now and that the dead man in France was the only person in the world with whom I connected. It had been a hellavah ride, and I was barely hanging on. I clammed up, though, as usual. I was the manifestation of their hopes and dreams, and I didn't want

15

them to know their dream was devolving into a nightmare.

"Hazel, I'm going to finish up some paperwork at the office tonight and leave directly from here for JFK. I got that bag in the file room already packed. I'll leave the keys to my condo in my top desk drawer. Go by and water my plants, read my mail and let the cleaning lady in on Wednesdays."

"Sho' nuff, massah, boss, sah!" Hazel responded sarcastically.

"OK, OK, would you *please* take care of those things for me?" I said slowly, carefully, and respectfully.

"Why, yes, I'd be glad to," she answered, overly gracious.

Sister Robinson from the church told Mama I'd meet my wife-to-be in my travels. According to Mama, Sister Robinson came into the world with a sheer veil of skin over her eyes that gave her second sight and her fortune telling instant credibility. At Mama's urging, I always kept a packed bag in the office in anticipation of the big event. Sometimes, though, I believe I kept that bag close by because it felt easier to leave from the office than from my empty condo. You don't expect a goodbye hug or a "we'll be waiting for you to get back home," leaving from the office.

I collapsed for another moment onto my familiar leather sofa to collect myself, to take an account of the last several weeks, and to contemplate my last journey with Uncle Roy. Every stick of furniture remained in place, my bank accounts were in balance, and I could still throw the rock step-for-step with the boys in Keney Park. But a few words about a man whom I spent much of my childhood fearing, whose body lay lifeless three thousand miles away, shook the remaining core of my being. Though my things remained in their proper places, grief muted their colors, dulled their edges, and sapped away at their coveted value.

I slept at the office more often than in my own bed it seems. I know that I absorbed more bad news on that sofa than anywhere else. So it only seemed natural to again sink deep into its well-designed folds and contemplate life without my uncle Roy. Two years passed since my last trip to France and the last time I saw Uncle Roy, but my mind wandered to that first trip we took to France together nearly twenty-five years ago. I smiled. It was the first of many such trips for me, but the one from which Uncle Roy never returned.

An hour later, I lifted my heavily medicated body from the sofa and made the obligatory calls to other relatives who might care about Roy's passing. I assumed the persona of the disinterested lawyer and reported his passing without emotion to his friends and relatives. I dutifully called those who would genuinely mourn his death and those who didn't give a rat's ass about him but for his money.

I called Aunt Ora Mae at the home place in Oklahoma first. She fell silent on the other end of the line after hearing the news. The receiver must have dropped from her hand because I heard it crash through her prized glass top coffee table. She covered that very table with blankets whenever I visited her house growing up. Uncle Roy sent it to her special delivery from France. I was twenty-seven years old before I saw that coffee table in the buff, and I found it unimpressive. But to Aunt Ora Mae, Uncle Roy and the table were one and the same.

I wanted to hang up the moment she dropped the receiver, but I thought it better to hold on and make sure that she was okay. Uncle Ruben picked up the receiver.

"Who in the hell is this?" he demanded.

"This is Chris, Uncle Ruben. Is Aunt Ora Mae alright?"

"She's fine. What did you say to upset her, boy?"

"Uncle Roy passed away in France. It happened this afternoon, or at least I got the call this afternoon."

"I see."

"How's Aunt Ora Mae?" I asked, again expecting more detail.

"She's a little shaken, as you can imagine. But she's a strong woman. She'll be all right. I'll take care of her. Look, Chris, I gottah 'tend to her now. You call us back later when the 'rangements is made and let us know what we kin do."

"All right, Uncle Ruben. Goodbye."

Next, I called my cousin Lisa in California who competes with me for the title of family success story. Lisa's success in life, though, contained more fiction than fact. Lisa directed traffic at the crossroads of the "I-couldn't-give-a-rat's-ass" branch of the family tree. She failed, by design I'm sure, to keep in close contact with much of the family. She needed the separation in order to maintain her illusion of West Coast happiness and sunny prosperity. She let me in on her hard times only during her divorce from her first husband. She needed free legal advice and a referral, both of which I provided. Apparently, he popped her in the mouth as often as the sun rose over Newport Beach. But he worked at a good job and owned a fat annuity, so she stayed with him as long as she could stand his hard right jab.

Lisa reminded me before every family gathering of the confidentiality that all lawyers must maintain with respect to their clients even if those clients are pretentious, self-important, and overbearing relatives. My life may have been bland, but hell rode roughshod over hers, and she knew my lawyer's oath would keep me quiet about it. She kept the familial competition going with quiet assurance that I would abide by attorney/client confidentiality. Most of the family doesn't know to this day that Lisa divorced Travon. I often wonder what else we don't know about her.

I only called Lisa to pass on news of a death or some other similar family milestone. Otherwise, I kept my distance because she always seemed more interested in money than people...living or dead.

"May I speak to Lisa, please?

"Who's callin'?"

"Lisa, this is Chris," I said recognizing her voice.

"Who died? Somebody musta since that's the only time I ever hear from my sorry ass, favorite cou'in."

"Uncle Roy pas--",

"You still driving that beat up '75 Benz?" she interrupted.

"Yeah, it's a classic, you know, still has the factory seats."

"Boy, that thang was burnt orange the natural way. Did you at least get them butt-ugly rust spots knocked out?"

"It gets me from A to B and I own it. But, anyway, about Uncle Roy, he passed sometime today in France."

"Oh, you know, I am truly sorry to hear that. I hope God blesses his tight-ass soul, or whatever knocked around inside 'im. Did he leave a will?"

"I don't know. I just found out today that he--"

"Did he make any money with that cheese stuff?"

"I was Uncle Roy's lawyer in the States, so even if I could answer that question, I couldn't tell you, Lisa. You understand attorney/client privilege better than anyone else in the family."

"I surely do, favorite cou'in. Just imagine...that crazy old bastard was probably sitting on a gold mine and nobody knew jackshit about it.

"You need to get saved, Lisa. This isn't about money."

"Shit, Chris, this is the United-fucking-States of America; everything is about money here. It's about money from sea to fucking shining sea and Uncle Sam will rob, rape, and kill from the Halls of Montezuma to the shores of Tripoli to get his hands on it. Not to change the subject, but you know that you're my lawyer, cou'in, so I can talk to you, right?"

"Lisa, I'll keep tight whatever you say."

"Then, what do you know about foreclosures?"

"I know some. But look, Lisa, I have to call Grandma and a few others. I'll call you when I get back in the country. Good bye."

I needed to end the conversation quickly to avoid becoming entangled in more of her family secrets. I already knew more about Lisa than I cared to. After our brief conversation, I could tell that she remained the same old Lisa.

I called Uncle Roy's friends and relatives all over the U.S. They were an odd collection of war buddies, preachers, and prostitutes. He lived in France for ten years before I even knew of his friends in the States. Up to that time, his life in America seemed miserably hermetic from my point of view.

* * * *

Mom and Dad arrived at Grandma's assisted living home later that evening. They wanted to be there to comfort her after I broke the news that her last living brother passed away. I arrived a half hour or so later.

"Grandma, how you doin'?" I asked.

"Fine, fine...how you?" she answered.

"I'm okay, Grandma. You keeping yourself busy?"

"Busy enough."

"You haven't been sparkin' at Mr. Davis again, have you?"

"Boy, yah thank I'm a damn fool? I don' want no dried up old goat like dat. Now, enough with the chit-chat. I knows y'al ain't just checkin' up on me. If'n you wanted to do that, y'all would ah been here last week *when I sang 'Amazing Grace' in the program*. And, *furthermo'*, I knows that a big time, silk suit-wearing, secretary-having, lawyer like you ain't here just to talk tah yo' crippled ass ol' grandma. Now, what in the hell is it? When yah ol' like me, yah cain't afford to waste too much time on silly manners and pleasantries."

"It's Uncle Roy, Grandma, I got a call from overseas this morning. He passed."

"Mama, it'll be alright. He's in a better place now," my mother said to Grandma.

Grandma didn't sob or break down in a storm of grief. A single, long-stowed tear trickled down between the deep creases in her quivering cheek. The tear landed on the arm of her wheelchair without splattering and rolled whole onto the carpeted floor below. The droplet came to rest on top of the plush carpet the way a crystal ball sits on an alabaster pedestal. It shimmered brilliantly in the sunlight breaking through her window and reflected its varied rays around the room. It then sank slowly into the carpet the way an earth sprinkled coffin descends into a freshly dug grave.

The old woman spoke.

"Number one: I ain't sad. And number two: he ain't in no bettah place 'less she's there too. I had gave my big brother up for dead some forty-five years ago anyway--I done my grieving then. These last forty-five years knowing he was alive is been grace for me. I 'member Mama gittin' the telegram from the service: '*Shot down in Europe Stop Remains not recovered Stop Presumed dead Stop.*' You know, the white folks who lost chillin in Okmulgee got a visit from two fine, sharply dressed servicemen with the telegram. Mama said that's what happened to the folks she worked for when they boy was killed. Colored folks, though, they just got the damn telegram."

Chapter Five

Life the hound
Equivocal
Comes at a bound
Either to rend me
Or to befriend me.

Robert Francis

Grandma had an Uncle Roy story to tell. She sat up straight in her chair, pulled the home's antiseptic-filled air deep inside of her lungs, and released it with Roy's story in tow.

"Roy was quite the man before Uncle Sam got ah hold of 'im. Growing up, I had more so-called friend girls than I could shake a stick at. Mostly though, they used me to git close to my big brother, Booker. Booker is Roy's birth name. To me, he was just my brother, so I didn't see what all the fuss was 'bout. The girls 'ould tell me how his smooth, crispy brown skin and deep baritone voice made their innards quiver, and how even the shadow cast by his six-foot frame reminded them of the warm rushing waters of a hot springs. He even smelled manly they said--not of the tar stench stuck to a body worn out from laying railroad ties all day or the smell of freshly cut grass clinging to men who worked the hay-field. Roy, they said, smelled of adventure and newness wrapped in sweet pleasure and bound with the courage of a lion. A whiff of 'im was enough to make a preacher's wife lose her salvation.

"He was a strong man too. All the mens in my daddy's family was strong. His powerful arms were tougher than the climbing limbs of a stout oak tree. He played tight end for the Dunbar High School Tigers. I 'member the time he ran down one of them boys from Muskogee who intercepted the ball. Roy's leg muscles flexed so in the chase that he tore through his purple and gold cotton football pants and left little more than a shredded skirt around his waist. He still tackled that boy, though. Coach House wrapped a towel around Roy's waist until they could get him a new pair of pants. The mens laughed at Roy's naked bottom streaking down the field, but the womens crossed they forearms over their breasts and bit their nails.

"The girls knew that he wouldn't spend his whole life in Okmulgee. He'd pack his stuff up one day, leave, and make a good life somewhere else. If they latched onto him, they thought they'd be safe in a better place up north or out west somewhere. I knew and understood that about Roy too. I wasn't much different than they was on that issue, and I wanted to go wherever he went 'cause I knew he'd protect me, keep me safe from the mean folks in this world, and help me to have a real life.

"He was a junior or senior in high school by the time he had a steady girlfriend; Avery Rose Rembert. Avery was a plain girl from what I knew of her. She was in one of them churches where the womens and girls couldn't wear make up, and it required them to wear dresses all the time. The athletic girls in that church surrendered their salvation to play basketball in skorts every spring, and then they'd get re-saved at the end of the season. They got saved, unsaved, and resaved year after year.

"I suppose Avery was pretty in her own way, and she was certainly smart. We young folks, though, scratched our heads in dismay over Roy and Avery. There were ten or fifteen other prettier, smarter and richer girls Roy could've picked before Avery. Grown folks, however, said that Roy made a *wise* choice with Avery. He didn't go for the prettiest girl, the richest girl or the 'ho, for that matter. They said he went for a good, solid, practical girl. Now, generally, her folks wouldn't have approved of Roy because he wasn't in the Holiness Church, but he being such a prize around town and all, I guess they thought the Lawd would make an exception.

"Avery's seven brothers and three sisters made sure that any other girls interested in Roy left her alone. A couple of her brothers went for bad, and the sisters would fight at the drop of a hat, and git saved agin afterwards. Everybody knew also that if you fought one Rembert, then you fought all the Remberts. So the girls that still liked Roy left him and Avery alone.

"Roy seemed content with Avery even though she couldn't do nothin' fun. She couldn't go to the movies, dancing or even listen to records 'lessen' it was gospel music. The Holiness thought anything fun was a sin. They didn't even have a radio from what I kin recall. They rarely walked outside of their gate 'less it was to go to a church function. I don't think she even saw Roy play football. He only saw her at their church, school, and at her house. He tol' me that he'd sit in the front room with Avery, and her mama sat on the divan right smack dab 'tween them. I didn't understand why Roy tolerated such a thing since he could've picked any girl 'round town he wanted. I thought he must really love Avery.

"The shit hit the fan, though, after they dated a year or so. I heard Mama in the back room crying quietly one morning, and Daddy slamming doors to beat the devil standing in the crack. Avery's daddy came over to the house with Avery in tow and their preacher, Rev. McFalls, flanking 'em. Avery's eyes were red and swollen for crying. Her face was spotted with reddish brown bruises and whelps from a ripe green switch marked her legs. She did her best to cover them, but they was too fresh to hide easily.

"Sweat poured down her father's high yellow face and the blood vessels in his neck were gorged to 'bout bustin'. He was a funny looking man, anyway, with a long torso and short stubby legs. He looked to have grown normally from his head to his waist, and then just stopped there leaving his legs short. But he was still an important-looking colored man to me because of his really light skin. We used to say the Rembert's were light, bright, almost white. The only dark-skinned colored men I knew that were important in town were the educated ones: doctors, preachers, and teachers. Men of Mr. Rembert's complexion, though, made themselves seem important, educated or not, 'cause they walked around with their heads held high and they only 'sociated with other light-skinned people.

"Daddy tol' me to go to Paulette's house next door 'cause the grown folks needed to talk about somethin' impo'tant. I could tell by his stern tone that Daddy was in no mood to hear me begging to stay, so I got to steppin' without 'changing a word. I left the house all right enough, but I planted myself in the damp grass right under the living room window where I could hear everything the *grown folks* said. All I needed was a bag of popcorn and a bottle of Nehi grape soda to make the moment perfect.

"'Let's just git right down to this thang. She is pregnant, and she done only been with yo' boy, Lankster. Your boy! Now what *you* gonna do about this thang?' said Mr. Rembert angrily.

"'I ain't gonna do nothin' 'bout nothin' 'till I have a chance to talk to my boy,' Daddy said calmly, sitting down in the lounge chair.

"'Well, what yah got to talk to 'im 'bout? Hits hisum and dat's all there is to the thang. Now, I brought Rev. McFalls here so he kin marry them 'fo the sun sets and maybe this baby still got chance to be born with the favor of God on him,' Mr. Rembert replied matter of factly.

"'We ain't gonna do no such thang. I'm gonna talk to my boy first, and den, after I hear what he have to say, I will call you,' again Daddy said calmly and rationally.

"They were quiet for a few seconds, so I raised my eyes just above the window sill to see what was going on. I saw Mr. Rembert's stubby legs carry his long torso across the living room, and he got right up in Daddy's face. You'd ah thought he was Daddy's boss man or somethin'.

"'Like I said, there ain't nothin' to talk about. That boy of yours is gonna marry my Avery today, and we gonna make sure dat happens, ain't we,' Mr. Rembert ordered.

"This time Daddy's neck bulged, and his wrinkled eyebrows lowered over the tops of his eyelids. He stood up over Mr. Rembert, and the words slide from his mouth with perfect pitch and clarity but with the force of a runaway Frisco freight train.

"'This is my house, Got dammit. And I don't give a shit how holy or how white you is, you don't talk to me like that in my house. Now, you kin take your daughter and your pastor and walk out that door under your own power, or I will drag you ass-first out that door and deposit you on that gov'ment paved road outside.' Daddy's words seemed to force Mr. Rembert to take a few steps back and drop his head down a notch or two.

"'Kin I git y'all somethin' to drank?' Mama asked.

"'They don't need nothin' to drank 'cause they 'bout to leave,' Daddy responded.

"'Now, we is all Christian folks here. If that means anything to any of us, we oughttah be able to work all this out bidoubt killing one another. That baby growing in Avery's belly is gonna need grandparents, 'cause Lawd knows the parents ain't old enough to take care of it,' Mama said.

"'You speaking the truth, Mrs. Lankster. You sho' 'nough is speaking the truth,' the pastor said in a quivering alto.

Pastor McFalls finally moved away from the door and guided Mr. Rembert and Avery to the sofa. Avery sat down between the two men with her head hung low the entire time. Her hair fell over her forehead and covered her face so I couldn't see her eyes. Her left arm lay along her side, and she grabbed its elbow with the hand of the other arm with its forearm crossing her midsection. She either wanted to hide her belly or protect it; I didn't know which one. I think she was ashamed, though. I know I wouldah been if'n I was in a family-way with no husband. But somethin' about her made me think that it wasn't the baby that shamed her.

"'Avery, sweetheart, did you tell my boy you is pregnant,' Mama asked.

"'Yes, M'am, I tol...' she responded.

"'She done said more now dan I could beat outtah her,' Mr. Rembert said, shutting Avery down.

Mamma looked at him with the kind of eyes that said 'you shut up, you done done enuff damage already.' He quieted down.

"'What did he say?' Mama asked.

"'He say he gonna take care of the situation. Just give him a little time to get thangs together and...' Avery answered.

"Again, Mr. Rembert broke in. 'He gonna take care of it by marrying you, that's how he gonna take care of it.'

"Daddy's chest deflated and his head dropped upon hearing Avery say Roy promised to take care of the baby. I suppose Daddy still hoped that Roy weren't the baby's daddy. He got used to the idea that one member of his family might go off to college and not be tied down with mouths to feed befo' he could pee straight. College was a new notion for our family. All we seemed to do up to that time was work, have babies, complain about the white folks, and die po' as dirt.

"I guess in one way or another we tied up all our hopes and dreams in Roy; rightly or wrongly. He was the plow clearing the field of the doubt and fear that blocked our way. He was our family's Moses, and we needed desperately for him to lead us out of Egypt. But Roy, I guessed, was no different than other boys. He had urges that couldn't wait for college, a good job, and our deliverance.

"I could tell by the way that Daddy turned his body to one side that he wanted to leave the room now. If he was a dog, he would've tucked his tail between his legs and crawled under the front porch. He dropped his head into the open palm of his left hand and massaged his temple and forehead in the midst of a long sigh. He did those same thangs whenever we went through money problems. And he surmised that we was 'bout to have money problems. I could see him calculating in his head how much the baby and Av-

25

ery would add to the family budget. He probably thought about where he could find another part-time job or how he didn't need to pay for coffee at the café on Saturday mornings anymore. His anger at Mr. Rembert's arrogance dissipated, and worry filled the hole it left. Daddy's blood ran through this unborn baby's veins, and to Daddy that meant that the baby was his responsibility.

"'It ain't like that.' Avery spoke for the first time without a pending question.

"'Shut up, just shut yo' mouth and let the grown folks work this out. You done done yo' hoing. Now we gonna straighten this mess out whether you like it or not,'" Mr. Rembert ordered.

"'But...' was all Avery said before Mr. Rembert stood up over her and raised his right hand to slap her down.

"'Spare the rod and spoil the chil'. That's what the Bible says,' the preacher affirmed and moved away from Avery to give Mr. Rembert more swinging room.

"Mr. Rembert's hand descended toward Avery's head, and I closed my eyes tight. I sho' nuff didn't want to see nobody git beat down. But a second or two passed, and I didn't hear the thump or slap. So I opened my eyes and saw Daddy holding Mr. Rembert's arm back at the wrist and saying something to him quietly. I pressed closer to the window.

"'This is still my house. You ain't gonna hit that chil' in *mah* house. And you listen real close, if that is my boy's baby growing in her belly, *you ain't gonna hit her in your house either.*'

"Mama's hand caressed the base of Daddy's neck, and she sat him and Mr. Rembert down.

"'How far along is yah, Avery?' Mama asked.

"'I ain't been visited by the old lady down south for three months now, Mrs. Lankster. I'm startin' to show a little,' Avery answered.

"'You got everything you need, girl? You done seen Dr. Anderson?' Daddy asked.

"'No, sir, I ain't seen no doctor,' Avery answered.

"'Well, then, dat's the first thang we got to do,' Daddy said softly.

"What a strange sight for me to witness. They was passing Avery from one family to the other without asking her what she wanted. She was *just* Roy's girlfriend less than an hour before. But now the gears were turning and she was becoming part of our

family with no engagement, wedding, or fancy reception to celebrate the occasion. It all happened because of a baby not yet born.
My family always took care of the babies no matter how they happen to come into this world. And neither the baby nor its teenaged
parents seemed to have any say in the matter.

"The negotiations that followed were a clear sign that the parents agreed that Roy was the father of Avery's baby. The preacher
seemed to perk up now that the hard part was over. He talked
about how in the Bible some number of asses and oxen, menser-
vants and maid servants, lambs and goats were always exchanged
between the families of newlyweds. Daddy wasn't much of a nego-
tiator, though.

"'Me and my boy will take care of this girl and the baby, irre-
gardless of asses and oxen. Dat's all that I got to say on dat. Y'all
need to understand something, though. I'm gonna tell my boy that
the right thang for him to do is to marry Avery and brang her into
dis house. I'm even gonna tell him that he *oughtah* marry her. But
I am not going to *make* him marry Avery. He gonna have to make
that decision hisself,' Daddy said.

"'I ain't gonna marry 'im,' Avery said softly. I heard her clearly,
but none of the adults seemed to hear her. She was no longer important to the discussion. She contributed all required of her by
naming Roy the baby's daddy.

"'As Gawd is my witness, Lankster, if you let that baby be born
a bastard, hit'll be on your head. I like your boy, and folks around
here say y'all is a good family. But if he leave my daughter with a
bastard, he ain't no different than these other no account niggahs
running 'round here,' said Mr. Rembert.

"Now I knew he and Daddy would go at it after that comment no matter what Mama did to calm Daddy down. Shit, I was
mad after he said that. I wanted Daddy to git him for talking that
way about Roy, and I wanted to climb through that window and
scratch his eyes out too. But Daddy just sat there saying and doing
nothing. The way Daddy was actin', or *not* actin', made me believe
he agreed with Mr. Rembert. He didn't move an inch or part his
lips a hair's width to speak. I couldn't take it anymore. I turned
away from the window sill and marched toward the front door to
get inside and give Mr. Rembert a piece of my mind.

"I s'pose Mr. Rembert simply tried to enforce same law they
forced on him. He was made to marry Mrs. Rembert, so he was

dead set on Roy marrying Avery. I understood him better in one way, but less well in another. He felt it his and Daddy's job to make Roy marry Avery. But I didn't understand why he didn't sympathize with Roy, considering his own situation. He, of all the folks in our living room that day, understood the agony of being forced to marry someone you don't love. He raised kids with Mrs. Rembert and the most 'tention he gave any of them was what he gave to Avery behind her pregnancy. Mr. Rembert seemed hell bent on Roy and Avery suffering the same fate. He seemed intent on out doing his own folks by listening less to Avery and threatening her more. I think he was mad enough to kill Roy, Avery, and the unborn child if they didn't do exactly what he wanted.

"I marched on ready to give him a big piece of my mind. I came around the corner of the house and pulled myself up on the wooden front porch by grippin' the wrought iron corner post. It weren't graceful or in the style of a proper lady gittin' up on a porch, but I was too mad to care about acting like a lady. He couldn't say that stuff 'bout my big brother and git away with it. I looked up the street while reaching for the screen door and saw Roy headin' home from two blocks away. He was half dragging somebody along with him. I jumped off the porch and ran to Roy.

"'They got Avery in there, and she say she carrying your baby and everybody is mad and fussin' and fightin' and Mr. Rembert say you is just a niggah if you don't marry Avery and Daddy let him say it and I wanna scratch his eyes out...' I rambled on until Roy pressed two fingers against my lips.

"'It'll be alright, li'l sis. I got the situation under control. Everybody gone be done right,' he said with perfect assurance while holding on tight to the other boy.

"I took a deep breath and wrapped my arms around my big brother's waist. I wanted to stand between him and the trouble brewing at our house. But he didn't seem worried.

"'OK, now, li'l sis, me and Jonathan here have to git on to the house,' Roy said.

"I forgot about Jonathan just that quick. He was Rev. McFalls' eighteen or nineteen year old son. He was not much older than Roy. He wasn't a normal McFalls child, though, because he was in and out of the church. Yah see, Jonathan *loved the devil's music*, and I heard he would sing and play the house down in Lula Mae's Joint on Fifth Street many ah Saturday night. Half the time he was so eaten up by guilt playing gut bucket music over the funny smoke, sweaty bodies, and the stench of corn whiskey in the air that he could only find his salvation at the bottom of a bottle of gin. He'd sober up every six months or so, and then find his way back down the center aisle of his father's church, to the mourner's bench and back to Jesus. He'd fall back into sin again a few months later upon hearing the sirens' wail of the jazz spirits.

"In or out of church, Jonathan was what we used to call a pretty boy. God didn't bless him with physical strength or natural beauty. But Jonathan sure knew how to dress and clean up the narrow frame he had. What he lacked in natural assets he made up for with manmade beauty products and the effortless coolness inherent to all jazz musicians.

"He made good money leading a sinner's life in backwoods joints all over Oklahoma and Arkansas. He'd spend that money for J.L Penner silk suits, two-toned wing-tipped loafers, and wide-brim Chicago-style hats. He bathed his body in Italian colognes that seemed to take possession of a woman's spirit whenever he passed by. His shimmering jet-black hair rolled in waves over his well-edged head. Jonathan was not the kind a man any woman with half a brain would want to marry, but any woman who didn't desire at least a night with him was either a liar or a fool. He was the kind of man you could spend a night with that you'd never forget and that you'd smile inside yourself about when overtaken by the boredom of everyday life.

"But the Jonathan at the end of Roy's powerful right hand seemed dispossessed of all the charms his worldly ways bestowed upon him. He neared the end of his latest dance with salvation because I could smell a hint of fresh drunk gin on his breath. He was covered in mud up to his thighs and his hair was a stringy wet mop hanging down around his head. His messy appearance was why I didn't recognized him until Roy mentioned his name. His pretty boy persona came out of cans and bottles, and Roy apparently didn't give him time to open them up.

"'Hi Jonathan,' I said.

"'Hey, little girl. Look here, little girl, tell your muscle- headed brother to let me go,' he replied. I was peeved that he called me little girl, 'cause I wanted him to see that I was a woman.

"'Roy, why are you dragging him along?' I asked.

"'Jon got something to say to Avery and her daddy. He was

having some trouble gittin' there, so I'm jus helping him along.'

"'What's wrong with you, man? I ain't got nothing...to say...to them,' Jonathan slurred, pointing his index finger to the sky.

"'I hope the baby look like you. Daddy is already trying to figure out how we gonna take care of it and Avery. It kin look like Avery I 'pose if it gonna be a girl. But she gotta be able to wear make up or something. I hope it don't have a long top and stubby legs like Mr. Rembert. A baby top heavy like that won't ever learn to walk right. I don't even know how Mr. Rembert walks without tipping over,' I rambled on.

"I calmed down some since I was walking with Roy back to the house. He didn't seem worried, so I didn't worry. I knew Roy would set Mr. Rembert straight in a flash.

"For every two steps Roy and I took, he dragged Jonathan three steps it seemed. Jonathan was definitely drunk. His eyes were bloodshot and half opened, and his clothes smelled like pee. I could tell he wanted to protest being dragged down the street, but he couldn't seem to form the right words in his mouth, and he didn't have enough muscle on his bones to fight Roy anyway.

"'What's wrong with him?' I asked Roy.

"'Oh, he drank a little too much 'shine last night down at Lula Mae's joint. Then he decided to go swimming in the Greezy Creek under the Fifth Street Bridge. So I crawled down the bank and pulled him out of the water not ten minutes ago,' Roy answered.

"'I don't think you oughtta take him in our house like that. Daddy will sho' 'nough hit the roof,' I said, mounting the front porch ungracefully again. 'His daddy is in the front room with Avery, Mr. Rembert, and our folks. We don't need to add anymo' kindlin' to the fire ragin' in there.'

"'He ain't kindling, li'l sis. He's the fireman. He's gonna put that fire out,' Roy said just before we walked through the front door.

"Roy walked into to the front room, dragging Jonathan a half step behind him. I flanked them with my ears and eyes wide open and my mouth shut tightly. I hoped then that me and Avery would be invisible to the grown folks. It hurt my heart to see the way Daddy looked at Roy after we came in. I could see the disappointment in Daddy's eyes and the increasing slump in his disposition. I noticed though that Roy made eye contact with Daddy right away and gave him one of them half winks where he raised his cheek and his eyelid came down part ways, but it didn't close completely. Daddy nodded his head slightly saying without words, 'OK, I'll wait to hear what you have to say before I go off on yo' ass.'

"Mr. Rembert spoke first. He looked through Jonathan and me and spoke directly to Roy. I guess I *was* invisible. I noticed right away that he was less sure of himself since Roy walked into the room. His voice sounded hollow, and he hesitated between words. *Maybe Daddy let him have it after all*, I thought.

"'Me and Rev. McFalls is here to make sure you do right by Avery.'

"Roy didn't say a word or even look in Mr. Rembert's direction. He looked lovingly at Avery instead. *That's my big brother*, I thought, *nobody has to tell him to do the right thang*. Avery eyes met Roy's, and she smiled a sly smile for the first time that day. She smiled with confidence, though not joy. Avery opened her mouth to speak again only to have Rev. McFalls interrupt her this time.

"'Boy, look at you! You look like you done been down in the mire and mud with the hogs. Stand up straight and speak to these folks in whose house you just entered like you got some home training,' he said to Jonathan.

"'Afternoon...I mean mornin' folks whose house I just entered,' Jonathan responded with a drunken sarcasm and the tip of an imaginary hat.

"'You are a disgrace,' Rev. McFalls said getting off the sofa and heading toward Jonathan. In a flash, he grabbed Jonathan's free arm and tried to pull him out the door. But Roy still held on tight to Jonathan's other arm, and Rev. McFalls' exit was halted suddenly and completely.

"'I've got something to say,' Avery was finally able to say and be heard.

"'I done told you...' was all Mr. Rembert could say before Avery raised her voice defiantly above his.

"'I've...got...some...thing...to say,'" she repeated with conviction.

"'Let the chil' talk,'" Daddy said.

"'This baby I'm carrying is my baby. It's mine to carry, to birth into this world, and to brang up,' Avery said.

"'What baby?' Jonathan asked. The rest of us looked at him like he had two tails.

"'Our baby, Jon. Our baby,' Avery answered.

"'Our baby?' Jonathan said clearly, seeming to sober up.

"'Yes.'

"Jonathan looked at Rev. McFalls with a kind of rage in his eyes that I hadn't seen before or since. Roy instinctively tightened his grip a split second before every muscle in Jonathan's body lunged for Rev. McFalls' un-collared neck. Rev. McFalls backed away. Jonathan sobered up completely in a few seconds right before our eyes. He reached into his pocket and pulled out a wad of cash bigger than my daddy's fist and threw it at Rev. McFalls.

"'Pop, I think I'll stay in town after all, at least for seven or eight months anyway. You can have your money and your mother-fuckin' blessings back,' Jonathan said contemptuously. Jonathan then addressed my daddy. 'You know, Mr. Lankster, Pop gave me all of last month's offering in cash to leave town. He said he was giving me my inheritance and that I should take it and never come back. He told me I was an embarrassment, and he and some of the men of the church would make life hard for me here if I ever tried to come back. Ain't that right, Mr. Rembert?' Jonathan concluded while turning his head toward Mr. Rembert.

"Mr. Rembert looked away into a small corner in the back of the room and hung his head. Jonathan turned to Avery.

"'Avery Rembert, you sweet, little thang. Will you marry me?'

"'I kin answer that for you. No! Hell no! She ain't gonna marry nobody like you while I'm alive.' Mr. Rembert answered.

"'Then just go ahead and die, you sawed off muthafucka, just die!' Jonathan replied

"'Rembert, be quiet and let the girl speak for herself. This is still my house,' Daddy said with a smile in his tone.

"Avery brushed both her hands from her forehead to the back of her neck, removing the hair from her face. Her hands then covered her mouth, and her eyes began to sparkle with fresh tears.

"'Yes. Yes, I'll marry you, Jonathan McFalls.'

"Mr. Rembert's face turned beet red. Rev. McFalls' face was red, too, I'm sure, but he was too black for it to show through. Daddy was smiling from ear to ear, and Roy let go of Jonathan for the first time in an hour. Jonathan grabbed hold of Avery and hugged and kissed her right there in front of all of us. I smiled at the pinched look spreading across Mr. Rembert's face.

"It took me a while to catch on to all that transpired on that day, but I did eventually. Of course, I got the fact that Avery was carrying Jonathan's baby. But it took me a few days of pondering and several overheard conversations to understand that Rev. Mc-Falls and Mr. Rembert conspired to marry Avery off to Roy. They knew all along that it was Jonathan's baby, but they decided that Roy would be a better husband than Jonathan. Rev. McFalls also wanted to protect the sanctified reputation of his congregation, even at the expense of his son and grandchild.

"Jonathan hooked up with Oscar Pettiford, Okmulgee's most famous jazz musician, about a year after the baby was born. He worked with all the top acts of the day and eventually, set up residence in Los Angeles, California. He sent for Avery and the baby a year or so later and brought her home to a small palace. They made four more kids and a lifetime of wonderful memories together. But Jonathan was about marriage the way he was about church, in and out.

"What I didn't figure out on my own was what was going on with Roy and Avery in high school. Some folks were saying that my big, strapping brother might be funny. So I went straight to the source for the answer, and I got right to the point.

"'Why wasn't you beatin' up Jonathan for gittin' *your* girlfriend pregnant?'

"'Cause she was just that *a girl friend*, in the platonic sense. You know what platonic means, right, li'l sis?'

"'Well...yeah...maybe...no. No, I'm pretty sure I don't know what that word means.'

"'It means that we were *just* friends. You see, both Avery and I were prisoners in a way. We were trapped in and trying to live up to other people's expectations. Our *relationship* freed us from some of those expectations. I'd sit in Rev. McFalls' church where Mr. Rembert could keep an eye on me, and Avery would experience life. She'd hold my hand in public, and keep other girls at bay. I was free...'

"'You know people round here saying that you are funny.'"

"'You didn't let me finish. Risa and I were free to experience life beyond expectations'"

"'Risa? Risa Roundtree? You mean you and Risa been a couple all this time?'

"Roy tapped his index finger against his lips and winked at me.

"'Let that be our little secret, sis,' he whispered.

"That's the Roy I'll remember.

"Fifteen years later, mo' or less, we thought that Roy was killed in the waw. Den he just shows up in Taft. He wasn't much of a man after they got through messing with his head in there. He was the walking dead--just a lump of flesh with no feelings at all. Then he was sort o' born again back over yondah, yah know, overseas. Yah know, even though he nevah came back here, Roy kept in touch; he wrote me nearly a letter a month. I knowed more about him since he been over there than I ever did living with him in the same Tower Avenue two-family here in Hartford. I knows he was happy. He lived more life than most folk twice his age. That's all I got to say on that."

The old woman wheeled herself to the mahogany cedar chest at the foot of her bed. That chest was her last true zone of privacy in the world outside of her deeply personal thoughts. She insisted that I padlock the lid shortly after we moved her in to the assisted living center. She wears the key on a chain around her neck and guards it with wild animal ferocity. She stapled one of those signs to the side of the chest that city drivers post in their car windows. "No Radio, No Money, Security System." Grandma added in her own hand, "and no graham crackers or peppermint sticks either!"

She opened the chest slowly so she would not stir up the aroma of cedar and mothballs well settled in its insides. She folded back a yellow and green handmade lone star quilt she stitched thirty years ago and pulled out several rubber-banded bundles of Roy's letters written to her over fifteen years.

"You young folks know so much about so many thangs, but you know so little about the stuff that matters most. Let me help you a little, son, everythang is 'bout love, some kind of love. Dat's why we still here. They done had they feet on our necks for all my life and den some, yet I got more joy in my heart than you. Why? 'Cause it when you ain't got nothing dat's when you can really see the somethin' dat matters. Roy's already been on the road you 'bout to tek. Find 'im and he can lead you home. Chris, you take these letters, read every one of 'em, and then burn 'em. Throw the ashes off the top of dat dere Eiffel Tower. Maybe, if'n we all lucky, the whole world will take in some o' Roy's heart and it'll be a bettah place.

"And the next time I see you on the Channel 6 news, you bettah have yo' nappy-ass hair cut and be clean shaved. I don't want mah friends here thanking I didn't raise you right. And don't come home with none o' them French gals.

"Listen to me, chil', Roy's heart is the cure for what's ailing you," the old woman finished.

Chapter Six

Our two souls therefore, which are one
Though I must go, endure not yet
A breach, but an expansion,
Like gold to airy thinness beat.

John Donne

Finding Roy's Letters

The next morning, I boarded the first Air France Concorde to Paris. I spent the first half of the transatlantic flight arranging Uncle Roy's letters to Grandma in chronological order. Some of the letters were so old that the envelopes were brown, frayed, and worn through. I borrowed a pair of tweezers from a passing flight attendant and peeled away layer after layer. Uncle Roy's writings became my family's Dead Sea Scrolls and they deserved the same care and attention. The flight attendant, speaking in African accented French, made me promise to return the tweezers or she would "have to take me out." Not really seeing her and only half listening, I agreed to return them to her satisfaction.

I deliberately focused on the dates Uncle Roy mailed the letters, so I just read the postmarks. Grandma inhabited these letters. Her scent rose generously from every page. She imbued them with that old woman smell: a mixture of graham crackers, peppermint, cedar, and mothballs. A vague impression of life radiated from the pages in a soothing warmth I couldn't quantify precisely. I sorted slowly through the years.

I could tell that Grandma read several of them numerous times. She wrote copious notes in the margins and highlighted certain sections apparently to reread at a later time. She cried over Uncle Roy's letters. Teardrop stains littered the pages and doubtless, she pressed them close to her heart to feel whatever he felt. She treasured his every word.

It is safe to say Uncle Roy's words became Roy to Grandma. What's that passage in the Bible? Oh yes, John 1:14: *the Word became flesh and dwelt among us.* He faded away from her in the flesh, and Grandma must have thought it was God's will to let his words pass also.

36

Uncle Roy made it clear in the earlier letters that he felt the need to explain himself to her. He wanted to explain why he came back from the war a basket case, why he spent all those years brooding, sullen and isolated in our basement, and why after thirty plus years he returned to Europe with me in tow and never again set foot in America.

So, I spent the next half of the flight dividing his letters into the three major periods of his life: during WWII, after WWII in America, and his last years in France. It took monumental discipline to resist the temptation to read entire letters while scanning the introductory paragraphs, but somehow I managed. I could credit my rigorous legal training for such restraint, or maybe I was just plain afraid that if I read the letters, I'd find my lonely self in them and a wretched genetic disposition favoring solitude. Or maybe I wasn't too anxious to read them in their entirety because I knew Grandma meant the letters for me more than anybody else, and I didn't know why. Grandma's wisdom often dwarfed my vaulted Ivy League education. I learned the hard way to respect it above all and to never take her words at face value. So I pressed on in search of my uncle Roy and maybe, just maybe, in search of myself.

The supersonic jet landed on time, and my driver waited just outside the baggage claim area. I left the letters packed in my bag and absorbed the French countryside on the final leg of my trip. We arrived at Uncle Roy's modest country cottage a couple of hours later. To my surprise, hundreds of bouquets of flowers lined the stone and beam fence around the cottage's grounds. Dozens of people were gathered outside of the fence along the road singing, crying, and holding burning candles apparently in vigil.

"We appreciate love in France!" someone shouted at my passing car.

A light fog settled over the valley, making it difficult to see more than ten or fifteen feet in front of me. The driver slowed to a stop before I realized that I did not desire to disembark in an unfamiliar place, hampered by poor visibility, and in the midst of a crowd of strangers. There is something about a crowd of white folks with fire that makes a black American man inherently uneasy anywhere in the world he might find himself.

The silent onlookers were a mixed lot: men and women, young and old, wealthy and poor. I wondered what common purpose brought together such a disparate group. Most stood in silence, staring at me with tired eyes and mist-covered faces. The driver slowed to a safe crawl to avoid hitting anyone in the crowd. The headlights from the car illuminated their faces, reflecting off the beaded mist. I remember asking myself, *Is this for my uncle Roy? He was an old man--surely his death could not have been unexpected to those who knew him or would even have been noteworthy to strangers.*

I felt a sudden and compelling urge to seek refuge while climbing out of the car. I know what I felt because all the signs were there: I could hear every distinct beat of my heart, my breaths shortened, I felt that itchiness in my armpits that precedes preflight sweating, and I felt every tiny unnoticed hair all over my body stand to attention. I admit to being frightened. Fear happens when dozens of strangers rub against you, pressing unspoken demands. Frankly, what I don't understand frightens me. That's only normal, I think.

I didn't understand why they were there or what they wanted. My lack of understanding in a moment of uncertainty on foreign soil led me to wild speculation. Maybe they came to make certain that this nastiest of nasty Americans whom they despised actually died. I considered the opposite proposition too difficult to believe at that time: that they came to mourn the loss of someone whom they loved and admired. I considered it especially difficult to believe if *my* crazy uncle figured into their affections.

I pushed my way inside the gate, refusing to look anyone directly in the eye. I rolled my hands in the air around my ears to indicate that I didn't understand French. It was an expedient lie. I approached the sculptured wrought iron gate when a low echoing chant rolled across the gathering. It was in French, and though I spoke very elegant French and understood the language even better, I focused my attention on getting to safety inside the house. So, their words passed between my ears uninterrupted, muddled and presumed to be hostile.

The housekeeper told me later that they were chanting, "Rest in peace, beloved one." *Beloved one? Who was that? Uncle Roy? Funny how fear can alter your perception of reality*, I thought.

After a long bath and a light lunch, I set myself up in the modest guest bedroom and began reading Uncle Roy's letters. The housekeeper came in and gave me a package from Uncle Roy's friend Daniel Cristol containing a file on Mancel Marchant. She also informed me that the lady of the house, Marie, adjourned to the farm of her birth and left it to me to make the arrangements for Uncle Roy's funeral. I found Marie's few requests written in perfect English on the dining room table in a short note.

Dear Chris:

Please accept my apologies for not being here to greet you upon your arrival in France. Know that such inhospitality is not the way of the French, but the expediencies of the moment have taken me away. I beg your forgiveness in this matter. I do not have much time, so I shall be brief. Monique will provide you with my simple requests for your uncle's funeral. I would be most appreciative if you would honor the same, but the decisions are all yours. Roy would have wanted it that way. I have adjourned to my birthplace to take care of several long overdue matters. I shall return to Rouen shortly before the services. Your uncle would say 'make yourself at home.' I say the same.
Love,
Marie

The housekeeper was prepared for my arrival. There was food and directions to the mortuary, church, graveyard, and the lawyer's office. She suggested that I see the lawyer first--"that's what your uncle said you should do." Apparently, Uncle Roy carefully arranged his earthly affairs before he passed. He seemed to know the end of his life neared even though he wasn't visibly ill.

I met with the lawyer the next day, and she gave me a copy of Uncle Roy's journal among other things. The journal was all about Marie. The first fifty pages provided a detailed account of the time they spent together during the war. The balance consisted of Uncle Roy's fictionalized accounts of Marie's life without him. He spun eight different scenarios, each more elaborate than the last. Each scenario ended melodramatically and neither included him in the end. The journal was a monument to Uncle Roy's intense despair written during his loneliest years in Hartford. For the first time, I realized that I misconstrued his bottomless sadness and pain for anger and belligerence all of those years. I realized also that I'd never really known my uncle.

Deep, brown leather with bold, gold lettering covered the

journal. At a casual glance, it could easily be confused for a bible. He filled every blank page and the open spaces, headings and margins on every page. He wrote from beginning to end in the margins, and then end to beginning outside the margins. Uncle Roy diligently recorded all of his sadness in a neat little package and filled it to overflowing.

I cross-referenced the early parts of the journal with the letters to Grandma and what I personally knew about his life. This is Uncle Roy's story.

Chapter Seven

Two roads diverged in a yellow wood,

Robert Frost

Dealing With Bullies

I have to take you back to my sixth grade year to begin my part in Uncle Roy's odyssey. We'll go back even further in his writings, but it began for me in middle school.

I was a good kid, mostly. Mom and Dad seldom needed to punish me, and the few bad habits I cultivated were generally tolerable. I lived the good life from a kid's perspective. Mama and Dad kept me well supplied with toys, friends, and lots of love. I suffered from only two major problems as far as my young and inexperienced mind discerned: an old crazy uncle and a bully named Dewayne Moten. You might say I lived with a bully from within and a bully from without. The latter of my problems I resolved decisively one day after school. The "resolution" taught me a life's lesson about my other bully.

The truth be told, I feared Mom more than Dewayne. She strictly forbade me from fighting. Consequently, I ran home from school most days in order to avoid the other bullies, including Dewayne who stalked me and a few other undesirables after the last bell. Though I felt I could take any of them in a one-on-one fight, Mom absolutely forbade it unless it was a last resort, and then, only in self-defense. I arrived at that age when girls mattered to me, and I thought running from bullies everyday made me matter less and less to the girls who mattered more and more to me. Faced with Mom's edict and also struggling to catch the eye of Shonda Jacobs, I was compelled to take matters into my own hands and use my well-developed brain for more than just schoolwork.

One day I'm gonna let Dewayne Moten corner me, and then I'm gonna kick his black ass. If I beat up Moten, the baddest of the bullies, then I'd be bad! I'd be smart and bad and den ain't nobody gonna mess with me. Or maybe I'd just be bad--the bad kids seem to have more fun anyway. Kids would fear me. I could rule the school, I remember thinking.

Mom also insisted that I wear the optional school uniform:

plain navy blue pants and a button down white oxford shirt. I owned exactly five pairs of plain navy blue pants and five white oxford shirts. Mom always bought my school clothes at least one size too big. She intended that they last for at least two school years. The ordinary uniform further detracted from my desired reputation. A part of me wanted to stand at the head of a crowded hallway and yell to everyone passing that I was more than that uniform, more than a coward, more than the sum of what they thought of me. But I attended a public school where uniforms were optional and, therefore, emblazoned with an invisible bull's-eye for those who were forced by their parents to wear them. Most other students dressed in more fashionable clothes at school, and some even left the sales tags hanging to show from where and for how much they purchased them. Back then trendy clothes on the outside that everybody recognized mattered more than the me on the inside that nobody knew.

My tenuous reputation suffered further because of my inexplicable passion for the French language and all things French. This suffering I willingly endured. I spoke better French than the native Haitians populating most of the class. Madam LeBlanc said that I was her best student ever, a "born Francophone!" I often covered my head with a black beret on cold days, which elicited mild approval from my finicky fashion conscious peers. I bragged about reading *The Three Musketeers* in the original French, corresponding with a French police detective, and being an avid fan of the Tour de France. I covered my bedroom walls with a thousand years of French maps and a world map with every French speaking country on the planet highlighted in yellow.

Mom and Dad went along with the "French thing" until a case of overpriced French wine arrived by overnight mail C.O.D. Though they enjoyed sharing a rare glass of it with special guests every now and then, my mailing privileges were severely restricted thereafter.

I will never run from a bully again, I declared to myself one morning. *I will not ask the teachers for protection or ride home with my mom. The day has come for Dewayne Moten to receive his long overdue ass-kicking.*

I walked out of the school building that afternoon be-bopping, shoulders rocking side-to-side, and sneering. I spotted Dewayne near the flagpole with his back to me before I was halfway out of the door. I strutted over to Dewayne and bumped him with enough force to send him face first into the dirt. A neatly tied blue box fell from his backpack on his way down. Dewayne was enraged. He picked up the box carefully, dusted it off, and tucked it away in his backpack again.

"I'm gonna kill you," warned Dewayne.

He came after me with all the blind ferocity I anticipated. He chased me through the schoolyard and out of the front gate.

A mass of other overly excited children followed Dewayne shouting in unison, "Fight! Fight! Fight!" I ran hard along a carefully pre-selected route guaranteed to assure I'd be cornered by Dewayne with no exits. I already figured it out, once cornered and in certain danger of bodily harm, I would have no choice but to fight in defense of my own precious life. No one, not even Mom, would fault me for fighting under such circumstances.

Sure enough, Dewayne cornered me two blocks from the school in the alley behind the Cantonese Take-out.

"Get ready for an ass-kickin', you dirty black frog," Dewayne warned.

Dewayne struck first. His open hands slammed against my chest knocking me back onto an open pile of rotting garbage. Confident in the sufficiency of his first strike, Dewayne turned away, raised his fists in victory in the air, and basked in the approval of the cheering throng. When he turned back, he barely glimpsed my tightly closed right fist that crushed the bridge of his nose. Dewayne's hands went immediately to nurse his bloodied, throbbing nose. I followed up in perfect time with a second blow to Dewayne's exposed midsection. He doubled over and fell to the ground, gasping for air and writhing in pain. Dewayne lay helpless before me. I wasn't finished.

"Who gone kick whose ass?" I shouted, standing over him pounding my chest like a silver back gorilla. My pointy-toed Oxford shoes then battered Dewayne's upper thigh until he begged for mercy. The fight was over before it really began. The decisiveness of my victory stunned the cheering crowd into silence. Dewayne, crying and still dripping blood, cast a knowing glance up at me from the wet pavement.

I ran through the stunned crowd, knocking several kids down on my way home. I ran all the way without stopping. I could feel the blood rushing through every vein and vessel in my body with every stride I took. I could hear and count the rhythmic beats of my fiercely pumping heart. Less than ten minutes passed, and the world around me shrunk rapidly and fit neatly into my tightly clasped fist. I was primed to fight again.

"Yes! I won! Dewayne and nobody else is ever gonna mess with me again. Should I go back and get the others now? No, enough for today. I will deal with them tomorrow," I vowed under my breath.

I barely slept that night. I couldn't wait to get back to school and bask in my newly earned respect.

But the day didn't take the path I expected. Not a single person spoke to me the next day during first period. My classmates steered clear of me. Shonda Jacobs stepped on my foot at the water fountain by accident and burst into tears after she saw it was me.

"Please don't hit me!" the terrified girl begged.

"Why would I hit you?" I began saying before she ran off. She didn't hear the rest. *"I wanted you to step on my foot. I placed it there to get your attention. I got respect now. Do you like me?"* was what I wanted to say. But she was gone before I could form the first word.

A note came from the main office, and my teacher sent me to the principal during third period. I walked into the office and sat down next to a smelly, old black man with tangled grey hair and a scruffy beard. He smelled sour, and his clothes were neat but old and reeked of mothballs. I assumed he was there to apply for the open janitor's job.

Dewayne and his foster mother sat on the other side of the room. Tears streamed down Dewayne's swollen and bandaged face, but he sat still and silent. He sat so still, in fact, that the flowing tears made him look like a simmering pot boiling over. He sat there as if he were the only one in the room and locked away safely in his own little world.

I never really looked carefully at Dewayne before that moment. I noticed his badly worn and dingy Converse high-tops for the first time. He was still dressed in the same bloodstained polyester shirt from our fight the day before. His oversized pants held onto his body only by the aid of a tightly drawn belt. His fade was overgrown and his ears dusty.

Somehow, Dewayne's ragged appearance never stood out before. I guess I never saw past the wall of intimidation and bravado he erected to insulate himself from the rest of us.

Dewayne's well-dressed foster mother sat next to him with her mouth perpetually open and thoroughly dressing him down.

"I cain't afford to miss work for no shit like this. I'm gonnah send yo black ass back to the state 'cause I can't handle no mo' foolishness like this. They oughttah send you back to yo junkie mama; you two deserve each other about now. Who do you think *you* are...causing *me* all this trouble? That little bit of a check every month sho' nuff ain't worth all this shit."

Dewayne sat silently with his head down staring at the floor.

Dewayne and his foster mother met with the principal first. I overheard the foster mother and Principal Harris yelling at Dewayne.

"I didn't start nothin'. He did," Dewayne argued.

"You shut up! Shut up and don't you say another word! We know *you* already, so don't try that stuff with me. You can't fool me because I've seen too many Dewaynes! This is it, boy. I'm calling the state today and having you transferred out of here. They have a school for kids like you downtown. We got too many like you anyway," yelled Principal Harris.

What have I done? He's gonna expel me, too, I thought. Part of me wanted Mom and Dad there between Principal Harris and me. Another part of me wanted them kept in the dark about the fight because my punishment at home would be far worse than what they dished out at school.

Dewayne and his foster mother came out, and Principal Harris invited me into his office. To my surprise the scruffy, smelly old man followed me. A smiling and slightly nervous Principal Harris started talking before we sat down.

"We know Chris is a *good* kid from a *good* home. I know that he didn't start this--he was only defending himself. We cannot expect a child not to defend himself when set upon by a hoodlum like that. I promise you, Mr. Lankster, that we will protect Chris and students like him from the likes of them. I want you to know that we don't have many of them here, but then it don't take but a few to stir up trouble. I beg of you not to withdraw him, leave him here, he'll be safe. We'll protect *him*. I understand that Chris is one of the best French students we've ever had at Quirk Middle School. How are you doing, son? Did he hurt you?"

Mr. Lankster? Oh my God, it's Uncle Roy, I thought. I turned suddenly and stared at him. I held thousands of stored memories that required filling-in with pictures of him. Each brain cell waited its turn to fill in the blank parts of the memory it held. I would have been embarrassed under normal circumstances, but I was too curious about him for embarrassment to take hold.

"Chris, are you okay?" Principal Harris asked again.

"Yes, sir, I was not injured," I answered in my best English, returning to the real time world.

I settled assuredly back in my chair after recovering from the shock of Uncle Roy's presence. The common wisdom prevailed and took its place at the top of the batting order. What's the common wisdom? It's the widely accepted notion that the bad kid is *always* bad and the good kid is *always* good. No red-blooded, close-minded adult was capable of suspecting the good kid of going bad or the bad kid of any good. I, a known good kid, was therefore not capable of contemplating, planning, and executing a fight with a street hoodlum. Dewayne, on the other hand, was capable of being nothing but a brute: a poor, black, fatherless brute.

I won a larger prize than I realized. *Carte blanche, that's an apropos French phrase*, I thought. I realized for the first time in my life that authority drones could not peer into my immortal soul and discover my hidden motives. I learned that the appearance of goodness is far more powerful to most people than actual goodness. The ecstasy of my absolute deception surged through my veins. The world around me now seemed much smaller and far more malleable than it did just twenty-four hours before. I also understood something about why the bad kids were bad. I enjoyed the tingly, floating, fearless sensation that accompanies escape from wrongdoing. In a word, I felt big, really big because I got away with it. Everything and everyone around me was small, and the fear of punishment faded from me like a cheap suit at high noon.

Principal Harris asked me to step outside so that he could speak with Uncle Roy in private. I sat in the waiting area and strained to hear what they were saying. While out, I overheard Ms. Mako, Mr. Harris' secretary, on the telephone with the state.

"This is Ms. Johneva Mako, Senior Administrative Assistant II, from the Quirk Middle School. I need to speak with Dewayne Moten's worker... Yes, hello... Well, Dewayne attacked and beat up one of our *good* students...the school wants him out... The boy is alright, but... Yes, she came, but she can't handle him, you know that... This afternoon? Good, he'll be waiting in the office."

He didn't beat me up. I beat him up! Get it right lipstick head woman! I wanted to blurt out, but dared not for fear of revealing my deception.

Ms. Mako called down to detention and asked that Dewayne be sent to the office with all of his "stuff." Principal Harris called Ms. Mako into his office, and I overheard the principal saying something about slam-dunks and laughing through the briefly opened door. Dewayne appeared at the office five minutes later. He carried all of his stuff: a dingy worn-out backpack, frayed books, and that small, neatly tied blue box. The box was so neat and elegant that it appeared out of place in Dewayne's hands. It was the kind of thing a kid with Dewayne's reputation would steal.

"What's in that box?" I asked him, getting personal now that my dominance was established.

"Nothing," Dewayne answered.

"Then why you carrying it?"

"It got the only thang dat's really mine in it."

"What's that?"

"My mama gave me a good luck charm 'fore she got too sick to keep me. She say if I keep it, then I can be sure she gone come back and git me."

"Where yah mama now?"

"She sick. But when she git better, she gone come get me."

"Where yah daddy, then?"

"None o' yah damn business where is mah daddy. Let me ask you somethin'--why you *let* me catch yah? I wasn't *gonna* catch yah. Why you *let* me catch yah?"

I did not answer. The world grew larger again on the heels of Dewayne's question, and it seemed to slip rapidly out of my control. I realized that my deception was not complete.

"You wanted to fight me, didn't you? I don't never want to fight nobody--but I gots to fight causn' I ain't got nobody to fight fah me. You don't got to fight," Dewayne said.

I slumped over in my chair staring at the floor now stunned at my eleven-year-old arrogance. My motives were transparent to Dewayne, the heretofore, mindless, dumb, bullying brute. Dewayne Moten, who lived in a transient world completely dependent on total strangers, saw through my ruse.

Crazy Ol' Uncle Roy is in there advocating for me. Someone is always there for me, I thought to myself. A creeping sense of guilt replaced the rush of the thrill of victory I felt just minutes before. My recently suppressed good nature emerged from the darkness of apathy.

I weighed the positives and negatives of coming clean--confessing. The good part of my nature required that I also consider the positive and negative effects on Dewayne if I came clean. My child's mind grasped the realization then, that considering the pains, pleasures, and sacrifices of others is what really separates the good among us from the bad. To state it succinctly: I understood the power of compassion that day.

Principal Harris' door swung open, and he came out smiling, exchanging pleasant goodbyes, and shaking hands with Uncle Roy.

I cleared my throat and spoke rapidly.

"I have something to say. Dewayne didn't start the fight... I did. I knocked him down on purpose, lured him into the alley, and hit 'im. He never wanted to fight, but I hit him first, and he just fought back--that's all he knew how to do."

I spoke quickly to get it all out uninterrupted and before my guilt faded away. Every adult head in the room, but Uncle Roy's, turned slowly and methodically in Dewayne's direction. The closed minds refused to open, and their prejudices kicked into high gear.

"Did he threaten you, Chris? Don't be afraid of him. He's on his way outtah here," said Principal Harris while leering angrily at Dewayne.

"That's why he fought back, 'cause he ain't got anybody to fight for him--not even you, Principal Harris. I ain't scared of Dewayne. I never was. I did this 'cause I wanted everybody to respect me," I said.

"My, my, my...what are we going to do about this strange turn of events?" said Ms. Mako.

"And by the way, Ms. Mako, *I* kicked his ass...I mean kicked his butt--look at him, not vice versa. Is that French?" I added with a weak smile.

"Now, Chris, you do not have to lie for Dewayne," said Principal Harris.

"Wait a minute...this boy doesn't lie, Principal Harris. At least he don't just come right out and tell lies. He may have a silly notion about how to earn respect every now and then, but he doesn't

48

just outright lie. Chris, apologize to Dewayne, then you get your stuff, because you're coming home with me," Uncle Roy said in an authoritative voice.

Uncle Roy spoke more words that day than I'd heard him speak at one time in my entire life. They were shockingly coherent, appropriately judgmental, and reasonably commanding. For the second time that day, I misjudged the intelligence and character of a person I thought I knew.

"I'm sorry, Dewayne. Please forgive me, man."

"It's alright, man. Thanks fo' stickin' up fo' me."

"Now, Principal Harris, let's go back into your office and discuss an appropriate at school punishment for my nephew. Chris, go back to class, and I'll deal with you when we get home," said Uncle Roy.

Uncle Roy never "dealt with" me, nor did he tell my parents. They found out from me during my explanation regarding my three days of in-school suspension. Dad gave me the last whipping of my life behind the fighting. I wasn't sure at the time, but I thought Dad was smiling behind every lick. I suppose there was a time when he doubted that I would be man enough to survive in the Hartford Public School System, especially with that "sissy French stuff" he'd complain about. My high grades, appreciation for all things French, and goody two-shoes reputation didn't give him much to brag about to his drinking buddies. But taking out the school bully with a couple of punches was something he understood. To his way of thinking, I finally joined that "boys will be boys" clique and confirmed my solid hold on manhood. Also, I finally did something that I knew Dad was proud of for the first time in my life. I knew this instinctively because his actions, though condemning and punitive, were executed with a definite wink.

Dad waited until I was in high school to finally "fess up." He told me how proud he was that I took charge of the situation even though he couldn't say so at the time. He asked me for a blow-by-blow account of the fight. He then said something that made me proud.

"Son, I've worked with my hands all my life. My daddy and all his peoples worked with they hands too. I been knowing for a long time that you gone be working with your head. I don't know nothing 'bout that; working with the head, I means. So I don't have nothing to tell you 'bout what to expect. But I want you to know

I'm proud of you, and I'm always gone be here for you, no matter what," Dad said.

Mom, however, was genuinely sadden and disappointed by my actions. She imagined me locked up with the other teenage boys she knew vanishing from our neighborhood. She conjured up visions of herself sitting in the ER while the doctors operated on my bullet-riddled body. She imagined the same for Dewayne for whom she developed a genuine concern. In fact, she picked Dewayne up later and took him to my pediatrician for treatment. She worked out an arrangement with his foster mother that allowed Dewayne to stay at our house. He never went back to his foster home except for the semi-annual visits from the social worker. His foster mother kept getting the welfare check, though. Dewayne lived in our house for four years until his mother cleaned herself up. Mama always tried to make things right, and she succeeded with Dewayne.

Dewayne recovered from his bumps and bruises, and I recovered from my walk on the wild side. I discovered that Dewayne spoke some Creole he learned from a Haitian foster family with whom he spent a couple of years. It wasn't quite continental French, but it was close enough for us to start with. We formed a lifelong friendship from that day forward. We are fond of saying about our friendship that we saved one another; I saved Dewayne from the unrelenting backhand of poverty, and he saved me from the poverty of arrogance.

I learned that my bullies often kept dark and nagging secrets. Their anger is often just a thorn-covered blanket they use to protect their secrets. I knew Dewayne's secrets; now I wondered about Uncle Roy's.

Chapter Eight

I took the [road] less traveled by
And that has made all the difference

Robert Frost

The Competition

I have to take some of the credit or the blame, whichever is appropriate, for Uncle Roy's self-imposed exile from the United States. I was a skinny thirteen-year-old kid whose only dream at that time was to visit France. In fact, I think I wished I were French.

I was in the eighth grade in 1976, and an honor student at Quirk Middle School. Jimmy Carter was the President, and America was celebrating its Bicentennial. My parents were just ordinary working people, my dear grandmother wheelchair bound, and the other member of our household, Uncle Roy, was crazy. He was crazy in both ways: certifiably and in the street sense of the word.

Uncle Roy spent much of the 50s and 60s confined to a mental institution, or what we called "the crazy house," in Taft, Oklahoma. I always think and speak those words, "the crazy house," in quiet, hushed tones with squinted eyes and a wrinkled nose for emphasis. I whisper because it was always in a whisper that Mom and Grandma discussed that period in Uncle Roy's life. He continued his odd behavior while living with my parents in Connecticut. He barricaded himself in our basement apartment for nearly a decade. My friends in the old neighborhood called him "The Hartford Hermit."

The neighborhood gossips had accused Uncle Roy of nearly every unsolved crime that occurred within a twenty-five mile radius of our house. The Hartford Police Department raided the house once on a tip from an informant accusing Uncle Roy of cooking dope in our basement. All they found was cheese, shelf after shelf of fancy French cheese. It turns out that Roy was supplying some of the finest restaurants in New York City with cheese made right in our basement.

I can recall only one person ever coming to our house in those days to visit Uncle Roy. He was a large, messy, and uncomfort-

51

able looking man with a French accent by the name of Marchant. He was from Corsica, or at least that's what he told us. His clothes never seemed to fit properly; his jacket collar was always half flipped up, his shoe heels worn down on the inside, and his long black hair was stringy and disordered.

Grandma often defended Uncle Roy's odd reclusive behavior to her interested girlfriends. She would, in her most proper voice, refer to the fine French-speaking businessman who visited Roy periodically. She made Uncle Roy appear highly selective about his friends rather than, in her non-public words, "Crazier than a Betsy Bug."

Miss Queen Ester Rogers, whom Grandma always said was desperate to get any man, took two years of intensive French lessons and studied continental manners in an effort to gain access to Uncle Roy's basement. She fared no better than the others. Uncle Roy's hostile and angry voice yelled at her from behind a freshly slammed door. She was thought better for her efforts--she married a prosperous Haitian plumbing supplier from New Haven. His money attracted her, and her U.S. citizenship interested him.

My relationship with Uncle Roy began to change on February 16, 1976. Mom, Dad, Grandma, and I attended the Black History Month assembly at my school, and that changed everything. The assembly was held in the auditorium where the principal was to speak, make a few awards presentations, Dewayne would perform the "I have a Dream" speech, and then the parents would visit our homerooms. Principal Harris did welcome everyone, and then he broke from the program and introduced Madame LeBlanc, the French teacher, for what he called "a very, very special announcement." French was my favorite class, and Madame LeBlanc was my favorite teacher for more reasons than I care to explain.

Madame LeBlanc began her special announcement in perfect French. I sunk down deep into my seat after Grandma, in a booming voice that echoed across the auditorium, asked Mom, "What is that woman babbling about?"

Grandma's use of *that woman* meant that she not only disliked Madame LeBlanc's inability to communicate clearly, but her low-cut, tight dress, and high heels also fell under disdain. I could already imagine the conversation in the van on the way home from the program.

"She ain't got no more French in her than I does. Lovie Dee

told me her birth name is Lucinda Jones, and she growed up in Tupelo, Mississippi. They was so po' they used to wipe they asses with newspaper. And she know she's *too* old to wear that short, tight-ass dress."

Several scattered amens affirmed Grandma's question, though, and brought me back to the land of the living. So I pulled my jacket down below my ears and sat up in my seat. It was clear that almost no one in the audience understood French. Madame LeBlanc stopped her announcement mid-sentence and in elegant French asked me to come up on the stage and translate for the parents. Mom asked me why I was getting up; "because she just asked me to translate into English for y'all," I answered. She looked to the stage and saw Madame LeBlanc beckoning in my direction and let me pass.

"Cette année le Collège de Quirk a reçu une grande honneur de la Société Internationale des Affaires Francophones."

"This year the Quirk Middle School has received a great honor from the International Society of Foreign French Speakers," I translated.

"Un de nos étudiants de langue français les plus brillants au Collège de Quirk ont été choisis par un essai français international écrivant et parler la compétition passer un an étudiant en Paris dans une école française."

"One of our sunlight...no....our most brilliant French Language students at Quirk Middle School has been selected through an essay writing and International French-speaking competition to spend a year studying in Paris in a French school."

"Seulement dix ancien huit classeurs d'autour du pays sont choisi pour cette honneur."

"Only ten former eighth graders from around the country are chosen for this honor."

"J'ai été choisi pour cette grande honneur."

"I was chosen for this great honor."

Madame LeBlanc looked at me. I looked back at her and smiled softly, seeking her approval on the accuracy of my translation. She then asked me to repeat her last statement. I thought I translated it wrong. I tried to repeat exactly what I thought she said, but this time a little less confidently.

"I...was...chosen for this great honor?"

"Again, repeat it again," she looked at me in that way again and said in English.

I started, but before I could finish, the audience began to clap and cheer wildly. I even heard Grandma say, "All right now!" Dad stood up and cheered, while Mom cried in her seat. The audience's jubilation was lost on me.

Madame LeBlanc grabbed my face with both her hands and kissed me on each cheek in what I thought was the style of the French.

"Congratulations, Christopher, we are very proud of you," she said in perfect French.

I still didn't get it but, frankly, after that kiss, I didn't know there was a message to get. I just wanted to ask her to marry me. I thought she was congratulating me for finally winning her heart. I glanced slyly at Dewayne because of our longstanding bet on which of us would marry Madame LeBlanc. But Dewayne behaved inappropriately for the moment. He stood on his feet clapping and cheering loudly.

I finally realized that *I* had won the competition. They had chosen me to spend a year in France. In that moment, I seemed lighter than air, and I jumped up and down on the stage for joy. It was one of the happiest days of my very young life and a beginning of the realization of a dream.

We received a notice in the mail a few weeks later regarding the prize and my itinerary. They suggested I arrive in France by the first week of September. They required an adult to accompany me and remain with me for the duration of my studies in France. Room and board were covered, and we'd receive a small monthly stipend on which to live.

The adult chaperone requirement was a problem I didn't recognize at first. We weren't rich. We got by all right enough, but only with both my parents working full-time jobs. Even with that, Grandma contributed from her retirement and Uncle Roy from his military benefits.

Whenever Mom called me "son," I knew bad news was coming.

"Son, you know that the honor is in winning the competition even if you can't go to France. You should be proud to know that of the thousands of kids from around the world who tried, your essay was one of the best."

"I can work to get more money, Mom. Please don't let that stop me from going."

"It's not that simple, Chris. Neither your father nor I can afford to walk away from our jobs right now. We've worked a lot of years in them, and we have obligations here. I'm sure Grandma would go if she was physically able, but she ain't. There's just no one to go with you."

"What about Uncle Roy?" I asked after several hours of anguish.

"Chris, you know that Uncle Roy has barely set foot outside our yard in the last fifteen years, and 'sides, he ain't right in the head. I don't think he'd be interested in flying on a plane and living in France for a year."

"Please, let me ask him, Mom. He has the time, and he's in good health, ain't he? Please, Mom, at least let me ask?"

"I will let you ask Uncle Roy, but I want you to promise me first that you won't be disappointed when he says no."

"I won't be disappointed."

"You promise me, now."

"I promise I won't be disappointed."

Despair and disappointment overtook me, though, before I descended the stairs to Uncle Roy's door. In all of my thirteen years of life up to that point, I was never able to say more than hello to Uncle Roy before his door slammed in my face. I used to make a game of it and practice my delivery. But I knew I must try this time to say more. I found the courage somewhere from deep inside of me to walk down those dark stairs. I stood at Uncle Roy's door for seconds that passed with seemingly years in between and gathered the strength to knock.

Before I knocked, I ran back upstairs and got one of Mom's cast iron frying pans and some of those fancy crackers Uncle Roy ate. I knew that on Tuesday evenings at 7:00 p. m. sharp, Uncle Roy expected his crackers. I crept back down the stairs with cats' paws, slowly and quietly. I stood at the door, placed the skillet on the floor against the sill of the door, and yelled, "Uncle Roy, I have your crackers."

He opened the door and reached for the box of crackers. He reached, and I slid the frying pan between the door and the doorframe so that he couldn't close it completely. Before he could yell at me, I yelled my request at him.

"Uncle Roy, I won a trip to France for an entire school year, and I need a grown up to go with me. Please go with me. I need you!"

I expended all of my remaining courage on the last word to leave my mouth. I held none in reserve to wait for his answer or the sure tongue-lashing I expected him to unleash. I pulled the skillet from the doorsill and ran up the stairs with all the speed I could manage. Time passed for which I could not account. The next thing I remembered was crying at the dining room table surrounded by Mom, Dad, and Grandma.

"There will be other times to go to France. You're still a boy with your whole life in front of you," Mom said.

Grandma suggested that if she were able, she'd "knock that crazy so-and-so upside his head for saying no." Dad promised that we'd take a vacation to France next year and spend a couple of weeks. Mom hugged me and whispered, "Be strong, my little man."

In all the sadness, none of us noticed the vague apparition standing in the doorway. A minute or two passed before our noses discerned the stench of sour milk and followed it across the room to the open doorway. There stood Uncle Roy. I saw more than his very familiar right hand for the first time since he came to my school. His longer, grayer, and now dreadlocked hair twisted down his back. A full snow-white beard rested on his chest. He dressed in a dingy white t-shirt and brown wool army pants. His eyes were cocked wide open, and his nostrils flared to their limit. Uncle Roy was more bizarre in his appearance than I ever imagined.

"What's wrong with you, boy? You ask a question, but don't wait for the answer," he said in a raspy, dusty, and seldom-used voice. "My answer is *yes*." He turned and walked back down the stairs to his lair.

* * * *

The flight from Hartford's Bradley International Airport to New York City lasted exactly twenty-five minutes. I was a teenager on an adventure with a man I considered dangerously crazy and unapproachable only a few months earlier. I considered whether I should engage him in a conversation on the first leg of the journey or wait until the long flight across the Atlantic Ocean. He surely couldn't change his mind and return to Hartford if I waited until we were over the ocean. But if I started on the flight to New York and determined that he was certifiably crazy, then *I* could back out in New York City and save myself from the anticipated humiliation.

I stared hard at Uncle Roy's now clean-shaven face, trying to match it with the bewhiskered, belligerent one I often only glimpsed from behind his slamming apartment door. I tried to superimpose this very ordinary human face over the one my child's mind conjured up to match that disembodied voice. I imagined him a noxious beast ready to pounce. More particularly, I conjured up a green-skinned, yellow-eyed, flesh-eating, acid-drooling, and barely human monster. But the man sitting next to me wasn't a beast at all. Still, I held my judgment on Uncle Roy's sanity in abeyance, knowing that appearances can be deceiving.

He seemed bald now after having shaved his beard and cutting his curly dreadlocks. He seemed human. He was small compared to my father, but sophisticated, bilingual and, apparently, well traveled in his day. I realized that I learned more about Uncle Roy in the last several months than the sum of what I knew about him in my entire life before.

Uncle Roy babysat me in my preschool days. Apparently, he and I only spoke French in the first four years of my life. French was such a strange language to my parents, and they considered it gibberish. A well-meaning child psychologist advised them to separate me from Uncle Roy. She said his reclusive behavior failed to reinforce my language centers leading to retarded development. I assumed that I discovered French on my own until I heard that story. I was wrong again.

"We're gonna spend a lot of time together, huh, Uncle Roy?" I asked.

"Maybe," he answered.

"I don't know the rules."

"What do you mean, you don't know the rules? What rules?"

"Well, lemme see. Okay, I got it. Mom always says don't talk when grown folks are talkin'--that's a rule. Eat all the food on your plate, no cussin' and burpin' at the table--those are rules. Those are some of Mom's rules. I know what I can and cain't do when Mom's around. With you, however, I don't know the rules. What are your rules?"

"Let's see. I ain't nevah had no kids, so I ain't nevah had to make no rules. Nevertheless, I suppose that you do need rules. Okay, here yah go. Rule #1: All of your mother's rules are still in effect until further notice; Rule #2: Don't do nothing crazy in France to get yourself hurt, maimed, or killed, lessen I'm doing the hurtin', maimin', and killin'; Rule #3: If you do the crime, you do the time; Rule #4: Your uncle's stuff is all his stuff, so don't mess with your uncle's stuff; Rule #5: Speak perfect French in your uncle's presence, or learn to sign; and Rule #6: Wait until you have lived, nephew, before you die. Good enough?"

"I guess. I mean *oui*."

"Fine then."

We landed in NYC without incident but experienced some difficulty getting past U.S. immigration officials at JFK. The government placed a hold on Uncle Roy's passport thirty years prior. They asked a lot of questions about who we were, where we were going, for how long and why. Uncle Roy was really nervous until he told them something the French Ambassador said, and he gave them a telephone number to call. I guess they called. All my little brain knew then was that we were waiting too long and would probably miss our transatlantic flight. The man got back and said, "Everything is a go." He saluted Uncle Roy and held the door open for us. Uncle Roy saluted back, and then they rushed us past the long lines of people to our waiting airplane.

"The government men *are* gone. They are finally gone, Chris," Uncle Roy said with a smile. That may have been the first time I saw him smile. He willingly displayed a positive emotion for the first time in my recollection. He was not just being polite or smirking from one side of his mouth. It was a genuine, honest-to-God expression of happiness. I didn't want to lose the moment so I didn't ask who the government men were and where they went. I chose to just smile myself instead.

We arrived in Paris nine hours later. An elderly one-eyed man named Daniel Cristol met us at the airport. Apparently, he and Uncle Roy were old friends. He was a small man, impeccably dressed, and very formal. His greeting was intimately ritualistic and well-rehearsed in the way of many cultures outside of the United States. By "rehearsed" I mean in a way that says "I'm giving you the best greeting that centuries of refinement have bestowed upon my people because I consider you a very dear friend."

The patch over Mr. Cristol's eye was covered in silk, dyed fire engine red. Its maker embedded a small, brilliant, white diamond in its center. The lights in the terminal reflected off the diamond and periodically sent colorful rays dancing around the cavernous room. I concluded that Mr. Cristol wanted people to notice the patch and even to ask about it because he wanted to tell them his story. I wanted desperately to inquire, but Mama's rules strictly prohibited me from asking people about their handicaps. So I resisted even though I got the impression he considered his handicap as a badge of honor rather than the mark of shame.

The one-eyed man ended his greeting by kissing Uncle Roy on the cheeks, and they embraced in a bear hug reserved for long lost friends. He took us directly to his home in Paris. We ate dinner with Mr. Cristol and his wife, and he and Uncle Roy conversed in French too fast and difficult for me to follow. I know that they spoke about the war and a woman Uncle Roy knew. Well, she was more than someone he knew. Apparently, he once loved this woman. I heard mention of Marie for the first time that night.

I fell asleep on Mr. Cristol's plush sofa and woke up the next morning in the school's family residence where I'd spend the next school year. The events of the night before and my memories of the highly mannered, one-eyed man had faded away like a common dream.

Chapter Nine

I know I shall meet my fate
Somewhere among the clouds above;

William Butler Yeats

Dear Lil Sis, I was a member of the all-colored 99th Pursuit Squadron of the U.S. Army Air Corp which merged with other colored squadrons to form the 332 Fighter Group. It was supposed to be an experiment to give colored men control of the most lethal machine in the army arsenal. Only we were certain the experiment would succeed. Before we got off the ground good, they declared us incompetent, and Congress tried to shut us down. But the undisputed facts and the desperate necessities of war kept us going. We trained at first in Illinois and later in segregated units in Tuskegee, Alabama. We were all college educated or experienced pilots which made us the smartest and best-trained squadron in the service. But, as with most things, we got half the credit for our successes and twice the hatred-laced blame for perceived screw ups real and imagined.

We saw our first action in North Africa in 1943 and made our way through Tunis, Italy, Eastern Europe, and into Germany without losing a single bomber to enemy planes. I personally shot down a sparkling brand new Nazi Me 262 jet. We didn't know from jets then, and the Me 262 was one fast and elusive machine. But it was my day when we met over the pale skies near the German border, and the dogfight was over before it started because I needed to get back to a pot of collard greens slow cooking at the base.

We flew P-40 Warhawks and the P-47 Thunderbolt, but hit our stride in the P-51 Mustang. The Germans called us "Schwarze Vogelmenschen" or the "Black Birdmen." The Allies called us "Redtails" or "Redtail Angels" because of the insignia red paint on our tails, the empennage, the trim tabs, nose spinners and our knack for delivering salvation. My sleek, highly engineered red tail was the last thing many German boys saw in this life.

I was pulled off the Italian campaign and ordered to report immediately to Britain near the end of August 1943. At no point during the war up to that time did the Army separate me from my squadron. I mean that literally and figuratively. Our physical seg-regation was convenient for the Air Corp in a number of ways, but mostly because it minimized our contact with white, enlisted men who would have to salute us. The requirement that they salute a colored officer was always a point of controversy and a direct challenge to the military command structure. So, they decided to cordon off the colored officers rather than enforce the command structure.

I was the proverbial fly in the buttermilk among the Army Air Corp in Britain, but each man of lower rank I encountered saluted me without hesitation and without regard to race. In fact, they waited on me hand and foot from the time I landed. The white folks treated me better on that short trip than at any time in my entire life. That kind of treatment made the whole experience sur-real and surprisingly enjoyable. I remember thinking: *this must be what respect feels like.* But I knew that their strict adherence even to the smallest of military protocol meant that they were un-der direct orders to treat me well. Still, I loved every minute of it, orders or no orders. The officer treatment made it patently clear to me that the mission I was called up to perform was one from which I was not expected to return.

The French Résistance asked for support repeatedly from American fighter pilots for several months. A French unit flew Mustangs for reconnaissance purposes over their homeland. They wanted badly to get into the fight, though, and they needed our help to do it. The U. S. Army Air Corp flatly refused to place Amer-ican pilots under the command of foreigners. So they decided on a compromise: send a colored American airman. No one on the home front would raise hell about a colored man under foreign command, and the colored newspapers might even brag about it. Furthermore, the French don't appear to find coloreds as distaste-ful, and the Nazis wouldn't give a shit one way or the other. That was the cover story.

President Roosevelt considered the French Résistance politi-cally important, but our army commanders thought its military worth minor. My color made me both expendable and stealthy. I learned that I was much more than a convenient compromise, however. I was the token American support to the Résistance, but I was also being recruited for a special mission that would, I was told, ensure the Allies uninterrupted march across Europe, through the Brandenburg Gate and right up the ass of the Reichstag.

They knew I was one of the best pilots in the Air Corp despite my coal black skin and hick town upbringing. The Tuskegee Airmen's red-tailed fighters never failed to chase Nazi pilots back home or into an early grave. We always accomplished our mission, and I was the best of the best.

General Jerome T. Zinny called me into his ornate Elizabethan era office exactly twenty-four hours after I landed in Britain. It was twelve hours after his personal cook, a black man from Thomasville, Georgia, fried chicken, boiled collard greens, and perlow rice and baked cracklin' cornbread for me. The general's words were direct, chilling, and frank.

"Our eggheads are working on a single bomb that will flatten an entire city in one blast, Lankster. We have reason to believe the enemy is, too. Whichever side gets it first will win this war and recreate the world in its own image. The French were researching such a bomb before the German invasion, and their research is now and has been in enemy hands since. The arrogant Nazi bastards don't know what they have, though, so their research has languished with little funding and support. And our sources say Hitler doesn't have enough heavy water or some such thing yet to create a viable test bomb. The Jerrys think that they can pound us man for man into submission and we want them to continue believing that. We need you to make sure that they never know the potential of what they have," he said.

He didn't use the words atomic bomb; he just told me this super bomb could take out whole cities and insure a German victory if they got it first. I didn't learn about atomic bombs until after Hiroshima and Nagasaki when everyone else did. Apparently, the Germans captured French researchers and were combining their research knowledge with their own. Fortunately, the project hadn't attracted Hitler's attention and, therefore, wasn't a priority, but it was too far along to risk promising research results or, God forbid, a successful test.

The Allies didn't consider the French/German project a threat until the American project began to show promising and devastating potential. They knew that one German bomb would change the course of the war, especially if it were delivered by an unmanned V-2 rocket. The Nazis could pull back to Berlin and blast Britain into submission with the flick of a switch. Such a weapon in Nazi hands would bring about a sudden and complete American retreat from Europe.

General Zinny wanted the research facility utterly destroyed, but he wanted it done without attracting a lot of attention. He wanted one pilot, one ace, in a flying bomb to hit it and cash in a one-way ticket to the afterlife. He also wanted a pilot America could self-righteously discredit with a straight face.

He was blunt. "The Nazis won't be suspicious of a Redtail flown by a nigger," he said.

Just when I was getting used to the feel of respect, "nigger" rolled with ease and familiarity off the tongue of the man in charge.

"We'll make a big deal in the colored papers about you being loaned to the Résistance. And when you don't return from this mission, we'll say publicly that we didn't have high expectations for a nigger anyway, using more polite terms, of course. You'll be a nigger before the mission, a nigger on the mission, and just a dead nigger after the mission. You'll stay a nigger until the war is over, these super bombs are public knowledge, and the enemy threat is no longer viable. What I'm asking you to do, Roy, is to save possibly millions of Allied lives on this mission, yet accept the fact that we will brand you an incompetent, inferior black. You see, not only must the target be completely destroyed, but we cannot afford to let that Nazi bastard Hitler think that the target was either important or intentional," he said.

"There are so many contradictions in what you just said, sir, that I am amazed I even understand it. I think that if I read between the lines, though, I can conclude that you believe in me. I think you're telling me that I'm the only man for the job because I am the best pilot you have, who, because of the color of my skin, will never get credit for his heroism from friend or foe. My stealth is the ignorance and racism of the masses, and you're counting on the masses to behave true to form," I said.

"That about sums it up," he said.

He gave me twenty-four hours to think about accepting the mission. Apparently, several others from the regular units refused the assignment. I began to understand what Crispus Attucks must have felt.

"I will go on this mission, sir, because, even though I hate Jim Crow, I still think America has a heart capable of redemption. I can't say the same about them Nazis. They must be eradicated, but I want something in return," I said.

"You are in the Army, Lankster. We don't bargain; we follow orders. Nonetheless, what do you want?" he asked.

"I want the colored pilots treated the same way the white pilots are treated. I want our officers' quarters to meet the same standards, our repairs done in order of arrival, and our victories celebrated publicly. I want those in the lower rank to salute them and those in the higher ranks to decorate them for their valor, honor, and courage. And finally for me, I want my folks to know I died a hero. I want Ben Davis to contact my parents personally and tell them I died a hero. Can you make that happen, sir?" I asked.

"I'll see what I can do, son," he said.

"Will you make it happen?"

"I will," he answered after a pensive pause and salute to me.

The Army decorated me in an odd pre-death ceremony before I left. General Zinny read proclamations from the President, Secretary of War, and the exiled French government. Each proclaimed me first a credit to my race, and then my country, though my good deed may never be known.

I inspected Lena (my P-51 Mustang) from the tip of her nose to the last flap of her tail for the last time. I pressed my hand against her silver side and ran it through the cool morning dew gathered on her sheet metal. She was the most beautiful fighter in the war. She was my steel fortress--impervious to enemy bullets and bombs as far as I was concerned. I wish you could have seen her close up. She was far more elegant than she looked in the newsreels. She fought me sometimes in the air, but when her guns opened up, she was my sword and shield.

Lena was especially lethal in the hands of a well-trained colored man with the burdens of his race and class on his shoulders. I believed I was invincible. Invincibility eliminated fear from the equation and added just enough recklessness to bring me to home base at the end of every mission. Further, I understood that my fight was bigger than this war; I was fighting against Nazis at home and abroad.

I took a deep breath and sighed, releasing my last claim to a long life. The grounds men packed Lena to the hilt with napalm, a new explosive designed to ignite an all-consuming fire. I meticulously built up the nerve to crash her into a secret bomb laboratory in the back woods of France. She always brought me home, yet I prepared to send us both to our doom.

* * * *

Twelve hours later

My last sight of Lena was of her plunging into and disintegrating an uninteresting building deep in the woods, guarded neither by men, sand bags, or flak batteries. I observed all this in my death spiral, and I wondered if it was the right target. It was the first thing I can recall destroying that wasn't fighting back.

"Goodbye, sweet Lena," I lamented. I ejected instinctively 150 feet above the target. I was close enough to insure that Lena struck her target and to ride the shockwave of the blast. I remember thinking that whatever bomb they built surely couldn't surpass the show that Lena just put on. *God have mercy on our souls if it could,* I thought. The major Oklahoma newspapers and those in Berlin posted virtually the same headline a week later: *Inept Negro Pilot Crashes Plane on First Mission.*

I prayed drifting back to Earth that I, too, would die on impact. My ego was simply too big to live the rest of my life on government handouts with a broken and disfigured body. The massive shockwave cleanly snapped my left shinbone in midair. It blew me over a mile away from the obliterated target. I don't remember much of what happened between the shockwave and my landing in a grove of trees.

For good and very definite reasons, I expected not to live through the night for the first time in my life. Lena was my protector, and she was gone, while I floated helplessly into enemy controlled territory. My parachute caught in a blighted and leafless oak tree in the French countryside, and I hung there helpless, barely able to move and without even the cover of mature summer leaves. I hung semi-conscious fifteen feet above the ground with a broken leg, hyper-extended shoulders, and blast burns around the midsection.

Hope appeared on the horizon some time later. A young French woman climbed the tree to cut me down. At first, I thought she was a teenage boy because she was dressed in men's clothing. Her heavy boots, a dark tweed overcoat, brown wool trousers, and a black hat pulled tightly over her head led to honest confusion on my part. I didn't realize she was a woman until I caught her scent. She smelled of the delicate and sweet honeysuckle that grew wild in Oklahoma. She removed two of the three straps holding me to the parachute before I passed out the first time.

I awoke to the calls of a Nazi SS officer emerging alone from the brush before she loosened the last buckle completely. He fired a single shot from his pistol directly into my Mae West. The sudden, sharp pain shocked me back into clear consciousness. I remember losing control over my head and arms and feeling the sensation of warm blood running into my boots. After that, I faded in and out of existence.

The bastard shouted something to his men that I didn't understand at the time. I learned later that he said that he killed one of the Americans and to fan out five kilometers in every direction and search for others in the area; he said nothing about the woman. I heard him between fainting spells ordering her down from the tree. Semi-conscious, I saw him gesturing for her to remove her clothing. She refused and stood at attention with everything but the blindfold waiting for him to shoot her too. I expected him to shoot her, and I couldn't do a damn thing to stop him. Instead, he took the butt of his MP-40 and struck her across the face.

She tried her best to fight back, but he was well trained, too strong, and unrelentingly ruthless. Even when she was helpless, he still struck her across the face repeatedly. Eventually, she fell to the ground. It was clear to me, then, that he was planning to do more that simply take this girl into custody.

I discovered later that semiconscious and unable to defend herself, the girl thought of past opportunities she forwent to make love to men of her choosing as the Nazi hovered over her.

She had defied the convention of her day. She reached the age of twenty and remained defiantly single. She aspired to go to university and study philosophy before the war. Her girlfriends were married at eighteen, and many were well experienced before marriage. She was a prude in a country filled with people of high passion. "Joan Duce" they called her.

"I am Gunter," the Nazi said. "It is very dangerous out here at night for a woman. Littler girls like you should stay inside with their fathers and be safe. Or better yet, you should entrust yourself to strong Aryan men like me. We know how to care for you."

Later, I learned that she didn't hear him. Her thoughts were of the mayor's son. The mayor's son loved her, or at least he repeatedly said he did. The mayor's son was a beautiful man, tall, broad shoulders, strong hands, jet-black hair, and hazel eyes. He was desirable, a well-to-do gentleman, and a passionate kisser. She refused him. Not because of him, per se, but because of his father. The mayor was a loud, bald, and wiry man with pasty gray skin-- the way she imagined the son would look some day. She refused to spend her old age the wife of a loud, bald, gray man.

She thought now that refusing to share herself with him seemed silly in light of what was about to happen to her. It was even a lost opportunity to experience first love from one who would at least recognize her face in a crowd, a lover who knew her name, who proclaimed his love for her.

"He's touching me. I can feel him. I want to scream, but I won't give him the satisfaction of hearing my suffering. AAAH! Did he hear that--no--no-why are you doing this? Please don't do this. I will look at his face, yes. I'll remember every crease, every inch of it. I'll sear your image in my mind, and someday I'll make you pay for what you're doing to me. Get your filthy hands off of me! Did I say that? Did he hear me? Okay, okay, I'm opening my eyes now. I see you! Can you see me? I am a person--I have feelings! No! No! Don't hit me. He doesn't want me to see his face. He's ashamed. How dare you be ashamed, you grotesque bastard. You have no right to show shame, none! I will look at you. I WILL LOOK AT YOU! No! Stop...stop hitting me! Stop! Close my eyes, pray to God in heaven--Mother Mary deliver me, Mother Mary deliver me...."

She thought of what she could do just to survive. "Lie still and maybe he won't hurt me. Maybe he'll do it and just leave. Maybe I will still be able to bear children. Oh my God. My God!--what if I bear his child? I will spew him out--there will be no innocent child. I will survive. This cannot be happening to me. I am a soldier at war--can't he see that? I am not a woman--I'm a soldier. He is supposed to kill me, like he did the American. Fire a bullet in my head, you sorry bastard, and be decorated by your treacherous Fuehrer. That's what I expect, that's the honorable way to die--not like this. I won't be a wayside convenience for a brute.

"I wish for an off button. I would push it to end my life right now. Maybe he'll kill me afterwards."

She contemplated the best place to aim a gun to kill herself--to her head to wipe out any memory even in a corpse of what he did to her or to her insides to wipe out any evidence of his presence and decimate his putrid seed.

"Maybe I'll provoke him when he's done. Tell him he's a lousy lover, small and uninteresting. I'll spit in the face of his Aryan arrogance. Challenge his manhood and surely then he'll destroy this soiled body. What are the German words I need?" she thought.

While all this was the girl's world, I barely clung to life, still hanging in the tree. I cut myself down in what I believed were my last few moments alive. I fell freely and collapsed into the ground like a piece of overripe fruit. I decided that I couldn't waste the strength to break my fall. I reserved it for something else. That bastard may have called in my numbers, but I'd be damned if I would let him ravage that girl while I still breathed. He should have planted that bullet between my eyes. That was his first mistake.

The fall should have hurt. It must've hurt, but I didn't feel anything when I hit the ground. Or at least, I didn't recognize any new pain on top of that already racking my wrecked body. I did feel my organs shutting down slowly. Death was a wild fire sweeping through my body one neighborhood at a time and leaving nothing in its wake. He heard me hit the ground. He looked up from his sin, but my crumpled, bloodied form barely registered in his mind. He obviously didn't believe in ghosts. That was his second mistake.

My hands were still strong, though, and I pulled myself across the ground in his direction. He was hungry, that one, so hungry that his senses were all directed toward her. He prepared to devour her completely and leave nothing worthy of humanity. I wondered why she didn't cry out or if I just couldn't hear her. Maybe the blood clotted in my ears and blocked my hearing. But then, I don't know that I wanted to hear. It angered me even more that he kept hitting her for no reason. The son-of-a-bitch just kept hitting her!

He ripped open her trousers and tore off her underwear with unrestrained ferocity. And then he removed his clothes calmly and methodically. You would've thought that he was preparing to crawl into a warm bed for a good night's sleep. The perfectly polished black boots came off first, and then he tucked his socks inside. He undressed without taking his eyes off of her. He studied her and planned his assault step by step. He folded the pants carefully to preserve the crease. He removed his jacket one arm at a time, pulling gently from the bottom of the sleeve. He laid it over a bush with care to avoid wrinkles.

He's done this before, I remember thinking. There was a certain ritualism about how he proceeded, about how he hit her, and about how he refused to look her in the eye. He sat fully astride her small hips and ran his hands over her exposed breasts before sliding his body down over hers. He reached down to place himself inside of her. I rose on my knees above him.

I was close enough to see the brown birthmark in the small of his back. I'd be damned if it didn't have the shape of a colored man's fist raised high and defiantly. I wondered how it got past Hitler's race purity crazies. The raised fist beckoned me. Warm drops of my free flowing colored blood splattered on the back of his Aryan neck. Only then did Gunter Schmidt, the blonde, blue-eyed, highly decorated Nazi SS Officer turn his head and his eyes towards me.

There is a kind of fear that enters a man's eyes when he knows death is imminent. Once you see it, you never forget it. I saw it for the first time that day. In an instant, his eyes went from disbelief, to sadness, to bitter anger, and finally to the fear that follows an instantaneous assessment of a life poorly lived. The final seconds of life may be the only time in our lives when having done good works actually counts for something.

This one, this man I could tell was a sexual predator by nature. He fought this war for the solitary purpose of hunting down and devouring women. He relished war because he didn't have to limit his victims to the weak. He could move freely among the people and prey on strong women--women who would otherwise have drawn strength and vengeance from a civilized society. What I saw in his eyes informed me that I couldn't blame Gunter Schmidt on the Nazis. Over his brief life, he left the wreckage of dozens of innocent German, Polish, and now French women in his wake. But the sum total of his victims' pain and anguish visited him in the last few seconds of his miserable life. Their shame and anguish became his shame and anguish.

"Your time is up, you fuckin' coward!" I said.

I fell on the butt of my field knife. I could feel the blade slicing through his spinal cord and finding its way to his decayed heart.

That was all I remembered of that day. That was all I ever expected to remember again.

The girl, Marie, told me the rest. She hid my broken body until she and her father could come for me. She told me that she dressed the SS Officer in my jumpsuit and bashed his face beyond recognition with a stone. She also strung my dog tags around his neck. I wanted to tell her he was already dead, but I couldn't. She wouldn't have heard me anyway. His unit will believe that he is the shot down American pilot when they retrieve the body. Maybe the Jerrys would label Schmidt a deserter, and he'd find no honor in Germany either.

They hid me in a four by four by eight crawl space under the floorboards of a cow barn on their farm for the next several months. Marie nursed me back to health hour by hour.

"Series of the World, 1943: the beginning game in the Bronx, Yankees of New York, 4, Cardinals of St. Louis, 2. Gordon ran home to Yankees. Series of the World game 2: stadium of the Yankees of New York, Cardinals of St. Louis, 4 and Yankees of New York, 3. Marion and Sanders ran home to Cardinals. 68,578 fanatics attend and Cooper of St. Louis pitches them out." She wrote down baseball scores picked up from American Armed forces radio and read them back to me daily while I lay in a coma. I especially remembered the 1943 World Series scores.

A doctor working for the Résistance visited me when he could and removed the bullet and eight ounces of shrapnel from my legs and torso. Though I lost a lot of blood, Gunter's bullet passed through my body and lodged in my back muscle without hitting any vital organs.

Marie's father insisted that she hide too whenever German soldiers were around. She and I shared a cramped crawl space under a vat of milk whenever a Nazi patrol was in the area. The strong smell of the sour milk threw off the dogs. The warmth of her body next to mine gave me comfort and peace. I spent the first few weeks in hiding falling in and out of consciousness.

Chapter Ten

We dance round in a ring and suppose
But the Secret sits in the middle and knows

Robert Frost

Visions from Uncle Roy's Journal

I dreamed without ceasing my first few weeks on that French farm.

I drifted in and out of long deep sleeps while my body healed itself. My mind was content to entertain itself when left alone by the impulses of unpredictable life. I didn't dream fantastic dreams, but blissful, peaceful ones that substituted for an unavailable waking reality. My body wasn't tired, just battered, torn and mangled by the inherent stupidity of war. So my dreams allowed me snatches of peace in the midst of unbearable agony and an escape while my body healed.

I recall one dream in particular. Maybe it wasn't a dream, but more of an encounter or a vision. That's the right word, vision. My eyelids floated open and closed, and my view of the outside world passed by similar to a poorly spliced movie reel. Images of the French countryside flickered by and were gradually replaced by scenes from my Oklahoma youth.

I floated disembodied above my dozing form in the town square of late 1930s Okmulgee, Oklahoma. My head bobbed up and down rhythmically while sitting on an ornate cast iron bench depicting the Oklahoma Land Rush. The bench sat on the edge of the lush, green lawn of the sandstone Creek Nation Council House. The cast iron work depicted covered wagons racing across the Oklahoma prairie leaving miles of dust in their wake. Dispassionate natives watched from the sidelines while the lands given them were being taken away again. I was never sure if that bench was condemning or celebrating the Oklahoma Land Rush.

The Creek Council House itself was the hall of government for a defanged Native American world capital. The seat of government of Muscogee-Creek Nation was the 19th century model for the 20th century's Bantu stands. The council house was neutral ground in Jim Crow's Oklahoma and that made it the perfect place

71

for a brown man to dawdle when a gentle corn sweetened prairie breeze swept through clacking pecan trees. The clean air and the bright sun over tree cast shade made the day a hair's breadth shy of Oklahoma perfect.

A familiar person sat down next to me.

"Nate...Nate Washington, is that you? What are you doing in Europe, man?" I asked.

"I'm looking for you," Nate replied.

"Looking for me? Where's your uniform? Is it over? Did those Nazi bastards finally give up the ghost? If it ain't over, man, they'll shoot you for being a spy...that's at least two reasons why they'll shoot yah black ass."

"You don't need a uniform here...look around," Nate said.

I looked carefully and the rest of 1940s Okmulgee came into sharp focus. The Creek Nation Counsel House Square, the oil boom banks and the purveyor's offices were all there just where I remembered them. The kind of people I knew for most of my life milled around filling up time with their daily routines. They flowed in streams of red, black, and white uniformly here and there but never mixing on the small town's streets. After a short time in Europe, I learned that America was unique in that way: united under one flag, yet divided and distinct similar to its shapes and colors. There were western people, Confederate babies, barely free Freedmen, homeless natives, and all sorts of self-anointed saints and sinners out and about.

"How are you doing, Roy? Is it alright to call you that, Roy, I mean? That's what she calls you," said Nate.

"You can call me dog, for all I care, man. It's just good to see a friendly face, somebody from home. I was one scared mutha'-fuckah out there, man. Who'd thought I'd be glad to git back in god-damned Jim Crow Land."

"It was good to hear from you the other day."

"You must be thinking of somebody else, man, 'cause I haven't seen you in years. Matter o' fact, the only time we ever spoke was in J. J. Newberry's shortly before you passed-ah..." I paused, and panic filled my voice.

"You' dead, man! O' my God! I didn't make it, did I, Nate? You come to get me? That's why this place seems alright now." I was frantic.

"I've come to talk to you, Roy, that's all. After all, like I said, you called me. I didn't call you, man.

"Don't you remember; just before you ejected from Lena Horne? Remember the scent of burning gasoline? Remember the sound of Lena's engine disintegrating into flying fragments of hot metal. Remember, you cried out to me from the very bottom of your soul. You called me in a way I couldn't ignore."

"Man, when that shit happened, I was praying my natu'al black ass off, something I hadn't even thought about doing in years. You shouldah heard me: Holy this, Most High that, Almighty so-and-so. I screamed like a woman; I mustah sounded like one of them ol' sisters gittin' happy in church. I said it all, but what I didn't do was call you, Nate."

"Oh, but you did. You see, I *am* Holy God, I am Most High God, and I am Almighty God. Roy, you called me all right. Or should I say you called *on* me."

"Too many impossibilities," I thought to myself. "Okay, okay... if you're God, where did you come from? Who created *you*?"

"You created me and every man, woman and child who ever believed in me."

"So what you're saying is that you are a figment of my imagination?"

"What I am saying is that I am the substance of human imagination."

"Well if we created you, then who created us."

"I created you. Time is irrelevant to me; that's the way you made me. I am in the beginning, and I am in the end."

"Oh, I get it; we created you so you could create us. I guess everything is just human imagination manifest. That's not much of a miracle."

"The miracle is that there are far more of you who imagine good in the universe than those who imagine evil, Roy."

I was being asked to believe that the Supreme Being, God in the form of Nate Washington, sat not more than two feet away from me. I contemplated the impossibility of a perfect, omnipotent God and a fatally flawed Nate Washington intersecting anywhere in time and space. It seemed highly unlikely, but then life itself is unlikely.

Nate Washington was perhaps the weakest example of a man I ever knew. Physically, he was a painfully thin man, less than five feet tall, sickly in appearance, and his voice registered high in a woman's range, which always sent him to the alto section of the church choir with the women. He didn't even bother to overcompensate. Most little guys did with a big mouth, bigger fists, and an extra large ego. He was just a little man with an even smaller spirit.

Betty, Nate's wife, on the other hand, towered over him at 6'2" tall; and she must have weighed well over 200lbs. The only thing bigger than Betty's bad-ass attitude was her actual fleshy big ass; hence her nickname Big Booty Betty. She publicly and privately dictated their relationship. Unlike the other dominant women of her day, she never felt the need to uphold a public pretense that Mr. Big Booty Betty was in charge.

The men of Okmulgee, at least those of us confined to the darker side of the color line, called him Peck behind his back. The under-employed sidewalk denizens of the day joked that the skull under his tightly processed hairdo was covered with knots left by Betty's frequent pecking. From time to time, even Nate's children, especially his boys, were ashamed of their father's apparent weakness. They were rarely seen in public with both their parents.

Beneath the surface, though, I discovered one day that Nate's only true failing was that Betty was a free woman in a time and place when men defined themselves by their domination over women and children. That single failing, though, was sufficient to guarantee his outcast status on the rugged dusty plains of depression era Okmulgee.

I talked to Nate only once before that day. The events surrounding that conversation were the kind that you never forget. It was a brutally hot August day. White milky sweat dripped from under Mr. Jones' horse's saddle, hot and irritated children whined in the distance, and I chased a dusty breeze from one block to the next.

Oklahoma in August is an irresistible and frequent resting place for intense summer heat and humidity. Unbroken by high elevations, heavily treed forests or cool ocean breezes, the heat lingers longer, burns hotter, and singes more already frayed tempers there than any place on Earth. On one particularly blistering August day, a tired and sweat-drenched Nate stumbled over his fatigue and accidentally dropped a bag of Betty's carefully selected groceries on the sidewalk outside Neal's Grocery.

I watched him kneel down apologetically and salvage what he

could from the steaming pavement. His efforts, however, went unrewarded. When Betty saw what happened, she raised her open hand above his head. Nate began to stand with several badly bruised apples cupped in his hands. When Nate's eyes met hers, Betty's powerful right hand came down hard across Nate's left cheek. Nate's head followed the force of the blow and crashed into a wall adjacent to the walkway. Heads for a block and a half turned toward the ringing sound of flesh crashing against flesh.

Nate tried to stand up quickly with his face torn and bloodied. He wanted people to think, "That didn't hurt *me*." But he held his balance for less than an instant. While staring pleadingly into Betty's eyes, his knees buckled, and he dropped to the concrete sidewalk. Betty then wedged her right foot against his ribs and push-kicked him over with the piercing force of her oversized pointy-heeled shoe.

I watched Betty turn and walk away from Nate without an ounce of regret or hesitation. I saw her climb into their pickup and drive off leaving him broken, bloodied, and whimpering on the sidewalk.

Stunned, semiconscious and pitiful, Nate buried his face in his hands and wept silently. I could hear him mumbling between sobs, "Please forgive me."

But Betty was far gone by then; she didn't hear his plea for forgiveness. I imagined she assumed that he begged for her forgiveness and whispered to herself driving away, "*Forgive* you, my big, fleshy, black ass."

Stunned townsfolk for two blocks around stared in quiet curiosity at Nate. He was as strange to their eyes as a twisted hapless circus freak. It was not uncommon in 1930s Oklahoma to see a man slap-down a woman in public, especially if she "got out of her place," or for a child to receive a corrective swat across the back of the head. But none of these rugged Sooners could recall ever seeing a woman slap down a man the way Betty did Nate. Many could still hear the echo of the blow. Not one of them could draw on a preprogrammed response to what they saw. They didn't know whether to laugh, cry, ridicule, applaud, or condemn. A few men did, however, cast warning glares at their wives. Glares that said with words, "expect a preemptive beating when you get home just so you won't get the wrong idea." But most people just stared blankly at the weeping man brought to his knees by the open hand of a barely provoked woman.

Driven by an impulse I neither wanted nor understood, I stepped outside of my private self that day. I buried the self that never gets involved and let the helpful me shine through. I went to Nate, lifted him from the sidewalk, brushed him off, straightened his clothes, and carried him away from the site of his humiliation. I didn't know why then, but I felt an irresistible compulsion to rescue Nate, to reassure him, to save him. Nate's bizarre, little world crumbled before him in a humiliating, public spectacle. Betty left him with only his biological essence.

Nate swore off the rest of the world for Betty. He was content to have only her in his universe until that day. Now Betty was gone--gone in a spectacular ball of fire, leaving his universe void and without form.

"Tha'...tha...that's it," Nate whispered to me in stuttered speech.

"What's it?" I asked.

"I...I...I don't know. But ain't that what you think I oughttah say?"

"I ain't you, Nate. I guess you oughtta say what it is you feel."

"Right now, I don't feel nothin'."

"Then, I think that's progress."

"Did you see which way she went?" asked Nate.

"Looks like she drove home."

Betty sacrificed his last bit of social capital on a very public altar. I took Nate to the colored section of the JJ Newberry's Restaurant and listened patiently while he talked about his marriage. It became increasingly clear to me that all of Nate's passions began and ended with Betty. Even then, within minutes of his gross public humiliation, Nate still adored her. He could not find, or at least he refused to admit, any fault in her.

"If I been more careful...she sho 'nough loves her some apples...I shouda been lookin' where I was goin'. If I was just more careful," Nate rambled.

Here's a man who's been condemned to do one thing, and one thing only in life: love that woman. How his daddy must've sinned against God for such a curse to befall his son. What manner of man is this? I asked myself.

My prairie-bred mind struggled to deconstruct Nate Washington and rearrange him in a way that I could comprehend.

The tide turned swiftly, and Nate decided he wanted Betty back.

"I need to comfort her...to let her know it's all right," he said.

I wondered, *How could such a simple man love any woman, and especially that one, so much?* Nate's love for Betty was endless, unconditional, and without demand. It was a vast ocean wider, fuller, and deeper than any man could possibly comprehend. He surrendered all advantage to her. Strangely, aside from the events of the day, I recall that Nate always seemed happy--happy despite being lambasted by the world around him. And Nate only regretted that he retained so little of himself to sacrifice on Betty's altar.

The pity and disgust I felt for Nate dissipated following that afternoon in Newberry's.

You pity people who are helpless and suffering, and he ain't suffering or helpless. He willingly and freely surrendered all to that woman, I thought.

What I began to feel was an unnatural mixture of admiration for and fear of Nate Washington. I admired his ability to love and trust so deeply despite the condemnation of the world around him. I feared that the insanity of Nate's ability to love and trust so deeply might infect me and break my tenuous hold on my already ill-defined manhood under Jim Crow.

The last three words I spoke to Nate, again driven by undeniable impulse, were, "Keep on loving."

Betty found us in the colored section of the JJ Newberry's restaurant at about 5:00 p.m. I heard that she searched most of downtown looking for Nate for several hours. She pursued him for the first time in their painfully unbalanced lives together. Every few minutes in her pursuit, she turned her head and looked down behind her where she no doubt expected to see Nate in his usual place. But he wasn't in his place hanging on her dress tail or ready to cater to her every desire. Betty must have experienced the horrifying specter of loneliness in Nate's brief absence for the first time in their unbalanced lives together.

"Have I finally gone too far? Has he finally left me?" She must've pondered over those questions in their hours of separation. The Betty that ran to our table was not the large and foreboding woman I remembered from a few hours earlier. I sized her up carefully, and I considered defending Nate from another onslaught. But Betty seemed to crumble before us instead of attacking. Her imposing largeness collapsed the way shattered glass falls from a window frame. She went down on her knees awash in tears and begged Nate to forgive her.

"I know you is a man, and I is a woman. And the Good Lawd knows I got no cause to treat you the way I do. Please find it in what's left of yah heart to forgive me," Betty pleaded in contrite and sincere words foreign to her tongue. I wasn't sure if I actually heard her speak the next three words, or I just felt them through the force of her sincerity, but I certainly thought she said, "I surrender too."

Nate finally won a long brutal war of attrition that he waged by surrendering to the rampaging enemy over and over again. Battlefield after battlefield was soaked with his blood alone. Finally, the enemy grew weary of war for its own sake and in awe of Nate's fortitude.

"There is nothing to forgive. You'll never again have to test my love for you. That makes this the happiest day of my life," Nate answered.

Nate embraced Betty with the kind of embrace that made it impossible to tell where one of them began or the other ended. They walked out into public Okmulgee again this time locked together by bonds that before the last four hours were invisible to me. They disembarked onto the street, and I overheard Nate whisper to Betty, "I love you so, my dear. I will until the end of time."

I thought to myself, *Maybe, just maybe, now Betty understands what he means.*

Now, there sat Almighty God, in every sense of the word, embodied in the paradoxical Nate Washington. Nate was perhaps the weakest, yet the strongest man I ever knew. There sat the creator of the universe in the fleshly form of a human mouse with the heart of a lion. My mind overflowed with questions I needed to ask Him.

"Why was I even born?" I asked God.

"You were born for Nate."

"I barely knew the man, and besides, I gave him nothing."

"You were there the day he suffered mortal humiliation. You answered my call, and you rescued him. You took his confession. You witnessed his testimony of love. You tempered his passions at a time when no one else dared. You saved a man who loved a woman on the order that I love all of creation. That's saying something," God said.

"I guess I got the Holy Ghost after all. You know they wouldn't let me be baptized 'cause I didn't get the Holy Ghost. I guess now I've served my purpose for living," I said.

"You have served my purpose for your living."

"What right have you to dictate my life?"

"What life do you have but that which I have given you?"

"Am I dead?"

"You are not dead. For you, death has no meaning."

"If I am not dead, but I've served your purpose for my life, then why am I still here?"

"As I said, you have served *my* purpose for your life. Everybody serves my purpose for their lives one way or the other, willingly or unwillingly. It's what they do with their life afterwards that makes the difference in perpetuity. Now, it's time for you to find your own reason for living."

"Wait a minute. You mean I'm free. I've paid my debt to the God of the universe for a second-class life in a belligerent backwards world?" I said excitedly if a bit sarcastic.

"You have always been free--everybody's free. The only obstacles in your life are those of your own making. I ask only one thing of every man, woman, and child. What I asked of you, you have done and done well. What you do from this day forward is for you to decide."

"Why was I...no, why is anyone born into such a cruel world?"

"Creation is viciously mean and exceedingly joyful, deadly and life giving, brutally ugly and shockingly beautiful. You see and know only that which you permit yourself to see and know. I have not determined your steps, but I will honor a journey well traveled."

"What does that mean? I don't understand," I pleaded. I never received an answer.

"Game 3 series of the World: Yankees of New York 6, Cardinals of St. Louis, 2, no one ran home. Game 4 of the Series of the World: Yankees of New York 2, Cardinals of St. Louis 1, no one ran home," Marie read.

I awoke from my long dream to a woman's soft, gentle hand stroking my face. The warmth emanating from her hand against my anguished face brought more pleasure to me than I'd ever experienced. I felt wanted, watched over, cared for and loved for the first time in a very long time in my brief passage from the world of dreams back to consequential reality. I opened my eyes and stared into the tear-filled blue eyes of my French caretaker, Marie. Her long, flowing, black hair fell across her shoulders and hung just above me. Again I inhaled the scent of wild Oklahoma honeysuckle about her, one of my pleasant memories of home.

I looked at her with everything that made me who I was. My natural eyes saw a woman underdressed due to the harshness of war, barely fed, and tired from a long struggle against her nation's invaders and against men who would invade her. The eyes of my heart, however, saw a soul mate, the other half of my unfinished self and every reason in the world to cling to life.

"I thought... I was losing...you," Marie said in halting English.

"I have lost myself. Please help me find my way back," I responded in a barely audible whisper. "Who won the series?" I asked.

She fumbled through some handwritten notes. "Game 5 of the Series of the World: Yankees of New York 2 and Cardinals of St. Louis 0. Dickey ran home for Yankee New Yorkers. Yankee New Yorkers are declared champions of the Series of the World!"

Marie nursed me back to health in the weeks that followed. I was in love with her from the moment I first opened my eyes, but I refused to acknowledge it. All my life informed me that what I was feeling for her was wrong, and possibly even dangerous. All the typical things kept us apart in my mind: race, class, religion, language, geography, culture, the Florence Nightingale Syndrome, and, above all, fear. If I could have cleansed the prejudices of the world from my mind, perhaps we could have cleansed the world itself. But I didn't. I wouldn't.

Chapter Eleven

Marching Across France, from Uncle Roy's Journal

On June 6, 1944, Allied forces landed in Normandy, and the German grip on France weakened. German forces began their retreat in the weeks that followed, after nearly four years of occupation. It was clear by July 1944, that Allied forces would soon take Paris. The very evident German preparations to retreat from Paris were all Philippe Renoir needed to reevaluate his current alliance.

He must have known that as a collaborator his battered and mutilated body would hang dead from the nearest lamppost long before the last Panzer rolled across Paris' border headed back to Germany. He had to leave before they stopped defending all but their exit route, closed their headquarters and, worst of all, abandoned their loyal collaborators. Philippe would be most vulnerable during the time when the collaborators were cast off and before the Allies arrived. It would be then that anarchy and the insanity of mob rule would cover Paris in a blood-soaked blanket revenge. Like Cinna the Poet, even the undeserving would plead in vain for their lives. Philippe was determined not to wait until then. Philippe told Marie that he left Paris quietly for their rural farm. Seven weeks later, thinner, ragged, and filthy, he walked the last few miles to his boyhood home, arriving unexpected and unannounced. He noticed his sister's regular morning visit to the barn from the hillside where he waited out the daylight to make sure the farm wasn't being watched. He saw Marie go in to the barn to milk the cows and return a few minutes later with full liters of milk. He realized they were already hiding someone. Philippe must have resented instantly this unseen person.

Philippe stumbled out of the woods and reached the perimeter of the farm by nightfall. He was too weak to make it to the main house, so he fell beside the empty pigpens where he hoped someone would find him.

"Papa, Papa, there is a man face down in the pen," Marie called to her father.

"I'm coming, little one. Is he hurt?" her father asked.

"I don't know."

Marie ran to the enclosure to provide whatever assistance she could to the stranger until her father arrived. He was a large man, but she managed to roll him over by pulling at his worn-out clothing.

"Brother? Is it you?" Marie asked, recognizing a hint of her brother in the sunken cheeks and darkened eyes.

"Yes," a barely audible voice answered.

"Papa, hurry, it is Brother," Marie shouted.

The old man rushed to the pen with water and a first aid kit. He did not recognize his emaciated son now covered in the filth of the pigpen. There was certainly something vaguely familiar about the man. The old man never saw his worldly son so vulnerable before. He recalled that arrogance, pride, and the love of money were the dominant traits of his only boy. Not since Philippe was a child was he vulnerable or at least open to the influence of his father. Not since before his mother died did he display any apparent need for family.

Marie and her father nursed Philippe back to relative health over the next few days. They fed him skimmed milk and bread only for the first couple. He grew stronger and began to ask questions about the man living in the barn. He followed Marie into the barn on his first morning out of bed.

"Where is he? I know you're here," he called out. "I can help you."

"There is no one in the barn but us, brother," Marie replied.

"Sister, don't lie to me. I watched you from the woods for several days before I came down. I waited until I was certain the farm was not being watched, something about which you were apparently not concerned. Cows do not milk themselves, and you certainly were not milking them in the short time you were in there." Again he called, "I know you are here. Come out, let us talk."

"He's gone. We sent him away because it was too dangerous to keep both of you here. We don't have enough to eat for four people, and you are family after all. These are dangerous times, especially for you, brother," Marie replied.

"So, you have some sisterly love left for me after all--yet you chose this spy, traitor, deserter over me? What is he?"

"He was Résistance, and he would have cut your throat the first night if he had any idea who you were. So we sent him away, brother. We sent him away to protect you."

"Résistance has value, sister. I need to get out of France; the Germans are on the retreat and the Americans and British are coming. Your generosity to this one could be my ticket to a new life."

"He is gone, I told you. I know nothing about him. It is not our way to ask names, family history, or about the comings and goings of such people. We give food, shelter, clothing, and a warm bed and pray they don't kill us in our sleep. You would know this if you had--"

"If I had what, sister?" Philip asked grabbing her by the arms.

"If you believed in filling something more than your belly and your pockets, brother. Now let me go. I am not a child anymore," Marie demanded.

Philippe stood over Marie; he was easily twice her size. His eyes suddenly darkened, his massive chest expanded, and his voice dropped to a low growl.

"I have something more important at stake, sister...my life! And let me be clear. I value my life more than anything else in this miserable world. I will do whatever I deem necessary to preserve it. Do not toy with me about this man. Where did he go?"

Marie loved and admired her big brother with all of her sisterly heart as a child. Though he was much older, he always made time for her in the old days. He'd tickle her until her eyes filled with water and read her stories about other places and times beyond their small village. But the brother she knew died suddenly and prematurely when their mother died. He lost all faith, all hope, and all pride. He drifted between bouts of intense despair and uncontrollable rage. But she'd never feared him, even during his rapid transformation. Something in his eyes that day, though, made her fear him. Something made her think that she was not his beloved, little sister anymore but an obstacle in his path to damnation. An obstacle he'd crush without reservation to get what he wanted.

A slow-moving tide of sadness swept over Marie. What she loved about her brother was apparently long dead in him. What stood before her were the worst parts of him that absolutely refused to die.

Marie pulled back from Philippe and fell over the milking stool onto the barn floor.

"Where is he, you stupid bitch!" shouted Philip.

He stood over her sweating from every pore in his body, and breathing heavily. Every vein in his wrinkled neck gorged with rushing blood. His brow and lids were violently angry, yet his eyes seemed cold and devoid of sympathy.

"He may very well be my ticket out of France. I will slice your brain with a scythe if I must to find his whereabouts. I refuse to die out here in this filth with dirt under my fingernails and the stench of disease in the air. I will not! " Philippe grabbed Marie's collar with his left hand and cocked his clenched right fist.

It was then that I, the hidden fugitive, launched my body down from the hayloft onto Philippe's back. The big man crumbled under the force of the impact. I raised myself from the dirt floor and set upon Philippe with powerful unrelenting blows to the head. I pounded Philippe's face into the dirt floor until his bloody features formed a cast in the soil.

Philippe was unconscious from the initial impact of my body and never knew what hit him, but I didn't stop the assault. I was in such a rage that I didn't realize that he wasn't resisting. It barely registered when I grabbed the spade from the rack and prepared to plunge it deep into 's exposed back.

"No, stop! He's my brother," Marie cried.

"Your brother is dead, Marie. If he were alive, he and I would be sharing a drink and catching up on the latest news from the front. This lump of flesh could not be your brother," I responded.

"But he is a man. And you do not have the power to give life or to take it away."

"This life I can take away. He would have killed you...this is war...he would have...you're all I have."

"And I'd be dead and there would be no one here to stop you from killing him but you. I would hope that you would decide to let him live and let justice be done where it is properly done."

I threw the shovel at the barn door with such force that I drove the blade six inches into the wood. I took Marie in my arms and inspected her body with anxious eyes and careful hands. I fawned over her like a parent counting the fingers and toes of a newborn and hoping for perfection. I wasn't satisfied until I accounted for all that was Marie before I took my next breath. I held her against my body whilst wishing there was no war, no Philippe, and nothing in the world between.

Sadly, we felt the specter of separation descending upon us. We knew that this embrace and kiss would be one to remember and cherish over a long and lonely separation.

I returned to the loft, having never actually having seen or wanting to see Philippe's face.

Marie and Papa dragged his unconscious body into the main house where he recuperated once again. I had to leave and get to the Allied lines before the Nazis discovered me. Marie packed me a couple of pounds of food and drew a crude map to the American front lines, which I memorized and destroyed. She rehearsed several key phrases with me that the Résistance would recognize in the event I needed their help.

Philippe left his home unannounced in the middle of the night seven days later. He notified the local German commander that there's a fugitive on the farm, perhaps an American spy holding his family hostage. He personally escorted them back to the farm and watched dispassionately while foot soldiers roughed up his father and ransacked his heritage. The old man stared at Philippe through the entire ordeal.

The Germans uncovered enough evidence of another person living there even though the "spy" wasn't found.

"Where is he?" they demanded.

"I do not have a son, so I hired a vagrant to help me around the place. We paid him with food and shelter. These are the things an old man must do in these times if he has no son. My son is dead. He died before the war from grief and greed," the old man said, staring directly and coldly into Philippe's unflinching eyes.

The farm in Giverny would never again be a refuge for Philippe. He returned to Paris reluctantly and was truly alone in the world for the first time in his life. The Allies marched toward Paris as the Germans retreated.

Thousands of French Communists joined the ranks of the Résistance on the heels of the German invasion of the Soviet Union. Again, Philippe would name names and hitch his wagon to the new rising power in France. In exchange, he got protection, freedom, and eventually, a new name and a life in America.

Chapter Twelve

The ceremony of innocence is drowned;
The best lack all conviction, while the worst
Are full of passionate intensity

William Butler Yeats

The Retreat

The British and American forces blasted their way through Normandy, sending the Germans in full retreat. The Allies dropped hundreds of tons of bombs in the weeks before the Normandy invasion on strategic targets in Vernon in an effort to cut off anticipated German retreats and weaken their resolve. The emboldened Résistance in Vernon engaged the Germans in ground combat in the streets of the city. The tide of the war was clearly turning, and Giverny was close enough to the battlefields to smell the powder of destruction heavy on the air. Uncle Roy wrote the following to Grandma about the upheaval of this time:

Dear Lil Sis, I made my way back to the American forces over seventeen weary days by weaving my way through Nazi lines and tagging along with war ravaged civilians. I owe my safe arrival to the assistance I received from the rejuvenated Résistance. They were fully engaged in the war effort and, for the first time, bent on destroying the German capacity to do war rather than simply being an irritant to it. Marie stayed behind at my insistence because I felt she would be safer at home and the Giverny cell needed her leadership. I believed that the war would be over soon anyway, and we could then be together and have a normal life.

Marie, however, was still the whole substance of my private thoughts. I'd often drift off into deep and elaborate daydreams about us at risk to my personal safety. I thought more about Marie in those seventeen days than I did about my hope of sanctuary behind the American lines. Part of me wanted to forgo a return to duty and run back to Marie. After all, I did my part for the war effort.

Reason informed me that the American lines were one step closer to the only home I ever knew. My heart told me, however, that each step closer to my countrymen took me further away from the new home where I truly belonged. But we were young, and the war was near its end, so I downplayed our separation.

"Mark my words, Marie, I will be back. It'll take more than a world war to keep us apart," I promised. Every word I spoke to her seemed wrong for the moment. I realized soon enough that it was the moment itself that was wrong. It was one of those times when the head ruled the heart, where duty trumped love and where concern for personal safety overrode the rightness of flesh embracing flesh. The words were wrong and the moment was wrong because I let the immediate circumstances dictate my actions when the urges of my heart should have ruled the day.

I spent most of the daylight in the dank cellars of private homes, rat-infested barns, and out-of-the-way Résistance hideouts. You might say the French version of the Underground Railroad shuttled me to safety from our common enemies. I remember the kindness and bravery of a one-eyed Frenchman named Daniel in particular. He seemed to move me through German lines with the efficiency and smoothness of a hot knife through butter. He harbored an intense and almost pathological disdain for the Germans. Daniel was the first person to share the rumors with me about the mass murder of Jews, Roma, homosexuals and others in German detention camps. He pledged to spend the rest of his life avenging his brothers if it were so.

Daniel led me the last few miles of the way to the American lines. We walked up to the American guard post on the base camp perimeter triumphantly one damp Sunday morning. We believed we were heroes.

"Lieutenant Booker T. Lankster, United States Army Air Corp, reporting for duty," I said standing smartly at attention and saluting the lower ranked guard.

"Hands up! Get them up now and hit the ground! Hit the ground now, god-damn-it!" the guards shouted while holding us in their sites.

Daniel didn't expect a reward for helping me, but he did expect a measure of praise and perhaps a hot meal and a flattering footnote in the war's history. I expected the same and maybe a high level debriefing on German troop movements, armaments and the capabilities of the Résistance. We were greeted instead with suspicion and contempt. We were separated at the gate, dragged to separate detention areas, and interrogated. Daniel was released hungry and disoriented sixteen hours later. Our shoddy treatment was enough to make him wonder if the Résistance chose the right ally.

I was officially detained and branded a deserter fifteen hours later. My interrogators didn't accept my explanation for how I got there. Colored soldiers weren't allowed in frontline combat positions alongside whites, and the battlefield commanders refused to believe that I could possibly be a downed fighter pilot. Suspicion turned into accusation and accusation into contempt when no army records listed me in their colored infantry ranks. They locked me in a temporary jail segregated from the white American deserters and the white Germans.

"I am in the Army Air Corps. I am a fighter pilot. Please contact General Zinny; he can identify me," I pleaded.

"How do you know Zinny? How many other American commanders do you know? How long were you watching us? Who plays first base for the Yankees? Zinny doesn't know you."

We American prisoners were forced to tag, identify, and haul dead civilian and Nazi bodies during our detention. Hauling those remains brought me closer to human carnage and destruction than at any time in the war. The other prisoners and I would jockey for position whenever the guard came to take us to work. We wanted to haul the freshly dead bodies--usually the last moved. They didn't smell of rotting, maggot-infested offal. And body parts were less likely to separate from the newly dead--that made them less dead to us and, therefore, more palatable.

Pilots hit distant targets, and we destroyed other machines. I rarely saw the actual faces of enemy pilots, and machines didn't cry out in pain or plead for mercy. They simply sputtered, flamed out, and fell from the sky. I never saw the final tragic results of my actions. But when my hands touched death on the ground, there was no escape from the tragic consequences of our actions.

I believed that this war was necessary to the extent that necessary is a word we can apply legitimately to war. Maybe of all wars we needed to fight this one and our side needed to win. The Nazis were far worse than Jim Crow's America on the scale of human evil. They combined the hate of the Klan with unrestrained legalized force and the lethal army of a modern nation state at their disposal. Our basic human dignity compelled us to stand between them and world conquest.

I took up arms in the service side-by-side with American seg-regationists in order to eliminate a madman determined to destroy or subjugate all races different than his own. Our common enemy moderated our tendencies. But with the scent of victory in the air, I saw America's ugliness raise its head from the mud yet again.

I heard and understood something I wasn't supposed to on a work detail deep in a heavily wooded forest. A firing squad of nine fresh-faced American GIs prepared to shoot seven blind-folded, French civilians to death. There are times in the heat of battle when such executions may have been permitted, but this was not such a time. We were able to hold them captive, and they posed no immediate threat to us. I lacked the status to question the rightness or wrongness of what was about to happen. I trusted that someone in command determined that it was the right thing to do under the circumstances. Status or the lack thereof can be a barrier to action.

"They ain't nothin' but red Jews anyway. They're the niggers of Europe and the brains of the Communist infestation of the French Résistance. We will not allow France to fall into the hands of the communists. We will not tolerate them," the colonel said in French to a hooded informer. I overheard, or more precisely, understood, since neither man considered that I might understand French.

The hooded informer seemed to agree, and he promised that he could identify others in time. The informer returned to the camp, leaving me with a shovel, the colonel, and seven hand-picked soldiers standing one hundred yards to the east with seven blindfolded Résistance members in their sights.

The colonel couldn't have known that I spoke French, or he would have been more careful in his conversation with the inform-er. The disgusted expression on my face though probably gave me away, and he called me over. I have never considered myself a par-ticularly moral person. Life is too short, and we were always too poor to stand as pillars of social morality. It seemed to me that morality left very little for poor folks to do with themselves except work for rich folks and insuring their daily lives were better. But I acted outside of myself again for the second time in my life that day. I took a moral stand.

I shuffled over to the colonel with my best full-toothy grin and low hung head. It was the best Step-'n-fetch-it impersonation in my repertoire. He probably would have told me to leave the shovel if he considered me a threat. He would have tied me up in the firing line too if he knew about the close kinship I formed with the Résistance over the last several months. His ignorance was my cloak.

"Boy, we gone execute these murderers, and I wants you to burn the bodies and bury the ashes in that pit over yonder."

"These men and men like them are my friends. I will not allow you to execute them," I whispered standing within two feet of him. "You will not hurt them," I ordered.

"Who do you--?" was all he managed to say before my right hand grabbed and squeezed closed his vocal chords and my left hand lifted his sidearm from its holster.

"You should always keep your sidearm snapped in its holster unless you plan to use it right away, sir. Otherwise a malcontent might lift it from the holster before you do. *Où vous étaient quand ils ont enseigné cette leçon dans l'entraînement fondamental?* (Where were you when they taught that lesson in basic training?)"

"Agh! Agh...."

"No, no, no...don't...try...to speak. They can't hear you and releasing air only allows me to tighten my grip. Your sidearm is now pointed at your frontal cortex. Did you know a bullet can pass through the frontal lobe, scramble it like eggs and, yet you can survive the trauma? That is, of course, assuming you don't bleed to death before help arrives. If you do survive, you'll be fed baby food for the balance of your miserable life from a veteran's hospital bed somewhere. Probably spoon fed by a busty blonde bombshell that you won't know what to do with anymore. You don't want that now, do you?"

(Shakes head no.)

"Fine, then this is what we're going to do. You're going to call your men and tell them to release the condemned men. Then tell them to let the releasees run for their lives. Tell them to fire all their rounds over the releassee's heads so they'll remember who's in charge now. Got it?"

(Shakes head affirmatively.)

"If you're a good boy and you do just what I said, I promise that instead of scrambled eggs for brains, you'll get out of this with just a small knot on the noodle and a few lost memories. Ready?"

(Shakes head yes.)

"Corporal Powell, remove the blindfolds and release the prisoners. We just wanted to teach them a lesson, boys. Let them go, but fire all your rounds over their heads so they'll know who's in charge now," said the colonel.

"Good, goooo...," were the last sounds the colonel heard for a few hours.

The colonel slipped into unconsciousness while his ad hoc firing squad squeezed off dozens of rounds into the air. I helped him safely to the ground and joined the fleeing prisoners passing nearby.

Hauling the dead bodies of German soldiers gave me some nominal value to the ongoing war effort. But even that value evaporated when I became an enemy of the American's secret war against alleged French Communists. The natural blackness of my skin would instantly discredit whatever I would say to the American power structure in my defense. The French might listen to me, though. They would want to know why we summarily executed members of the Résistance. The French wouldn't understand the American disdain for Communists even if they were allies.

I spent most my life concerned about the prospect of being dragged out of my home in the middle of the night by Oklahoma Klansmen and lynched over some perceived slight to a white woman. I feared it might happen even more during flight training in Tuskegee, Alabama. Now, I feared being hunted down in the dark forests of France and executed by my own army to cover up the crimes of others. I was now officially an enemy of the greatest military power on Earth. The only refuge left to me was a free France and the waiting arms of Marie.

I returned to Giverny and Marie in the late summer of 1944, under the protection and guidance of my new blood brothers in the Résistance. I knew then that my home was with Marie. The circumstances and my heart now left me with no other choices. I spent most of my days in hiding, and we split our nights between hastening the German retreat and laying the foundation for an eternity together.

Chapter Thirteen

...I am here
Or there, or elsewhere. In my beginning.

T.S. Eliot

A Garden for a Blind Man

Dear Lil Sis, Marie led me by the hand through a break in the wall and into a small corner of the old man's garden two weeks after we were reunited. She tended sections of the garden while its caretakers laid their lives on the line in the war. She said that she wanted me to meet a trusted, old friend who frequented the garden. She led me over the Japanese Bridge and into a thicket of lush green shrubs ringed by radiant purple irises. Six-foot tall shrubs encircled an area half canopied at the top by tall, leaning trees on the other side of the thicket. In the middle of the enclosure sat a blind man on a stump with a sketchpad in his lap.

Marie began a conversation with the man. He sat in the midst of the enclosure seemingly absorbing its essence through his pores. He sensed Marie's presence before she actually spoke, and I sensed he knew I was there also. I knew he was blind because his eyes rolled around in his head without any focus or direction and a pair of darkened glasses sat at his side. His wandering eyes proved he was never trained for seeing or the pretense of sight. He sat upright in his chair in heavily mended clothes absorbing what he could of the surroundings with his remaining senses. Marie told me his caretaker brother was in London, flying bombing missions over his French homeland in American planes.

Marie fussed over the blind man's clothing during their exchange of friendly greetings.

"I have a visitor with me today...he is a seer. You must therefore look presentable," she explained while smoothing out wrinkles in his shirt. He smiled and straightened his body to make her task easier.

"And what are you doing to make this seer more presentable to me?" he asked sarcastically.

"I have insisted that he stand before you naked so he would

not waste fine clothing that could otherwise be worn in company that would appreciate his stellar sense of fashion and taste," she answered.

"If this seer has such a sense of fashion and taste, then it begs the question, my sweet, what is he doing in the company of a woman who prefers to dress in men's clothing and fancies herself a warrior?" he responded.

"A warrior indeed, sweet flower. It takes a warrior to strip a man to his bare bottom and bring him before you...," she said.

"Indeed?" he concluded. They laughed at themselves, and then exchanged kisses and a long hug.

He smelled much better than he appeared. His scent was that of freshly cut lilacs. I was tempted to ask if he slept among the lilacs or maybe ate the petals for supper. I decided not to ask, though, until I got to know him better.

"This is the gateway to Eden. On rare occasions, the mind of a man reflects the beauty of God," he said in broken, uneducated French. He intended for her to translate for my benefit.

I supposed he meant that Claude Monet tapped into the mind of God when he created this garden. But, again I did not ask him what he meant exactly.

"How long have you been blind?" I did ask, regrettably. I realized after the words left my mouth that a stranger addressing a person's physical maladies wasn't an appropriate way to begin a new friendship. But the dirty deed was done, and I decided to live with the poor first impression I created.

"I have never been able to see with *these* eyes. Yet I can see this garden and you cannot," he responded in perfect French.

He knew I was a foreigner before I spoke. I sensed that he even knew I was an American and, therefore, he concluded most likely not a francophone. So he didn't see the need to speak his best French when he assumed Marie was the only French speaker. But when I answered him in his native language, he felt the need to formalize his elocution in my presence. He apologized to me for using his colloquial dialect with a slight forward nod of his head.

Okay, so we both blew the first impressions; I guess we're even, I thought.

An artist's sketchpad lay on his lap, and his fingers were blackened from the charcoal pencils he apparently used on the pad. His face was that of a thin man; sunken cheeks, darkened, and hollow eye sockets and a white shade across the bottom third of his face created by a thin beard. But his body below the shoulders spread out in under-inflated balloon layers and seemed to rest on an invisible waist. He fit into that garden as if Claude Monet himself painted him permanently into the landscape.

Even though I stood there staring at him, I felt that I was only seeing an impression of the man behind the blindness.

Marie was always careful to take me places where we were alone or among trusted members of the Résistance. Black skin in occupied France at that time was a one-way ticket to a POW camp, or worse, a concentration camp. She never left me alone even with trusted allies. Consequently, I rarely came out in the daytime unless the occupiers were otherwise occupied and the townspeople still in their beds. But she left me alone with the blind man without hesitation or even a goodbye.

I was concerned that she would bring me to the old man's garden, and then leave me in the presence of a stranger, even a helpless blind stranger. Nevertheless, there was part of me that expected to find the blind man or someone similarly strange, dressed the way he was dressed, sitting where he sat and doing something beyond human expectation. This blind man drew on a sketchpad with charcoal pencils. I would never again think of Monet's Garden without thinking of him in its midst.

He gestured for me to sit down. I soon discovered that his living senses were formidable. He smelled America on me, and I was certain that he could count the beats of my heart. I looked around for a chair; there was none. I looked for a stump; there was none. I couldn't even find a suitable mound of dirt that would raise me to his level. So I sat on the ground in the middle of a crushed stone path below the eye level of a man who could not see me and, therefore, could not appreciate my subordinate position. In good but simple French, the blind man told me a fairy tale while he scribbled on the pad with the charcoal pencils. Because Marie cared about this man and Mama raised a son respectful to his elders, I took a deep breath, settled in, and listened patiently to his tale.

"The Great Green Wizard ruled the Land of Sol. He made no demand on the village leaders except that they harvest all the love of the people and give it to him. In exchange, he promised security from their enemies and prosperity from their fields. So the villagers gave eagerly the love of all to the wizard freely. The

leaders of the village realized much too late, however, that a life without love is no life at all. Without love, the Land of Sol was a hot, dry, wind beaten desert of the heart, devoid of hope, promise, and joy.

"One day, Jacques the treehopper from a faraway land, passed over the Land of Sol. He cast a glance down on the beautiful maiden Ose' gathering mushrooms from the base of the trees. He was so taken by her rare beauty that he lost his footing, hopped onto a dead branch of an oak tree, and fell from the treetops to the forest floor. Ose', though without most of her love, hid a sliver of sympathy and a dollop of nurture in her bosom. She used them gladly to tend to the injured treehopper. She raised his head from the soil and rested it in her lap. She washed the dirt from his face with her tears and toweled away the dampness with her hair. When his eyes opened and met hers, his love became her love, and their hearts were bonded together.

"The Great Green Wizard, sensing a disturbance in his heart, stuck his pointed narrow nose in the air in the direction of the East Wind, his only willing ally. The East Wind brought to him the jasmine scent of love free in the air. The wizard, in his loudest voice, commanded his imperial guard to bring Ose' and Jacques to his palace.

"The wizard, too, was captivated instantly by Ose's rare beauty and gentle spirit. He greatly desired to have her for himself. He knew from the moment he laid eyes on her that he had never possessed all of her love. Of all the women in the Land of Sol, he declared that Ose' would be queen. He stretched forth his hand and offered her a portion of his bartered love and the throne at his side in exchange for her willing hand in marriage.

"So little time had passed since Jacques and Ose' met, yet both knew that their hearts were bound together long ago.

"'Our hearts are one, dark wizard,' Jacques proclaimed, 'look elsewhere for your queen.'

"'You are less than a fly in my presence, treehopper. Release her, or I will vanquish you into eternity!' the Great Green Wizard demanded of Jacques.

"'I love the treehopper,' Ose' responded.

"'And I love this girl who gathers mushrooms in the forest,' Jacques added, neither yet knowing the others name.

"'Who is he, next to me? Share your love with me, or I will

95

vanquish him to the end of existence,' the Great Green Wizard demanded of Ose'.

"'You have the love of all these people, and still you want more. Have you not learned that love not freely given is no love at all?' Ose' responded in a respectful whisper.

"'Then freely you shall give.'

"The Great Green Wizard cried out in a voice of summons to the underworld. From there arose a fiery chariot driven by a fallen angel and drawn by seven demons. The minions of darkness set upon Jacques and lashed him to the golden wheel of the damned chariot. They drove the chariot out and into the darkness howling like a pack of wolves at the moonlight.

"Ose' ran after the chariot proclaiming her love for Jacques until she reached the edge of the land. She prepared to throw herself into the sea for her love but the men of the Land of Sol restrained her with ropes of hemp and covered her eyes with a silk blindfold. Ose' would have pursued the chariot into the sea, but, instead, she wept for her treehopper.

"The demon drawn chariot lifted Jacques into the darkness of space, passed the sun, and traveled beyond the stars. It stopped at the end of all that exists, turned, and headed back toward Earth through the back alleys of the universe. The minions released Jacques in the exact place from which they took him earlier, but he did not see Ose'. Jacques stood among all the people of the Land of Sol, yet the people did not stand with Jacques.

"Only the Great Green Wizard could see Jacques.

"'Release her love or you will never see her again,' the Great Green Wizard demanded with his words out of sync with his mouth.

"'I will not. I...cannot,' Jacques answered

"'Then you shall remain where you are for all eternity,' the wizard proclaimed. 'Turn around boy and look behind you.'

"Jacques did what the wizard instructed and caught the barest glimpse of Ose' in a mirror on her bedroom wall. She was just behind him, within his reach and the sound of his voice, he thought. He turned and called to her but he did not see her, nor did she answer his call. The Great Green Wizard spoke again.

"'She is there, boy, directly behind you but a universe away. She will always be just behind you, but there are galaxies between you and her that only I can transverse. Your arms are too

short to reach across eternity, and your voice too weak for her to hear. Your mind is too pathetic to touch hers. Your years too few to journey back here without my help. Release her boy, and I will give you the riches of a king!'

"'No, I will not, and she will never release me. Your power has been wasted, wizard.'

"Jacques wept for the mushroom gatherer. She was closer to him than a whisper, yet farther from his touch than there is space in the universe. He waited in that place for ten years for her to turn around and see him. Ose' never did. Her world's back turned away from him forever. He only caught glimpses of her face in the mirrors of her world.

"However, the wizard grew concerned because Ose' began to sense Jacques's presence. He was a wizard of cunning, not of craft, so he needed Jacques to move from Ose's presence without harming him. His twisted mind conjured up an idea.

"'You can see her again without my help,' he told Jacques. 'You have always been free to leave where you are whenever you chose. You may travel back along the path that brought you there and reunite with Ose'. But be aware that time is not your friend. You shall age naturally and so shall she. Every step you take for half your journey will take her further from your sight though bringing you closer to her touch. If you leave now, you will have one minute of life left in your body to spend with her.'

"Jacques considered whether he was content merely to look upon glimpses of his love from the other end of the universe or whether a minute's embrace with her would be worth a lifetime journey. Jacques responded to the wizard.

"'You have made the choice for me, Evil One! You possess love, but it is clear to me that you do not know love. I know love. One minute in the arms of my beloved, even if I'm a decayed old man, is worth an eternity alive in this place.'

"And so Jacques began his trek.

"Ose' had seen glimpses of Jacques in the mirror. For a time, a glimpse of his love sustained her. But then a day came when she did not catch glimpses of Jacques and she did not sense his warm, soothing breath on the back of her neck. She mourned for him.

"'The treehopper would never trade my love for anything that you could offer him. You have killed him. For that I will never *forgive you. I still love him, and I will until I join him in death.'*

"In time, the Great Green Wizard grew weak because of jealously, bitterness, and unfulfilled desire. The people rose up and deposed him. Much of his evil was undone, but Jacques was not heard from in that time.

"Ose' bore the burden of unrequited love for Jacques for eighty years. She lay down upon her deathbed a wrinkled and tired old woman in the darkness of winter. An ancient, frost-covered man in ragged clothes shuffled to her bedside while the last remnants of life ebbed from her body. Her eyes knew him not, but her heart rejoiced.

"'Say nothing, sweet mushroom gatherer,' Jacques said in a soft voice. 'We only have a minute together. I want to spend it holding you, caressing you, kissing you.' And so they did.

"The townspeople found their lifeless bodies locked together in an unbreakable embrace. They buried them together that way in a heart-shaped grave."

The blind man drew wildly on the sketchpad with the charcoal pencils. Dust rose from the pad in pillars. He'd break out in violent coughing spells from time to time, stop the story, and then resume after clearing his throat. I doubted very much that his wild scribbling on the sketchpad amounted to anything sensible to a sighted person. This man had been blind from birth, after all, and painting is ninety-five percent visual and five percent coordination. He possessed neither ability particularly well, from what I observed. Nevertheless, he handed me the pad when he finished, and I accepted it politely.

"What do you think of my work?" he asked.

That was the one question I dreaded. I didn't want to respond directly because it would certainly require some dishonesty on my part to answer. But then he knew he was blind.

"Look, I'm sure you already know this, but here I go: you are blind. You have been blind since birth and I doubt that you have any idea what visual art is, much less how to draw."

"I am an artist. I don't draw. Just *look* at my work. It is especially for you," he responded insistently.

I saw what I expected to see at first: chaos in stark black and white on paper. The sheet was filled with disconnected lines and random spaces going nowhere, doing nothing and totally without meaning to my eyes. But before I could completely dismiss his work and manufacture a polite if insincere thank you, I saw a woman's hand on the canvas out of the corner of my eye. I focused on that section of the drawing, and I swear to you, Sis, something was there.

They came into focus when I really looked for them. Jacques and Ose' were there on the page locked in an eternal embrace. Ose' danced around the canvas in a candy apple red dress with a white chiffon collar and pleats below the waist. Her black hair was tied in a ball and pressed against the back of her head. Jacques' pants were midnight blue and creased along the sides. His shirt was baggy at the sleeves, yellow and buttoned to the chin. His arms were wrapped around her, one to the back of her neck and the other in the small of her back. Their foreheads were touching. They stared at one another longingly and finally embraced. Around Jacques and Ose' roared the chaos of the entire universe. Suns exploded, comets whisked by, and planets collided.

The blind man spoke to me one last time. "I can see you too. Some things are beyond us and simply meant to be. Remember, my friend, it is only when you cease walking that a journey is not completed."

The rational part of me had no idea what he meant. His words were the foolish ramblings of an eccentric as far as I was concerned. Another part of me, however, knew exactly what he was saying and acknowledged his wisdom. I believed I was superior to this raggedy, old, blind man when I walked into his hideaway in Monet's Garden. I was decidedly inferior after our meeting.

Two hours passed before I could extract myself from the sketching. The blind man was gone. His stump was just a stump again. The colors of the garden were duller than I remembered from earlier that day. Part of me wanted to run away and destroy his art. You see, I only recently began to really believe in God.... I was not ready to believe in black magic also. Another part of me wanted to track down the blind man and ask him what it all meant. *Be straight with me, damn it...what does it mean?*" I imagined myself asking. I compromised: I hastily exited the clearing in the middle of the thicket, but I kept the sketch.

Marie found me wandering around the edge of the lily pond staring at my reflection in the water. Someday, I hoped to see more of the garden.

"Why did you leave me with him?" I asked.

"He's like a second father to me," she answered.

"You needed his blessing for us?"

"Yes."

"What is he?"

"He's just a man whose eyes work in a different way than ours. Did he sketch for you?"

"He did," I answered. She seemed relieved. I assumed that I gained his acceptance.

"What did you see?" she asked.

"I saw just what I expected to see; wild, undisciplined chaos." She seemed disappointed at my answer. I continued. "At least, that's what I saw at first. Then I saw what *he* wanted me to see. Two star-crossed lovers from an implausible fairytale locked in an eternal embrace. Come here, let me show you." I pulled the rolled sheet from under my arm.

"No, it will only make sense to you," she responded.

"I assume that you have one?" I asked.

"I do, from my childhood. I was only ten years old," she replied.

"Can I see yours?" I asked.

"You may if you insist. But, please allow me to keep this one secret for now," she requested.

"I will," I promised.

Chapter Fourteen

Bring her up to th' high alter, that she may
The sacred ceremonies there partake
The which do endless matrimony make
That all the woods may answer and their echo ring.

Edmund Spenser

The Marriage

Dear Lil Sis, Marie wanted to get married right away, but there were no priests available in all of Giverny. I wanted to marry Marie right away, but there were no priests available in all of Giverny. (I wanted to add my desire here also so you'd know that our desires were one and the same, even in those early days.) I'm sure that if we found a priest with idle time on his hands, he would have gladly filled his time with a common wedding for two common people in love. He would have welcomed us. We would have been a respite from his tending to the many dead and dying littering Normandy. You see, the younger local priests left the parish for service behind the advancing frontline of the victorious Allied armies. The Archbishop of Normandy charged his priests to pray over death on a scale never imagined in all of human history. More men died at the hands of other men in Normandy than male babies born in all of France the previous year.

A blessed wedding in the midst of war was another of those contradictions that seemed to characterize my relationship with Marie. I suppose we could have just dispensed with a wedding ceremony and taken each other in the heat of the moment and without vows. Everyone would have understood that with the war raging and other exigent circumstances. But we wanted to do right by each other and leave no shade of doubt to sap even an ounce of legitimacy from our union. We were compelled to stand before God alone if need be and proclaim in a ceremony of our own creation our love for and commitment to one another for an eternity without demand or condition.

Mutual love and commitment without demand or condition sounds surreal even to me now putting this pen to paper, but that's what we had. Frankly, it didn't seem real then either. But isn't that a symptom of genuine love; it's a warm, cozy blanket between you and harsh, cold reality. It sustained and nurtured us when we were apart for over thirty years through countless desperate nights and thousands of lonely miles. Every single day we were together thereafter was the best day of our lives. In fact, we were so anxious to start each new day that we rarely slept through the night. If you remember anything I write in these letters, remember this: mutual love and commitment without demand or condition is the true and whole meaning of life. I believe in the truth of this for all even if it takes a lifetime to find.

"Come on, Roy, follow me. I know the perfect place," Marie said.

"Slow down, Marie, let me catch my breath."

"Come on, we can marry *ourselves* in paradise. Creation will be our witness. I know the perfect place in the old man's garden."

"I hope the old man doesn't have a shotgun!"

Marie's choice of words intrigued me. You see, paradise to me was elusive on the order of God. Paradise is without form, beyond my ability to even imagine, of extraordinary beauty and complexity and unapproachable by mere men. When we again crawled through a jagged hole in the wall separating the old man's garden from the mortal world, paradise suddenly took on form, substance, color and shape to me. I stood on the edge of a garden of such magnificent beauty that a blind man *could* see it, I thought. I meant that in both ways: with his inner spiritual eyes and with his cursed natural eyes. The shapes, textures, and smells were so brilliant and alive that they would suggest color even to one who never saw color.

We knew our time was limited, and we professed our love for one another. We married ourselves in a ceremony of our own creation.

"Breath of my breath, heart of my heart, life of my life, soul of my soul. Before the eyes of God and all of creation, I wed myself to you freely, faithfully, and forever. It is good for a man to take a wife. It is good for a woman to take a husband. Let us two become one. So it has been ordained since the beginning.

"What I do today, I do with my whole heart. What I do today, I do forever."

It was late summer and the colors in Monet's Garden were deeper and richer than the day was long. The most destructive war in the history of the Earth raged on, but the Old Man's garden remained peaceful. A white-spotted doe burst through the brush into the small circular clearing where we were and ran leaping around us a couple of times, and then left the same way she entered. The purple iris petals Marie spread about floated in the air in the doe's wake and settled gently around us as its presence faded. We were content then that God acknowledged and blessed our union.

We tied our right and left wrists together with a vine of daisies and consummated our union on a blanket of rose petals.

Chapter Fifteen

How could our love die?
Like a lotus on water I live for you.

Kabir

Six Months Together

I could see that writing letters was a kind of therapy for Uncle Roy. The happier he was, the shorter the letters were and the longer the periods of time between each letter. He and Marie shared six months together after his escape from the detention camp. He recalled some of that time in the following letter:

Dear Lil Sis, Marie's father taught me how to make his family's signature cheese following a century old recipe. I was casual about the whole affair and indulged him the first couple of times around until Marie pulled me aside one day.

"Food is very important in our culture. It is very important to Papa. My mother passed away when I was a child before she could teach me the recipes of her family. Papa packed me up two weeks later and sent me off to my maternal grandmother. I pleaded with him to let me stay...I thought I was never coming back. But he wanted me to learn the recipes that my mother was not able to teach me. It was important to him that I learn them exactly the way she learned them.

"Master cheese makers have been a part of our family for six generations. He wants nothing more than to pass on what he knows to his son. You, my dear, are the only son he has left," she said.

I began to take the whole cheese thing more seriously after that. Back home cheese was just cheese when I was growing up. One kind was not much different from another. But under Papa's tutelage, I learned to appreciate the finest aspects of many different kinds of cheese in Giverny. Cheese became an indispensable aspect of nearly every meal for me.

Learning to make it was an exquisite art. My new father-in-law condensed years of subtlety and training into a few weeks for me. He apparently thought long and hard about how he'd teach it to someone. He said that once I knew the taste, he would be satisfied.

"You'll find the right ingredients if you know the taste," he said.

I *would* find the right ingredients in time. I hoped that he would be proud of my Carré de Roucq.

All I really wanted to do was spend time with Marie before the cheese making took hold. Before, during, and after we worked the farm, though. I did chores on that farm that I would not even consider doing in Oklahoma. I would have considered it too close to slave work for my tastes. In France, it was work that assured I'd be close to Marie, and that's all I cared about.

Gasoline was still in short supply, so I hitched a mule to one side of the tiller, and I pulled the other while Marie guided it. I spread seed by hand and dragged my knees through the dirt planting saplings. I hauled milk in fifty-liter drums on my back and tossed bales of hay down from the barn loft. I learned that there was no shame in hard work done of your own free will.

Marie and I still talked long into the evening. She introduced me to French cooking, and I introduced her to Count Basie. The locals were aware of our relationship, but we still avoided the U.S. patrols.

Chapter Sixteen

And please forget
About justice it doesn't exist
About brotherhood it's deceit
About love it has no right

Ingrid Jonker

Leaving France, from my research

Hundreds of American lives were allegedly saved by the information Mancel Marchant obtained from the Nazi's in their hasty retreat from Paris. He was mentioned in the footnotes of several war documents declassified in the 1990s chronicling intelligence efforts during the French campaign. I learned from those documents strung together with other bits and pieces of my research that Mancel Marchant was a name he adopted for a new life outside of France. He knew he'd remain safe in Europe only in the exclusive company of the American military.

Marchant's given name, Philippe Renoir, appeared on another and far more ignoble list. The Mossad, the new Israeli intelligence agency, compiled a list of Frenchmen believed to have committed crimes against the French Jewry during the war. Marchant was known to have identified numerous so-called French Communists who were rounded up by American forces and never heard from again. The Americans assumed his information was credible because of some value of the Nazi documents he supplied. They were wrong.

Marchant noticed almost immediately that the Americans handling him equated French intellectuals with either communism or communist sympathizers. He knew many people who fit the profile who often gathered at his bar and debated the issues of the day for hours on end before the invasion. Several surfaced in Paris after the war from years spent underground hiding and fighting with the Résistance. Many of these men and women formed crucial elements of the Résistance. Marchant exhibited no hesitation in identifying suspected communists whether or not the evidence supported him. The secret war waged against French communists in the waning days of the Third Reich devolved into a proxy war against particularly French Jewish intellectuals.

Naming names did not endear him to the Résistance, nor did his flawed methodology persuade the Mossad years later of his innocence. U.S. Army Intelligence promised him a new identity for his "valuable contributions to the war effort" and secret passage to a new home in the United States.

Before leaving France, Marchant wanted to see Giverny and his home one last time. In particular, he wanted to visit his mother's grave and say goodbye to Marie. He was not generally given to sentimentality, but he was all but certain he'd never set foot in France again. It was difficult even for Marchant to bid farewell to his homeland forever. So he hitched a ride with a couple of happy American GIs on leave and anxious to see Monet's famed garden. They dropped him off along the roadside a half-mile from his ancestral farm and promised to pick him up from that spot at nightfall.

Uncle wrote about this time.

He recalled moving freely about the farm with the comfort of a one who owned the land. So much had relaxed since the Germans left and he was no longer a secret. He wasn't just working the farm, but he was part of the farm. He entered the house without announcing himself and his clothing hung from the line drying in the sunlight next to Papa's and Marie's. He worked like a man invested in the soil, not one working for a wage at the end of the week. Marchant must have witnessed some of this and resented Roy instantly.

The records indicate Marchant saw Uncle Roy working in the vegetable garden and rubbed the still tender knot on the back of his head. He hitched a ride to the old man's garden to find his traveling companions. He told the two young soldiers about the colored American deserter he just learned was hiding out in the countryside. He reminded them of the great sacrifice they made to fight the war and that the blood of their comrades still wet the sands of Normandy. Finally, he sealed Roy's fate by telling them of several unsolved rapes in the village.

"My family has been part of this village for over three hundred years. I may never lay eyes on it again, but I will not see it given over to such a savage. I must ask a personal favor of you. Seize this man and make sure that he is tried, convicted and incarcerated for the balance of his life. He is not worthy of life, yet a quick death would be too easy on him."

The soldiers flung Roy's battered and unconscious body head first into the bed of their uncovered jeep exactly two hours later. Roy never saw them coming. He never raised his head from tending to the tomato saplings barely clinging to life in the vegetable garden.

The jeep bumped along the pothole-strewn road for twenty-five miles before Marie missed the chopping sound of Roy's hoe. Roy lay hog-tied and semi-unconscious in the jeep's bed bumping up and down like a sack of soggy potatoes. Marchant, sitting precariously on the sidewall of the jeep's bed, must have studied every inch of Roy's face. He seared the contours of Roy's chiseled cheekbones and ebony brow onto every cell in his calculating brain. He probably had never been this close to a colored man before. He noticed the strange texture of his hair and the squat and rounded nose on his brown face. I suspect Marchant wanted to reach out and touch the hair to register its texture in his mind as well.

If Marchant understood the intricacies of American race relations in the 40's, then he would have followed through on the homicidal urge welling up inside his gut. He would have reached for standard issue field knife sheathed in the driver's utility belt. He would have grabbed hold of it, raised it high, and cried out in anguished tones for justice and virginity for the little, pigtailed French girls this man victimized. And then he would have plunged serrated blade repeatedly into soft tissue of Roy's unconscious body until the strength left his hands and no more blood flowed for the man's body. If he had known about the true status of colored men in America, then he would have known a trial wasn't necessary to judge Roy's guilt or innocence; mere suspicion of wrongdoing cast upon a colored man served as sufficient justification of any punishment no matter how disproportionate. But Marchant knew nothing about American race relations. So, he probably just stared at the helpless man and smiled under his lips as he manufactured the tale in his head that would assure Roy's never say the light of day again.

Circumstances beyond their control separated Roy and Marie for the second time in their brief lives together.

Roy surfaced six months later languishing in a brig still under construction at the recently established Tinker Air Force Base in Oklahoma City. The Army waited until after the Germans surrendered to schedule his first hearing (from what I could gather). The few records I found from the hearings were sparse and redacted of any substantive witness testimony. The army tribunal scheduled at about the same time that the Allies discovered the awful extent of the Final Solution, and consequently, the United States became especially sensitive to the "Jewish Question."

Roy wrote the following to Grandma:

Dear Lil Sis, They accused me of striking an officer, colluding with the enemy, desertion from my duties at the detention camp during wartime and raping several unnamed French women and girls. I didn't desert! I escaped. There's a difference between the two. The officer deserved to die, but I showed him mercy, and for that they should give me a medal. The victims reported the last of the alleged rapes two days before my mission. I think I know the real culprit. But they wielded wide latitude and could try me under arbitrary standards since the war still raged in the Pacific. Nobody seems to care about the facts, especially when undesirables are being accused and when we're fighting a war. I faced summary execution on all counts if found guilty. I prepared myself for execution.

The A-bomb was still a secret then, and I was told that the war depended on keeping that secret. So General Zinny wasn't much help, but he at least acknowledged via an affidavit that I was loaned to the Résistance. But he maintained the cover story that I was an incompetent fighter pilot. He played it to the hilt with all the passion I knew he would implore. He even suggested that I be ordered to pay restitution for Lena, in addition to whatever other punishment the tribunal meted out. I kept my pledge not to divulge the true nature of my mission, but I'm not sure why. The Army didn't seem to care about me, so why did I care about their secrets. The truth is, I didn't believe that man was capable of building a bomb that could wipe a whole city anyway. At the time, I thought only God possessed that kind of power. So I wasn't about to run off at the mouth like a fool about some fantastical doomsday bomb and my secret mission to save the world.

But I witnessed atrocities in that makeshift brig in France that were not national secrets or too fantastical to believe. On that point, I reserved the right to tell the world. I told my JAG lawyer, Captain Carl Boykin, what I knew about G.I. firing squads and the Résistance members in their sites. I intended to testify about those non-secrets. I was sad about my situation, but I felt strangely free to speak my mind. I knew that the military would at least give me a chance to speak my mind, and a highly trained government stenographer would record my every word. So if I couldn't get any justice in my lifetime, at least somebody in the future would know the truth.

I told my lawyer, "They lined them up and shot them down like mangy ol' dogs...no hearings...no trials...nothing. They said it was because they were Jews and communist--'the niggers of Europe' they said. But the people they were murdering were the same people who helped me. As far as I was concerned, the colonel's actions made us no better than the Nazis.

"I've been reading about that Final Solution thing--some folks are calling it a Jewish holocaust. I never wanted to believe that people were born without hearts, but it isn't hard now to believe that people are capable of any atrocity. What I saw let me know that America has its share of heartless folks too.

"I want counter-charges brought against them, my accusers. I want the world to know what they did to those Frenchmen. They are the deserters, not me. They deserted justice and freedom while I held it high!" I explained.

"But it's your word against a highly decorated officer. You must know that we can't win. Let me plea bargain and I think I can at least keep you alive."

"*We* can't win? I like you. But, I too am a highly decorated officer."

"You know what I mean."

"You want a fancy legal argument? Did you read Zinny's affidavit? I was under the command of the Résistance per his direct orders. My defense of the Résistance, therefore, was well within my duty by the direct orders from my commanders. I just followed orders.

"Look, I just want to tell the truth. There was this one-eyed man, a member of the Résistance, who helped me. Daniel--I think his name was Daniel. But he went by the name Prometheus. I believe he lived somewhere around Vernon. Find him and he can tell you what happened to his colleagues when our people took control. Ask him this...ask him if more members of the Résistance died at the hands of the Germans or at the hands of Americans. Then you just let us get on the stand and tell the truth."

Captain Boykin found Daniel Cristol studying ornithology in London about a month later. What Daniel told him made him ashamed. Americans liberated Europe one village at a time with a tremendous loss of life on all sides. Our enlisted men fought with honor, pride, and justice firmly rooted on their side. Yet a handful of men steeped in ignorance and driven by their petty prejudices acted out in a way that tarnished aspects of our victory. They terrorized and murdered indiscriminately some of the very people we fought to free.

Captain Boykin prepared to defend my case with a new vigor armed with Daniel's affidavit and those of several other members of the Résistance. He requested and was granted a pretrial hearing. He suggested to the tribunal that it conduct an *in camera* examination of his evidence before it sent the case to a jury trial.

"This case has no national security implications, gentlemen. The public, therefore, will know whatever my client knows about his time in France. I have summarized my client's account in a pretrial motion to dismiss, and I ask you to consider them in light of Belzec, Sobibor, Treblinka, and Auschwitz-Birkenau," Captain Boykin told them.

I waited silently and readied myself to testify in the courtroom for two and a half hours. The MPs guarding me were told by the clerk to escort me back to my cell six hours into the day.

"Why? What's going on here? Let me speak to Captain Boykin....that's my right," I pleaded when they guided me out.

I did not get answers until Captain Boykin came to my cell seven days later.

"I'm going to say it to you straight. I've been offered a promotion to a Pentagon job if I resign as your counsel and forget everything I know about this case. Frankly, I'd probably be in here with you or we'd both be very dead if my father-in-law wasn't a United States Senator. They don't want your story told...not today, not tomorrow, not ever," he said.

"Well, what are you gonna do?"

"I'm going to stand my ground. I was a lawyer before I was a soldier. I promised to defend you to the best of my ability, and I take this justice thing seriously."

"I won't hold you...."

"What? Where is all that fire you had?"

"I won't hold you if you promise to take that job and do everything in your power to make the military the one place in America where a colored man can get a fair shake. Have your father talk to the President--you talk to the President, whatever. Colored men are fightin' and dying just like ya'll...bullets and cluster bombs don't just kill white soldiers so why should the military make a difference. You and I know that they will get me one way or the other, you or no you. There is no one out there missing me with enough power to stop them. The least I can do is to help some of my folks have a better way if I can. Make me that promise and you need never even think my name again."

Captain Boykin accepted reluctantly. I read many years later that President Truman personally selected then Major Boykin to bring about the new, integrated, merit-based military.

They offered me an honorable discharge if I agreed to drop my counter charges against the officers and agreed never to return to France or speak of the executions again. General Zinny told the tribunal that he was completely confident that I could be trusted to keep my mouth shut. He also told them that I was an American hero and my life must be preserved. They made the offer through a legal clerk before I received new counsel. I refused their terms because I needed to return to France. Marie was in France, and she was the sole reason I drew breath from one moment to the next.

An Army head doctor came to my cell four months after Captain Boykin left for the Pentagon. I still hadn't been assigned new counsel. The doctor spent forty-five minutes, asking me yes or no questions about my childhood, my relationship with Mama and Daddy, and my time in hiding in France. He asked questions, one after the other in rapid succession and made checks on a pad he carried. I discovered later that his official assignment was to evaluate my competence to stand trial. Needless to say, he found me incompetent and dangerously delusional. The tribunal promptly accepted his findings and concluded that I was unfit to stand trial because I could not competently assist counsel in my own defense. The tribunal ordered me committed to an asylum for the insane where I would be treated by trained medical professionals until I became legally competent. My court martial would resume when and if such a time came.

The head doctor reported the tribunal's decision to me.

"You are a danger to yourself and others. You must be subdued and committed without hesitation until you are competent. We can help you to get better. Come get him and hold him down," he ordered the MPs standing by.

It all happened so fast that I don't remember whether I protested. I do remember feeling that my life was no longer my own. They usurped my power to make even the most basic decisions about it merely to save a few politicians from embarrassment and difficult explanations. I didn't give up, but I didn't fight back either. I did not know how to fight back.

The head doctor shot the first of many doses of Lysergic Acid Diethylamide into a vein in my right arm while four MPs held me to the floor. It would be decades before I knew that drug by its common name, LSD. It was an up and coming form of victim humiliation used by our intelligence services. LSD propelled me into a pit of utter darkness that day from which it took me nearly thirty years to emerge.

Chapter Seventeen

They cannot scare me with their empty spaces
Between stars – on stars where no human race is.
I have it in me so much nearer home
To scare myself with my own desert places.

Robert Frost

On Being Crazy

Dear Lil Sis, Colored folks in Oklahoma spoke one word for crazy – *Taft*. Taft, Oklahoma, was a one-horse town and the home to the state insane asylum for coloreds. Crazy white folks went to the state institution in Vinita, Oklahoma, but crazy coloreds went to Taft. Yes, even we crazies in Oklahoma were segregated, which I think illuminates who the real crazies were. Nonetheless, the "crazy house" for colored folks was in Taft, and I was one of the Taft institution's chief residents for fourteen long, elusive years.

Some folks around Okmulgee thought I was destined for Taft anyway from a very young age. Southern country folks believed that really smart colored men all go crazy at some point in their lives. In fact, in some circles, being too smart and colored was synonymous with being crazy. We spent so many years pretending we weren't conspicuously smarter than whites that we forgot we were just pretending. I certainly fit the profile of one destined for colored craziness. Sadly, I can't say now, in retrospect, that I fully disagree with the belief.

You see, there were two kinds of smart colored folks: the kind who recognized the heavy hand of Jim Crow crushing their ambition and fled to the friendlier North, and the kind that stayed and were pounded into submission by the sledge hammer of segregation. Being too smart, understanding too deeply, and believing too much in merit under the strictures of Jim Crow was enough to drive any smart colored man crazy.

Half the town turned out to send me off to join the Tuskegee Airmen when I left Okmulgee. Mama baked sixteen sweet potato pies, and the Oklahoma Eagle ran a full-page story about me and the other Oklahoma boys who joined the unit. But there was no celebration, no pies, and no one I knew to greet me when I returned from the war to a padded holding cell in Taft.

I remember a great deal about being crazy. I hesitate to say that I suffered constant indignities, though most people would not subject a dog to the treatment I experienced there. Indignities, however, are relative and only matter if you give a shit about something. The weekly doses of LSD made sure I didn't give a shit about anything. I didn't care about nothing when I was crazy, and no one holds crazy folks accountable for not caring.

I'll admit I've wanted badly to forget being Taft, to wipe the slate clean and start those years over from scratch. I wanted to crawl back into Mama's womb and be born to someone else, somewhere else, and somehow else. But since I could not, I've tried to lock my memories of being crazy in the same faraway place I keep unwanted dreams. They resided in that "hell yes it was fuckin' unpleasant, but just repeat over and over to yourself that it wasn't real" place. But it simply hasn't worked because I still remember.

I have never told anyone in the family about those days. I have never written a word regarding them before this letter. I've thought about them an awful lot lately, and I'm hoping very badly that by finally writing about them here, I can exorcise those memories from my mind.

I talked crazy, walked crazy, and, above all, thought crazy in the asylum. My tongue was swollen constantly, and my mouth always seemed dry from the drugs, though I drooled more than an overfed newborn. The only fleshly desires left in me were eating and sleeping. Sometimes I didn't even want those. When other desires did show themselves, I became obsessed with fulfilling them. I couldn't stop myself once they started.

One day I decided that I could no longer tolerate the hospital green paint covering the concrete block walls in my room, so I started taking it off one chip at a time in the places hidden from the orderlies' view. I chipped away perfect concrete gray silhouettes behind the bed, the dresser and the toilet. I chipped away in the shaded areas in the corner of my room that couldn't be seen from the door, and I took all the paint off the inside of the door itself. I chipped, peeled, and scraped until the spoon I used dulled and my raw fingers bled.

When I ran out of hidden places to chip away at, I chipped away my image standing against the open space directly in view from the door. I stood in that spot whenever they conducted room checks. The room checkers came in and looked around carelessly per their norm, and then moved on to the next room. They failed to notice the chipped away green paint, and I laughed inside.

My work remained hidden until lights out. I couldn't get in that bed for the last check. There was still more of that paint to remove. And if I did, then they would see it before I was done and probably bring in more green paint. If they saw the room with all the green paint gone, then they'd know that it needed to go. So I stood there through first call, second call, and finally bed check.

"Get in the bed, Lankster."

"No, no, I can't do that."

"Get in the bed, you fuckin' idiot. Don't make me have to earn my government money tonight."

"No, no...can't do that."

"Johnson, bring me the keys. Lankster won't get in the bed... no, no, he's just standing against the wall...a motherfuckin' Statute of Liberty."

I *was* the Statue of Liberty...permanent and immovable. I folded one hand across my chest and the other rose to the sky. Behind me were green-free, bare, cinder block walls. It took five orderlies to get me off the wall and onto the floor. Three held me down until the night doctor came and shot something into my arm. The night doctor was the most pleasant of all the doctors at the facility. He was from a wealthy New York family and decided to give back to society by working with po' colored folks in a government facility.

"Mr. Lankster, why didn't you go to bed when you were told?" the doctor asked.

"It's everywhere. It gottah come off."

"What has to come off, Mr. Lankster?"

"You know. Cain't you see it? It's all ovah, and it's gonnah bring us all down. Let me up from here so I kin git it, Mr. Doctor."

"Hold on, hold on. Tell me what it is you see."

"Are you blind, man? Can't you see it? It's all over this place, a plague covering the walls. We gottah take it down 'fore it's too late.'

"Before what's too late?"

"It's too late for the world, planet earth, people."

"What's going to happen to them?"

"No, not them...what's going to happen to you, me, to us? I tol' yah already, we're gonnah die. Thangs is out of balance, and they cain't stay that way for long. That stuff is keeping it off, and I got-tah take it down now."

Again the doctor looked around the room for the stuff I spoke about. None of them noticed the concrete gray silhouette of my profile on the wall or the bare shaded areas of the room. They focused solely on subduing me.

"Mr. Lankster, how do you know so much?"

"I don't know. Look, Mr. Doc, I'll tell you what...I'll say my prayers at bedtime. Eat my vegetables, play first base for the Dodgers, and screw the girl next door if you just let me up this one time."

"How do you know so much, Mr. Lankster, while *we* know nothing about our impending doom?"

"I just know, that's all."

"If I said to you, Mr. Lankster, that 'I just know you are wrong,' would you accept that response from me?"

"No."

"Then how do you know the world is about to end?"

"He told me."

"Are you talking to God again, Mr. Lankster?"

"No, he ain't that big. He is sort of a fix-it man for the world. When thangs ain't happening right or at least how they are suppose to, he fixes 'em. There's a lot of thangs wrong with the world these days, and he ain't got time to get to them all. So he asked me if I could help with some of the small stuff that be going wrong around this place. Small stuff goin' wrong...that...um, green paint on these walls. It's been sucking happiness out of life around here for a long time. It gottah go...."

I drifted off into a long deep sleep. They noticed my good works after I passed out. They noticed the perfect silhouettes of the toilet, bed, dresser and the shadowed places around the room. On the third day, they painted over my work with white paint, and I was satisfied.

About a year before Mother Hadie Mae's visit, Little Miss Ann stopped visiting me. That was, coincidently, about the same time that Alphonso the orderly became a dope pusher.

Alphonso decided that I wasn't crazy enough for my heavy drug regimen, so he took it upon himself to wean me off of it. He found a better use for my prescriptions, especially the LSD. He knew people in Oklahoma City and Tulsa who'd pay good money for "the stuff" being wasted on me. Alphonso and I arrived at an understanding: I would continue to act just crazy enough to keep the prescriptions flowing, but not so crazy that the nurse would recommend that my drug protocol be reevaluated. He promised in exchange to do his part to get me released.

Little Miss Ann didn't like it when I stopped taking my medicine.

Little Miss Ann visited me every night for exactly 4900 nights or 13.4 years. She came into my room in the pitch-blackness of the night, long after the lights went out and we were told to go to bed. She would pass through the southern wall in my room always seemingly on her way somewhere else. She'd stop just before reaching the foot of my bed, turn slowly, and seem to study me... her prey. There was no childlike curiosity or playfulness in her study, just careful intense inspection.

"Hey, ol' uncle, may I have a nickel for a pop?" she asked the very first night.

"I don't have no money, little girl. You should run along home."

"You cannot say no to me. I am Little Miss Ann. I am going to forgive you this time--that is number one," she responded starting to keep count.

I noticed two things about Miss Ann after a few visits. She never used contractions when speaking, and she counted every time she forgave me for some wrong she perceived I committed against her.

Miss Ann was about eight years old, and her curly and well-kept blonde hair fell half way down her back. Her piercing blue eyes followed me around the room no matter where I went. She always dressed in the same lacy, layered, off-white dress tied around the waist with a pink ribbon. The neck and hem of the dress was sewn with pink irises on a bed of lace. A woman's pearl necklace hung around her tiny neck. Her tone was always sweet and childlike, but her words were demanding and authoritative. She displayed exquisite manners though such manners were, in her words, "not always suitable for an old uncle."

"They don't 'low us to have guests in our rooms, Little Miss Ann. You gottah stop coming here, or we both gone git in trouble."

"I am your guest, Uncle. You are behaving very rudely by asking me to leave. But I can forgive your bad manners. I am very good that way. Number 5...5...2.

"Do you know how to scream, Uncle? Sometimes me and my friends go off into the woods and just scream to the top of our lungs. We scream until we cannot scream anymore. It makes me feel free, Uncle. I am a bird in flight. Let us scream, Uncle--you and me."

"Please don't scream, Little Miss Ann. Somebody might think I'm trying to hurt you. Please don't scream."

"I am going to scream, Uncle. Please join me, or I might just think you are being rude again."

"No, please don't," I pleaded.

Little Miss Ann screamed. It wasn't a fun happy kid enjoying herself scream. It was the terror-filled scream of folks dying and dying slowly at the hands of other folks. So, I had no choice but to scream too. I needed to scream louder, longer, and with more terror to drown out Little Miss Ann's screams. I screamed because my life was at stake.

The whole ward erupted into a chorus of screams after I began. The sound echoed off the bare concrete walls until it reached ear-piercing decibels. The night orderlies turned on the lights in the green ward first, and then one after the other throughout the building on the wake of a wave of screams sweeping rapidly through the residential quarters. The time soon came for the orderlies and nurses to scream.

"Shut up, you crazy fools. Go back to sleep!"

"Which one started it? Number 31? I'll take care of his ass right now."

They beat on my door while I sucked in air to let loose again. I continued to scream louder and longer because Little Miss Ann still screamed. I continued to scream when the attendant's keys clanged in the heavy iron lock of my door. I screamed so that I didn't hear the familiar squeaks the door made when it opened. I didn't hear the orderly's hard shoes pounding on the floor, and I didn't hear the displaced air from his backhand coming across my face. I still screamed from the floor with his knee in my back. I screamed until the pinch in my arm sent me off into Indian dreams.

Little Miss Ann came again and again.

"Can you dance, Uncle? Please dance for me," Little Miss Ann asked once.

"Naw, I cain't dance, Little Miss Ann. I got a bum leg from the waw."

She turned her head down and away from me. I thought she wanted to cry. And then she said calmly, "My daddy says that all I have to do is ask you to dance, and you will dance. He said that if you will not dance, then you are broken and he will make sure you get fixed. Do I need to call my daddy?" she asked with her left hand on her hip.

I danced because she wanted me to dance. I didn't care about what her daddy said. At least, that's what I told myself in a whisper in the dark of the night.

"Why, you *can* dance, Uncle. I forgive you for lying to me. Number 3,562. Smile like you all do when you dance, Uncle."

I learned to smile displaying all of my front teeth and the whites of my eyes simultaneously. Little Miss Ann enjoyed that kind of smile. In time, I mastered shuffling my feet while raising and dropping my shoulders to the beat of the music. I tried to make Little Miss Ann happy, and she continued to speak without contractions and count the number of times she forgave me.

"Is dis whatcha yah wants, Miss Ann?"

"Stop all the talking and keep dancing, Uncle. Hey, Teddy wants to dance too."

She handed me her stuffed brown bear. That bear and I promenaded around the room, tapped our heels on the floor, and threw our heads back in a dancing fervor.

The dancing marathon ended with me drenched in sweat and one of the green smocked orderlies with his knee grinding in my back and his right hand pushing my face into the white tiled floor.

Dancing for Little Miss Ann sent the blood rushing through parts of my body I forgot about long ago. I felt strong and vibrant physically. Emotionally though, I didn't feel at all. I shut that part of myself down whenever Little Miss Ann visited. It became increasingly hard to restart it after she'd leave. After a while, I just stopped trying to restart it. I didn't need to feel, and I didn't need to consider whether Miss Ann's visits mattered to me. I just simply needed to do whatever I could to make Little Miss Ann happy, and her happiness had nothing to do with my happiness.

"I forgive you. That is number 4,899, Uncle."

Alphonso, the orderly, gave up his street job right before Miss Ann forgave me the 4,899th time. It was Christmas Day. The very next day, I started my walk back across the universe.

"No, no! That is not what I want, Uncle. This is boring. Okay, stand over there in the corner with your back to the wall. Do not move. You are a Christmas tree, and I am going to decorate you," said Little Miss Ann.

"But I's don' thank I kin be a Christmas tree, Miss Ann."

"You can be a Christmas tree. If I say you can be a Christmas tree, then you can be a Christmas tree. I forgive you, Uncle, for the last time, number 4,900. That is all the forgiveness you are entitled: 70 x 70."

"I's kin be a tree if'n y'all says I kin, Little Miss Ann."

I stood at attention and tried not to flinch when she pressed the ornament hooks into my flesh. I stood perfectly erect when she strung the lights around my body from head to toe. I held my head high when she covered it with the flowing white gown of the tree-top angel. I closed my eyes when she plugged the lights into that outlet at the foot of my bed that I didn't know was there. The warm lights soothed my cold body. The stark dry cinder blocks of my room radiated with the reflected colors and shapes of the season. I turned slowly to take in the whole room and enjoy an experience with Little Miss Ann for a change.

"Do not move! Christmas trees do not move!"

"I ain't gonna move no mo', Little Miss Ann."

"Do not talk! I told you that Christmas trees do not talk. You are done. I cannot forgive you for being a bad Christmas tree. Bad Christmas trees must be chopped down. Number 4,901."

The swirling lights vanished. The room darkened. I couldn't see what was going on around me.

"I bees a good Christmas tree. Please, please give me anotha chance," I cried.

I heard unfamiliar voices discussing me all around me.

"Fine timber...firewood...chop it...mill it."

Then I heard the spinning stone wheel of a blade sharpener. I could feel the moving air whishing around the spinning wheel and the rise and fall of the foot pedal driving the wheel. I heard the sounds of the blade grinding against the rotating stone. I smelled the sparks flying from the friction.

"I can be a good Christmas tree, see?"

But I ceased being a Christmas tree. I became merely a tree standing in the middle of a crazy man's room where no tree should stand. I became what most trees are to most men: worth more dead than alive.

"Whatcha doin', Little Miss Ann?" I asked nervously.

"Trees do not talk. I already told you that, *Mr. Hard Head*!"

"I ain's gonna talk much. I jes needs tah know what's gonna happen nex'. Yah see, I wants to be ready to do the right thang for yah."

"That is it! I think that I do not like trees anymore. They talk too much. I think that I will chop this old, stupid, talking tree down."

"No, please! Please don' cut the tree down."

I begged through the first swing of the ax. I remember wanting to scream in pain and step to the left to get away from the warm, wet blood pooling at my feet. But Little Miss Ann kept reminding me that trees couldn't move. I stood through that blow and several others before I fell without resistance to the floor. I didn't cry out because a tree wouldn't cry. I lay still on the floor in a shallow pool of blood because a tree would lay still.

I lay on my back with my face to the ceiling. There were 756 peeling, white paint chips up there. I looked around and noticed the absence of life from the room. There was no geranium on the windowsill, no green mold in the damp corners, and no hearty cockroaches scampering around bedposts. A hidden vortex sucked all other life out of that room. I wanted to find it and be sucked out also. I thought about Marie and wondered whether she was still waiting for me. I wondered if there would be enough of me left for her to love if I ever returned to France. For the second time in my life, my body crashed to Earth, and I did not feel the pain of the fall. My old pain left no room for new pain to take up residence.

Alphonso rolled me over and buried his left knee in my back. His right hand pushed my face into the white tile covered floor and a needle punctured my left shoulder. He tied-off my wrists before I drifted into unconsciousness.

"You stupid son-of-a-bitch. This is too damn crazy," Alphonso whispered in my ear while his co-workers applied first aid. I never saw Little Miss Ann again.

Chapter Eighteen

Mother Hadie Mae

Dear Lil Sis, I was reborn the day Mother Hadie Mae Robinson from the Macedonia Baptist Church came expecting to visit her son, Junior. Junior and I happened to have the same given first name, Booker. We were part of a whole generation of colored babies named for the famous Booker T. Washington. Junior was never "*too* smart," so you might wonder how he ended up in Taft. The rumormongers said that he got a hold of some bad corn whiskey that sent him running stark naked and screaming bloody murder down Main Street. I think it's more likely that Junior was a schizophrenic. Nevertheless, his being there brought Mother Hadie Mae, and with Mother Hadie Mae came my salvation.

Mother Hadie Mae asked the desk attendant if they would bring her son Booker from Okmulgee out front to visit with her for a spell.

Alphonso intercepted the page and brought me out instead. He decided a few weeks before that the fast life of a dope pusher was too dangerous for his tastes. He preferred the womanizing life of a pretty boy over the gun slinging of a street hood. Alphonso simply didn't have the ruthless nature of a dope pusher, and he was never quite the same after one of his regular customers pistol-whipped him over a $2 bag. Afterwards, he dumped his entire stash into a deep channel in the Arkansas River, spread the word around on the street that he was out of business for good, and found Jesus post haste.

"This is it, man. This is the day I pay my debt to you. Befo' I take you out d'here, I just want you to know that I'm sorry for anytime I did you wrong. I'm really sorry and, man, I'm asking you to forgive me if you can. I want you to know something else too: *you ain't crazy and you nevah wuz crazy.* I know that for a fact, and it don't take no doctor to know it. I got to see your file in Dr. Taylor's office, and they stuck an orange sticker on the folder jacket. The orange sticker files is gov'ment files. Them gov'ment files is all about secrets, man. They either 'bout tryin' to git somethin' outtah your head or 'bout tryin' to keep somethin' in your head from gittin' out. I knew you must be someone special when I seen that dot on your file. You...ain't...crazy...you nevah' was crazy," Alphonso

123

told me while escorting me down the green-walled hallway to the visitors' area.

Mother Hadie Mae burst into tears when she laid eyes on me. I must admit that I didn't recognize her. Too many years passed since I last saw her, and they injected too much shit into my veins for me to recognize someone so distant in my past. She cried from the moment she saw me until she turned and ran from the visiting area. She came back a few minutes later, marginally composed, and tried to talk to me, but she couldn't get the words out, and I was in no condition to help her.

Mother Hadie Mae was my Sunday school teacher. She used to tell Mama that I was the one the Lord would use to make life better for colored folks in Okmulgee. Ironically, she expected that I would save all the colored folks in town, yet she saved me. She mourned for me, the savior she doted on, when she heard that I died in the war. But I stood before her that day, half dressed, hung over, and anxious for her to deliver me from Taft.

Mother Hadie Mae called Mama on the telephone the minute she returned to Okmulgee. She never did see her Booker on that visit. She left the place happy that I was alive, sad that I was in such a poor state, and angry at my folks for not telling her where I was.

"Why didn't you tell me yah boy was up there? It almos' kilt me to death when I seed 'im," Mother Hadie Mae asked Mama.

"George been in Tulsa for nearly the past two years, Mother Hadie Mae. If'n I knew that y'all was goin' up dhere, I would've made dat boy pick yah up at the train station. Yah know he got a brand new truck and...."

"Ah tain't talkin' 'bout George. I'm takin' 'bout Booker! Yah boy, Booker, girl!

"Mother Hadie Mae, yah knows Booker is dead. He was kilt in the waw, nigh-on fourteen or fifteen years ago."

"Well, when I went to Taft lookin' to visit my Booker--yah know he dranks too much corn whiskey--they brought out your boy. It was him sho as the Lawd is in Heaven. I even set a while and tried to talk to him. He looks bad and all, sho nuff, but it was yah boy."

"Mother, now I don't mean to sass yah, but when we lost Booker, it like tah kilt me. Now I don't think what you doin' is at all funny. I'll go to Pastor on you 'bout this if yah don't cut it out now!"

"Yah really don' know he's dhere, do yah, chil'?

"Booker's dead. He been dead a long time now, and it's all I kin do jus' to call his name every now an' dhen. I got a letter from General Eisenhower that says he's dead. I keeps 'em right here in the dresser drawer for anybody tah see. What yah saw, if'n yah saw anybody ah tall was somebody dat looked like Booker."

"Lawd, Lawd, Lawd, what done happened here? Bernie, I'm gon' have Jimmy drive me over to yah house first thang tomorrow mornin'. You and Willie get dressed in yah Sunday clothes and find someone to sit with them grands. We gone take you to see yah boy."

Mama, Daddy, Mother Hadie Mae, and Jimmy drove to Taft on June 17, 1959. Dwight Eisenhower ruled in the White House, Elvis sang the blues on the radio, and the Russians developed their own bomb. I stayed locked away in the Oklahoma State Institute for the Colored Lunatics--courtesy of the United States Military over the "Jewish Question." They arrived just after noon. Mother Hadie Mae went to the same front desk attendant and this time asked to see both boys named Booker from Okmulgee. Alphonso brought me to the visitors' room for the second time in fourteen years. I saw my mama's face for the first time in nearly twenty years. I desperately wanted to speak, but my throat knotted up, and tears poured down my face.

"No more Indian dreams, I prayed. No more Indian dreams," I pleaded. "Mama, kin y'all git me outta here?" I finally asked. That was all I could say.

Chapter Nineteen

Walking

Dear Lil Sis, I never knew whether the A-bomb, the executions or both kept me in Taft. In either case, enough time apparently passed to make them no longer vital national security secrets. They finally freed me from that place. They released me with no words of apology and no instruction on managing in the modern world. But that's just my retrospective view of the situation. The truth of the matter is that I did not care one way or the other how or why I was released or that the world was now virtually unrecognizable. I cared simply that I was free. I cared about reorienting myself to the world and beginning my journey back to Marie. I remained enlisted and on active duty in the army during my stay in the Taft Institution, so the government accumulated quite a nest egg for me and paid it within 60 days. That and a monthly Army Air Corp pension check established me far better than most folks in Okmulgee.

I didn't understand money at that time because I hadn't used it for decades. I ignored it, and it accumulated in bank accounts in my name. It was there and available when I began to consider money again.

I went back home and slept in the same bed I did before leaving for Tuskegee. The same hole in the center of the mattress caused my back to ache again in the same spot. I was probably the only man in my squadron who slept better on a stiff, coarse Army Air Corp bunk than he did at home. I laid my head on the same homemade goose feather pillow and crawled back into my mama's welcoming womb. I was Mama's little boy again, and she gladly took care of me. Mama rejoiced at having any part of her son back. To her way of thinking, I rose from the dead and wiped away the pain, sorrow, and guilt she felt believing she outlived one of her children.

I could take care of my body: shower, shave, and shine. Even in the crazy house, they expected some of us to take care of our own personal hygiene. But Mama cooked, cleaned, took me for haircuts, and deposited money in my hand tied tightly in a red bandana to pay the barber. She bought my clothes, told me what to wear, and when to eat, get up from the table, sleep, arise, and speak to people.

I dragged around town close behind her on an invisible leash. My head hung out low seemingly detached from the top of my body. I shuffled with my feet spread wide along behind her taking dozens of tiny steps to each of her long, graceful strides. I'm convinced that she tried to lose me in town a few times. To her, it was akin to throwing a beginning swimmer into the deep end of the pool. "He'll find his way back, and then he'll start to cut the umbilical cord," she must've thought. I was onto her, though, and I did everything I could to hang on, everything short of sewing myself to the hem of her pleated paisley dress.

Mama never seemed to notice the whispers of mean folks, and for some unknown reason, they never felt the need to whisper in my presence. "Yeah, she used to strut 'round here with her nose stuck in the air talkin' 'bout her boy flying them aeroplanes. Look at her boy now; he ain't flying nothing but crazy." Mama never hid me in the back room or chained me to the fence post in the backyard. I was her boy, and she proudly paraded me and my craziness all over town.

Mama's style wasn't usually characterized by patience and trickery. I remembered her more as blunt and demanding where it concerned me before the war. When I was a "mannish teenager," she'd plant one hand on her hip, shake her index finger in my face, raise her voice loud enough to hear next door, and dare me to cross her for fear of death. "Git out from under me, boy. Git outta dhis here house and do something with yah friends. Yah need to do for yahself, 'cause I ain't got no mo' babies," she'd say. I would do exactly what she said without protest. I think I wanted to retreat from her space and set about creating my own.

Mama didn't say that to me after I got out of the crazy house, though. Mama was patient with me, gentle, kind, and even deferential. I didn't really recognize that side of Mama. I began to think that maybe she was afraid of me, weary of the stench of institutionalization still lingering in the space I inhabited. Was she afraid that she didn't know me anymore, or how I might react? Whatever the case, it was unnatural for a mother to fear her child, I thought. So, I began to drift back from the hem of her garment. I began to confront my fears and inhibitions; I didn't want Mama afraid of me. I finally thought about cutting the umbilical cord and drawing myself from the warmth and security of her womb.

Several months passed before I mustered up the courage to leave my room alone. Weeks more passed before I roamed freely about the house, and even more time before I ventured into the yard in the daylight. Mama then began gradually insisting that I go outside and get some fresh air.

"You is a grown man. You don't need to sit undah yah mama like you's a lil' kid," she said in a soft understanding voice.

Those idle and common words expressed in a sweet and understanding tone brought me great joy. I could see the day just on the horizon when she'd raise her voice and shake her finger in my face again. If I was lucky, she might even suck her teeth and roll her neck a time or two.

Gaining a nation's freedom requires sacrifices of blood and tears. I contributed my share of both during the war. Using freedom requires trust and confidence, both of which I began to reacquire cautiously over the next several months. I used my imagination in the interim.

"Two or three pounds of confidence today, Mr. Lankster?" the clerk asked.

"No, I don't think I'm ready for that much today, Haven. How's about...a half pound of confidence and a gallon of trust?" I responded.

"It's all up to you, Mr. Lankster. It's all up to you. Paper or plastic, paper in plastic or will you be having them here?" Haven asked.

"Paper in plastic. That way I'll have a good grip on them," I answered.

Haven called to me just before I got to the door, "We're running a special next week on love and happiness--buy one get one free, Mr. Lankster. If you're interested, I'll put some aside for you."

"No thanks. I got plenty of love, but, ya know, I think I'll take all the happiness I can get."

"Happiness it is then. Good choice, Mr. Lankster."

"I think so, Haven. I *think* so."

I dreamed that same thing for weeks. I'd wake up at 3:30 a.m. every time, sit on the edge of the bed, stretch my aching back, and then muster the courage to get to the bathroom and back alone and in the dark.

Fear ran rampant in my life in those days more so than at any time I could remember. I knew that staying close to home was safe, but I also knew that I wanted Marie and she was somewhere out in the world. Mama gave me the last bit of motivation I needed one cool summer afternoon.

Miss Lula Mae Barnett dropped by to talk to Mama about me. Mama called me into the room and told me to sit in the big chair in the corner while they talked. Miss Lula Mae considered herself a gifted matchmaker. She injected herself boldly into nearly everybody's love life on our side of town and sometimes on the other side too.

Miss Lula Mae was the oddest dresser in the entire county. She covered herself under layer upon layer of clothes. She was an introvert working a profession reserved for extroverts. She covered her body in multiple slips, aprons and long dresses that scraped the ground with every step she took. She layered two or three men's vests on top of the dresses and a woman's heavy wool shawl and black cloth gloves, no matter the weather. She covered her head with an extra large and very black wig and tied it up in a red bandana. She framed her eyes with oversized glasses that hid the top half of her face and distorted the size of her pupils. She habitually raised the glasses to her brow and looked under them if she needed to read small print. I could never tell how tall, short, fat, skinny, yellow, black or pink she was. I knew Miss Lula Mae only by her moving mounds of clothing, her grinding whisky voice, and the pungent smell of snuff always lingering about her person.

She accepted the mantle of town expert on matters of the heart, though she never married or, apparently, had even been in love. We thought she was a witch when we were kids. She kept the shades drawn on her dilapidated shotgun shack and always kept a massive kettle simmering in the backyard. Fifteen or twenty cats shared her home and not a single blade of grass grew anywhere in her yard. Yet, weeds grew up to six feet tall around the edge of the house and formed the giant nest in which it sat.

"I have the perfect match for yah boy, Bernice," Miss Lula Mae said, looking in my direction but talking to Mama. Mama never gave her much credit for being a matchmaker, but I sensed that she thought I needed help even if it came from Miss Lula Mae. She was willing to tolerate Miss Lula Mae for a few minutes.

"Yah knows Queen Ester Jones, don't yah? She live o'er on Sioux by the chu'ch. She married to Solomon Jones and they got them seven kids, all girls," Miss Lula Mae continued.

"I knows Queen Ester well, and me an' Solomon growed up together, Lula Mae. What about her?" Mama responded.

"Well, you know her middle child, Yahlanda? She the one with the baby by Low Boy."

"Yeah, I knows that gal some, but I knows her sisters, Margaret and Inola, better." Mama responded. Mama's use of "gal" instead of "girl" was a clear signal to Miss Lula Mae that she was already heading down the wrong path. Yolanda's sisters, Margaret and Inola, however, were worth at least considering.

"Well, *Yahlanda* and yah boy is perfect for one another," Miss Lula Mae persisted, despite the warning and attendant recommendations.

"Lula Mae, ain't somethin' wrong with that gal?"

"She a little off. They say hah mama held her in too long waiting for the midwife. Anyway, yah knows after she spit out that kid for Low Boy, Dr. Anderson fixed her so she cain't have no mo' babies. There ain't no chance of 'em branging any mo' crazy younguns in the world," Miss Lula Mae whispered, to keep it from me, I suppose.

"Why would I wants *her* for my boy, Lula Mae? She ain't nevah been no where or done nothing but spit out that baby and sit undah her mama and daddy. 'Sides, that gal ain't got the sense to rub two plug nickels togethah."

"Bernice, you need to take a good look at this boy of yourn. He ain't that much different than Yahlanda. Sho' nuff he done been overseas and all and served in the waw, but thas it. He ain't nevah gonna leave this town again. He gon' stay rat here and rot like the rest of dem. Now, the onless good thang about the situation is that the gov'ment pays him eve'y month, and they will from here on out."

"But *Yo'landa*, Lula Mae?" Mama asked incredulously.

"He and Yahlanda is jus' about the same speed, and his gov'ment money oughtta keep him, her, and that baby jus' fine. Besides, she 'bout the bes' he gone do the way he is now. Anybody else be marryin' him jus' fo' the money. Some ah these nasty gals around here would marry ah jackass for the money and run around on him sho' as my feets is black."

Are they black? I wondered, staring in her direction about where her feet should be.

"There's other good girls interested in him that don't care

nothin' 'bout that little money from the gov'ment," Mama lied, or if true I didn't know who they were.

"Bernice, there ain't nothin' that goes on around here in the way of marryin' that I don't knows about. Now, before the waw, yah boy was a good catch. With dat degree from Langston, he was good as they gits, for a colored girl anyways. He could've married one o' them high yellow Creole girls out south of town. He was smart and as purty as a wet summer morning. But now, he cain't do nothing bi'dout somebody doing it for 'im. You probably even got to hold his thang for him to piss straight. Dhere ain't too many womens 'round here, least among them that got choices anyhows, who's gone tolerate shit like that. Wake up, woman, and face the truth. Either that boy gonna git with Yahlanda or somebody not very much different from Yahlanda. I'm telling you, at leas' she's a good girl, who gone try to do him right. Otherwise, alls he got left is to stay up under you 'til one of you is dead and buried, or have some gold diggin' ho' take him for all he got."

Mama sat still and quiet. Her reason told her that there was some truth to what Miss Lula Mae said. Her pride told her to stand up for her boy and not to sell him short. I sat quietly in my chair in the corner, not caring about the words coming from Miss Lula Mae's mouth. I would have stood up for myself, if I remembered that I was a grown man who saw more of the world than most people do in their dreams. I would have said something if I remembered that most of the time what people think of you does matter.

Was it pride that got me here? Mama must've thought to herself. She was so proud when I became a Tuskegee Airman. We were amongst the best of the best educated and trained of all the colored soldiers. She showed off my picture with Eleanor Roosevelt to anybody she could snatch a second from. She knew some folks around there were jealous. After all, their boys were digging ditches and serving food to the white boys in the war while I was a pilot flying the most sophisticated planes in the world and shooting down white and yellow boys overseas. Now, she seriously considered marrying her pride and joy off to a simpleton who shared her body with Low Boy Kelly, the least desirable man in town.

"Why don't she marry Low Boy?" Mama asked weakly. I sensed her resistance fading.

"Her daddy jus' 'bout killed her rodeo night when he found out the little bastard was Low Boy's. I believes Low Boy mightah came up from behind and took her when she wasn't looking. She just didn't have sense enough to stop him. Anyway, Low Boy ain't no good in no kindah way, and he ain't been seen since her daddy got after him. That's why they ask me tah find somebody for her."

"So you came here?" Mama asked.

"I got to thanking about a good clean man, 'bout somebody on her level who got something to offer. It must be somebody that won't do her no harm and she won't do him no harm. Yo' boy is the one I thought of. Neither Yahlanda nor yah boy got any descent prospects around here. And if he ain't nothing else no mo', he's a good clean man," Lula Mae responded.

"There's a woman out there somewhere who'd marry my boy jus' like he is and treat 'im right," Mama said after a long silence.

"Like I said, Bernice, tain't nobody 'round here like dhat." Miss Lula Mae dug in. "Yah boy *was* somebody. Dhat's more pride than most colored folks can expect to have in they chillins...what he *was* I means. He ain't nobody now. Sis. Roosevelt ain't gonna take no mo' pictures with him. Sweetie, you gottah thank long term and 'bout what happiness he can git outta what's left of him."

Mama took a deep breath, clasped her hands together, and rubbed them over the bridge of her nose in a praying motion. She spoke slowly and deliberately with her eyes closed and her head angled down slightly.

"She ain't from 'round here. There was dis French girl. She came all the way to America, to Okmulgee, right here to Lafayette Street, and stood right on dat po'ch out dere looking for my boy. Dey told us he was dead. I still got the telegram from General Eisenhower. One of them generals even called me to say that my boy died a genuine hero no matter what the white papers was saying. So that's what we told her; he died in the waw a hero. That girl cried in my arms like a baby. She tol' me she loved my boy, and part of her died with him...."

I didn't hear another word Mama said after that. My entire world collapsed in on itself, shifted from black and white to static, and began to rebuild itself one line at a time in living color. Marie came to Oklahoma looking for me? I felt something inside again. The emotional numbness that characterized my life since returning to America began to fade away.

"Marie was here?" I asked Mama.

I thought I yelled the question to her. I felt a torrent rushing from my insides, but Mama didn't respond. She and Miss Lula Mae kept talking, barely aware that I was still in the room.

"Marie was here?" I asked again. This time I knew I screamed at the top of my lungs. Mama turned her head and looked curiously in my direction.

"Did you say somethin', son?" she asked rising from her seat and walking over to me. She bent over and brought her ear close to my mouth

"Marie was here?" I repeated.

Mama said later that those were the first words she heard me speak since they brought me home. My voice sounded low and rough from disuse, but it was there and my mama heard it.

"The tomb holdin' my boy's mind is finally opening up. Thank yah, Lawd Jesus," she cried out.

I was confused. Hadn't we spoken dozens of times a day since I returned home? Hadn't I told her on numerous occasions about Marie, the Tuskegee Airmen, and the crazy house? Hadn't I wished her a good morning, exchanged pleasantries over meals, and bid her a good night at the end of countless days? Or was I silent all that time, thinking volumes to myself, but speaking to no one?

"Marie *was* here, son. I hadn't even thought about her 'til Miss Lula Mae got to yapping 'bout what woman would want you. That was a long time ago, and I nearly forgot about her. She loved you, son," Mama finally answered.

She then turned to Miss Lula Mae.

"Lulu Mae, you kin git the hell outta my house now," she said calmly and with absolute clarity of intent.

Miss Lula Mae didn't exchange a word; she just quietly lifted her mounds of clothes from the sofa and left without saying good-bye.

Decades of raw and unfiltered human emotion rushed to the surface of my consciousness. I remember collapsing to the floor and sobbing uncontrollably. I remember laughing with great joy and wrapping myself in a welcome back bear hug. I remember moaning in pain and agony over decades of mistreatment and physical abuse. I vaguely remember Mama comforting me through it all, and then everything fading to black. I woke up two days later in my bed refreshed and wanting to talk again in a way that solicited answers from real people. The urge to find Marie in the flesh this time began to overtake me again. Mama told me that

Marie spent a week in Okmulgee walking the places I walked and absorbing my world.

Chapter Twenty

The Long Walk Back to Self

Dear Lil Sis, It wasn't easy breaking away from the narrow boundaries Taft programmed into me. I began by walking outside the fenced yard the next day, exactly eight months to the day after returning home. I was hoping to place my feet where Marie might have walked. I started slowly and sang those lines from *Santa Claus is Coming to Town* about putting one foot in front of the other. I set a goal to tread on every inch of the yard and leave my staggered and connected footprints from one end to the other.

Next, I walked the neighborhood. I couldn't walk in private yards, so I focused on covering the streets and sidewalks for three blocks in every direction. I learned the neighborhood streets cold. I gave names to the potholes, breaks in the sidewalks, intersections, and street signs.

I walked in circles for eight-hour stretches in the beginning. The strain on my out-of-shape body nearly killed me on the first day. I hadn't eaten or drunk liquid the entire time. I heaved and collapsed in the front yard just inside the gate. I lay there for several hours simmering in my own stomach acids before Mama came home and found me. She called our neighbor, Mr. Jerry, and they both carried me inside.

"You need to call the amalance to take dhis boy to the hosspital, girl. He mightah had ah sunstroke," advised Mr. Jerry.

"No, I ain't. They might not give him back, and Lawd knows I don't wanna git ugly over there," Mama answered.

I recuperated at home, in the house where I was born, under the soft breeze of a rotary fan that cooled my overheated body and the sure hand of the other woman in the world who loved me. I couldn't stand too much heat after that.

I was a benign mystery in the neighborhood as long as I stayed in the house and close to Mama. Our good neighbors became increasingly alarmed, however, seeing more of me on the street unaccompanied and wandering aimlessly. Upright Christian values and small town manners faded away quickly where I was concerned. The good people of the neighborhood replaced apathy with venomous gossip fueled by irrational fears.

Mama interceded on my behalf. "He's a touch shell-shocked from the waw, but he ain't thankin' 'bout hurt'n nobody. He was one of the colored pilots in the Army Air Corp Sis. Roosevelt brought on, and he got shot down overseas. They say he took three or four of them with him befo' he went down. They don't know what happened to him o'er there when them folks got him. My boy's a hero, though, sho' nuff. They say if'n he ever gets his mind straight, the president gonna wanna see him. Them Nazis, they took something from him o'er there and Lawd knows I hopes he finds it and comes back to us. But he won't do nobody here no harm, so don't pay him no mind. Jus' let him walk in peace."

I kept walking. Men ignored me. Single women avoided me. Mothers with children warned against me, and I just walked. Some white folks considered me normal for a colored. Coloreds considered me an example of what happens when a colored man gets "too big." Mama prayed for me. Sis, I don't know what you thought; of course you and Roger were in Connecticut by then. I walked anyway.

I walked farther each day. I walked farther away the next day from the place I stopped the day before without losing sight of it. This worked for me. The flat rolling plains of Oklahoma meant that I could sometimes walk several miles on a clear day and not lose sight of my last stopping point. I took comfort in the belief that the last place I stopped was a safe haven because I walked there before and no harm befell me. In time, I packed food and water and ate at the many safe spots I identified along the way. I minimized my contact with people that way. I slipped out of their consciousness.

A part of me expected to find Marie around every blind corner, on the other side of every hill, and from the underside of every tree. I knew that she came to look for me in Oklahoma. That's exactly what I would have done. She couldn't find me, of course, and no one who gave a shit about me knew where I was to tell her. They told her I was dead. She would know in her heart that I wasn't dead. She'd hear the same inner voice that told me she was not dead. Nonetheless, such news from a credible source would have been devastating in the beginning, and it would take time for her to regain her bearings. Part of me hoped that she set up residence nearby and awaited my return. I wanted to believe that she was just around the next corner.

There were times when I thought I saw her off in the distance, especially under a fully starred Oklahoma night sky. She dressed in a man's clothes. I remembered her with baggy pants drawn tightly at the waist, a dust-colored cotton shirt with two buttoned flap pockets and a wrinkled brown suit jacket. The jacket barely touched her shoulders, its hem came to her knees and billowed cape high in the wind. She tucked her hair under a black beret pulled halfway down her forehead. Strands of her hair fell out, suggesting she was someone other than whom she portrayed. I swore I saw her in mud splattered, well-used work boots laced halfway up with tattered strings. She dressed that way when she rescued me.

It was always someone or something else I saw. Sometimes it was a shadow, and other times a reified sun glare or the side effects of extreme fatigue. Each time I saw what I thought was Marie, the anticipation of holding her, talking to her, and looking into her eyes overwhelmed me. Equally, the disappointment of the illusion crushed me every time.

The mountain of fear I built up in the institution began to crumble in the familiar places proportional to a pile of worn-out shoes growing in my closet. It was difficult to take that next step beyond the places I knew already, but somehow I did. Fifteen months into my freedom, I walked twelve hours out and twelve hours back home. I was tired afterwards, but my body didn't ache for long, and sleep cured whatever physical ailments I had. A day, a night and day again passed, and I survived out in the free world. I traveled the entire spectrum of the day, farther than at any time since my return. I survived. The shackles of fear continued to fall away.

My familiar stops along the way became too numerous and distant from Okmulgee to remember. There were simply too many of them to hold in my head. I decided to buy a map, therefore, and plot every stopping place along my way. The closer I was to Okmulgee, the closer the dots were on the map. The farther I traveled from Okmulgee, the greater the distance between each dot. The farthest point I passed fifty times would become my new home base. This allowed me to gradually extend my journey far beyond Okmulgee. That was my plan.

I learned to use the maps to precisely plan my journey beyond the familiar places. It reminded me of discovering reading for the first time. The world lay before me undressed, exposed, and almost comprehensible in a map. I became obsessed with maps. Maps gave me the town, city, state, and nation in just a few pages. I could run my finger across Oklahoma, Arkansas, Tennessee, Kentucky, Ohio, Wisconsin, Pennsylvania, New Jersey, New York, the Atlantic Ocean, England, France, and Giverny. I could do it in a few seconds and without fear or sweat. I ran my index finger across unfamiliar places, and I did not fear them. A red dot with a name attached to it seemed far less menacing than asphalt, bricks, and mortar.

I bought an atlas of the United States from the IGA just off Wood Drive, which was approximately 2.58 miles from Mama's house. I wrote to fifty chambers of commerce in cities and small towns roughly fifty miles apart and requested maps of their communities. I bought maps of Canada, Iceland, and Greenland from the Sears & Roebuck catalogue. I even bought a navigation chart of the Atlantic Ocean from an army surplus store in Redbird, Oklahoma.

"A man could make it across the Atlantic Ocean without a boat and without being noticed. It's easy, if you know how," a WWI navy veteran told me in Choosky Bottom, Oklahoma.

I bought maps of England and France from the travel agency on Sixth Street, approximately 3.8 miles from Mama's house. I acquired maps of every town, city, and village in between every state and nation that interested me. I planned a journey on foot, averaging 30 miles a day. I could walk where I could walk and swim where I must swim and even fly if it came to that.

The last walk from which I returned to Okmulgee was exactly 150.4 miles. It took me twenty-four days round-trip. I had a surprising amount of human contact over those twenty-four days, mostly with the police, hobos, and prostitutes. Of the three, prostitutes treated me the best and were generally safe. They were safe because they were less likely to knock me over the head. There was a 50/50 chance that I'd be rolled by a policeman or a hobo, so I avoided contact with both. I never ate any food I didn't prepare or use a bathroom with a toilet, roof or four walls between respites.

The Okmulgee Police stopped me two miles inside the city line on my way back home for the last time. They warned me very politely at first not to let the sun set on me in the city, because they didn't allow hobos there.

"We don't 'low no hobos here," he said.

"I live here," I responded. Not believing me, they ordered me to get in the back of the car and suggested they could give me a lift home.

"I prefer to walk, sir," I responded politely.

"Well, you don't walk fast enough for us. Now you can get in this car and show us where you claim to live, or we can haul you head first into this car and run you in for vagrancy and lying to the police," the younger one responded.

I climbed into the back of the police cruiser without another word.

"What's your name?" they asked, and I told them.

They called in my name to their headquarters. "Well, well, well, seems you do live here. We have a missing persons report on you, boy. Where have you been for the last month?"

"I've been walking."

"Walking?"

"Just walking."

"You been walking all that time. You oughtta have holes worn in your ass," one responded with a snicker.

I did not respond.

"Let me see your feet, Mr. Walking Man," the other demanded contemptuously.

I lifted my left foot up on the back of the seat. The younger one's face turned red, his brow wrinkled, and the glimmer in his eyes faded to blank. He tapped his partner on the shoulder and pointed to my feet.

"Oh shit!" his partner yelled and the car swerved into the on-coming lane.

The looks on their faces told me not to look at my foot. Somewhere along the way, I walked through the leather soles of my shoes. I guessed how my feet must have looked when they called the hospital.

"Sharon, we're bringing in a bad one. He's gonna need ya'll to work on his right foot. I don't know...I didn't look at the left. Yeah, the right. It looks like hamburger. Blood, scabbing, and maybe some infection building up... No, we have not applied first aid."

The exposed parts of my bare feet were raw, bloody, and tender. They were burned from the hot pavement and punctured by gravel and dirt. I felt no pain in my feet until the moment I finally looked at them. The OPD officers decided to take me straight to the hospital rather than home.

"Why don' you jus' take the train like normal folks do?" the younger officer asked me after he calmed down.

"The train has too many people on it," I responded.

The truth was, though, until that very moment, passenger trains, buses, and airplanes had slipped out of my consciousness.

Two weeks passed. My feet healed enough that I could walk on them with only slight discomfort. I learned to use Mama's new telephone to call the train station downtown. The man told me that I could get to NYC for $150.00 round trip. I gave him my name and told him I'd be there the next day to pick up my ticket.

That was when I first noticed the government men. They began to watch me regularly and openly after my twenty-four days of absence. They took particular interest in me after my call to the train station. It was still about those days the army held me prisoner. It was about those executions.

I could spot a government man on the head of a straight pin. Everything about the government men was plain. They drove plain brown four-door Ford automobiles with black-walled tires and standard factory-issued hubcaps. Their cars were always clean inside and out like rich folks' cars, but they were not the kind of cars rich folks drove. That meant that someone in the motor pool was doing the cleaning. Government cars came straight from the factory. No dealer stickers, nameplates, or other extraneous accessories decorated the body of a government man's car.

Government men draped their bodies in plain dark suits, white shirts, and perfectly tied dark ties. A suit is a suit for the most part. But on a government man, a suit is a uniform with its perfectly creased pants and lint-free lapels. Brown or black wingtip shoes covered average sized, well-arched feet. Those feet supported regular shaped bodies fed on bacon, eggs, baked potatoes, and pork chops.

Government men were generally white with military style haircuts. Even so, since that Martin Luther King fellow started raising cane, I noticed a few colored government men here and there. Government men slept in the cars parked across the street and down the block from where I slept. They ate at the window table of the restaurant across the way from where I ate. They whispered in the ears of people to whom I just spoke. Sometimes government men wanted me to see them and sometimes they didn't. But they always saw me.

I tried buying train tickets at the station downtown, but I could not. I couldn't even get a ticket for a Greyhound bus out of town. It was a small town, and they all said my mama told them not to sell me a ticket, but I knew better than that. They noticed that the government men took a particular interest in me. I wasn't brewing moonshine in the outhouse, so the people made up stories to fill in the blanks. The colored folks thought I was a guinea pig in a program to put smart colored men in "their place." The white folks thought I was a civil rights agitator. They weren't sure, though, whether the government was spying on me or protecting me. Regardless, I couldn't buy my way out of town.

They watched the Greyhound bus station, the train station, and even the Tulsa airport. I could buy a coke and a hotdog, but not a ticket and a seat. All of a sudden, I didn't feel so free anymore.

I devised a plan. I stayed in the house with the shades drawn, the doors locked, and plotted my trek to France. "Put one foot in front of the other," rang in my ears. "I'll walk to France," I decided. I needed to travel about 4,500 miles on the Earth's surface, traveling generally west to east and mostly on foot. Those chamber of commerce maps contained lots of handy information. Banks and funeral parlors existed in every town big enough to have a chamber of commerce. I would need money, but it was too dangerous to carry any on me. So I got fifty-two money orders for $100.00 each and used them to open accounts in small town banks all across America. It took me several weeks to accumulate the money. I purchased seven money orders for a penny and one for $100. The clerk only talked about the seven one-cent money orders. "He paid more for the money order than its face value. He is just plain crazy."

They were the crazy ones, just sitting on their asses while their soul mates wandered aimlessly out in the world. They were obsessed with clothes, make up, pickup trucks, guns, and movie stars, while their hearts starved for genuine fulfillment. They dug themselves deep, narrow trenches in their own backyard, while the true miracles of life could be found one inch below the surface all over the planet. They only saw themselves through the reflections in mirrors distorted by notions of physical beauty. I saw Marie in my heart's eye. I didn't care if people laughed at me. I felt sorry for them. *I knew* what was important.

It was the last cold day of winter in Oklahoma. Scattered blades of green grass showed themselves among the masses of dead yellow grasses of a long winter. I planned every step of the first 150 miles of the journey upon which I was about to embark. I drew heavy dotted lines on paper and plotted on experience the last 1,400 new miles. I knew that I was leaving Oklahoma for the last time and never returning again.

I was formed from the damp red clay and soft sandstone of Oklahoma. For most of my life, I only ate the fruits of its rolling plains and cattle strewn ranges. If I passed back into the Oklahoma dust, it would be more of the same, and no one would notice. My destiny was to pass into the dust of some other place, where I would be different, where it would be mixed with Marie's.

Mama was in the kitchen when I walked through the house for the last time. She hauled water to the ringer washer on the back porch and fried chicken for dinner in her favorite cast iron skillet. It was the same ringer type washer I hauled hot or cold water from the faucet to many cold mornings before going off to school. We cured that cast iron skillet in a homemade fire pit I dug in the backyard. I grew up accustomed to the smell of washing bleach and frying chicken in the early morning air. The bleach drove me out of the house many mornings, and the chicken brought me home in the afternoons. The sizzle of the chicken and the slosh of the washer played the moody blues that morning because I needed to tell Mama that I was leaving and never coming back.

"Don't wait up for me, Mama," I said.

She didn't answer. She didn't even look at me. She just kept hauling the water to the washer and turning the chicken in the pan.

"Did you hear me, Mama? You don't have to wait up for me tonight?"

"I hears yah, son," she responded, and then paused. "Are yah sho *she* still waitin' up for you, son?" she asked slowly and deliberately, already knowing the answer.

"Yeah, Mama, I'm sure."

"Are you sho she still waitin' for you likes you is for her?"

"I believe she is, Mama. She's like me in that way, we's all there is for one another. It's kinda like the difference between eatin' your chicken hot outta the pan or eatin' chicken raw. One will brang you joy, and the other just might kill you. So if you cain't have it right, you don't have it atall. We are right for one another."

Mama turned, looked me up and down, and smiled. "You sho is a fine boy. You always been a fine boy. I knows the Lawd is given me mo' time with yah than a mama oughts to have with a son. Maybe that's why it's so hard to let you chilluns go. Thank yah, son, and when yah finds her--*Marie*...When you finds Marie, yah thanks her for lettin' me have this time with yah."

Mama took off her apron, folded it neatly, and laid it on the kitchen table. She pulled Daddy's old railroad lunchbox from under the counter already packed with homemade preserves, peanut butter, and hard biscuits. She wrapped some of her freshly cooked chicken in wax paper and placed it in the box.

"I knowed dis time was coming soon. Here's a little somethin' for you to have along the way...."

Mama handed me the silver, molded tin box. She looked me in the eye and said, "You is a fine boy, and yah got a good heart. Jus' cause them Nazis is gone, don't mean the world is ready fo' what you and her got. And what I say ain't got nothin' to do with how you two looks on the outside. The worl' wasn't ready for what Jesus had in 'im, and it ain't ready for yall neither. You be careful, and don't ever forgets where you come from."

Mama hugged me for the last time and kissed me in the center of my forehead. She took her the dish towel hanging from her apron strings and wiped her red lipstick from my furrowed brow. Whatever it is that a parent is supposed to impart to a child, she gave me the last of that day.

"Gwine, boy, now you gits outta heah befo' I burns the rest of my chicken," she said with tears streaming down her face.

Chapter Twenty-One

In The Lion's Den

I never questioned my belief that a man could really walk to France across the Atlantic Ocean. I didn't think too much about the probability of my success either. I found myself in a place emotionally where I was determined to do it no matter how outrageous it seemed. So I walked and walked and walked some more. I'd find a safe place to rest when my body couldn't stand for another foot to hit the pavement in front of me. Sometimes, I'd rest only a few hours and, at other times, for days or weeks depending on how safe the place and how tired my well used limbs. I walked for two years, Sis, before you all rescued me from Bellevue Hospital. A lotta stuff happened betwixt Okmulgee and New York.

I found Southern whorehouses particularly welcoming to me since I knew my way up and down a piano. I'd play jazz and bebop in dark, smoky bars and the over-decorated ballrooms of former plantation mansions. The people in these places behaved completely free in a way that I never before experienced. Sure, illicit sex drew them together, but for reasons beyond that, they seemed to check out of the norms of society all together. Good and bad didn't exist in a whorehouse. Grown men danced without inhibition, cross-dressed, drugged up, mixed races, and even openly discussed politics outside of the reach of the backhand of race and class. Many a white man sidestepping social norms and guzzling a fifth of Jack Daniels became especially honest when cloistered in these dens of moral ambiguity.

"Deep in my heart, I don't believe you niggers is inferior to us white folks. After all, y'all didn't volunteer for slavery--you didn't even ask to come here. But, there's expectations on a white man out there that you know nothin' 'bout. Expectations that we gonna keep what our forefathers left us. Expectations set down and maintained by folks with more guns, more money, and more smart words than I got. I gottah feed my family, I gottah walk the same streets and sit in the same pews my neighbors do, so I gottah git along," the white man's monologue would often start.

"Sometimes, I wish I was a colored man. You don't know how good you got it. Y'all don't got nothing that a white man can't take. Therefore, what you got to worry 'bout? You can do whatever you want, and if you just stay with other coloreds ain't nothing gonna be done to yah. Nobody expects nothin' of yah. Nobody expectin' you to have anything of substance in your head or have a good job. Nobody expectin' you to take care o' no wife and kids. You kin just roam like a wild tiger up and down the jungle, devouring here and there and doin' whatever the hell you feel like doin', an' nobody gonna say you ain't living up to yah promise.

"The hard cold truth is I wish I *wasn't* always burdened by superiority. There's a lotta pressure in being superior all the time. You can go here and do this, but you can't go there and do the other 'cause that's nigger stuff. You can't ask a nigger for help and you gottah beat his ass if'n he do help you when you need it 'cause he being uppity. You can't be a po' white man, 'cause then you is po' white trash. In my book, white trash is worse than being a black nigger. A nigger is property at least--property *somebody* wants. Don't nobody want no trash. Trash ain't fit for nothin' but to throwin' away and burnin' or buryin' in a heap with other trash.

"My world is just the way it is and I can't do nothing 'bout that. I cain't be a nigger with no 'sponsibility and I cain't be po' white trash squandering the privileges granted by my whiteness.

"Let me tell you somethin', boy. If you peoples really wants somethin', then you gottah be willing to die for it. What I got, I'm willing to die to keep it, and I'm even willing to die to git mo'. That's the American way. If'n you ain't willing to die for it, you ain't gonna git it. That's why we got stuff and y'all ain't got shit. You know what? It really ain't gonna make no difference in my life if nigger kids go to school with my kids, or I ride on the same bus and sit next to you. It ain't gonna matter to crackers like me. You think my grandpappy's pappy owned slaves, boy? He got his leg blowed off in the Civil Waw, but he damn sho' didn't own no slaves. Most po' white people didn't, yet they fought a war for them handful of rich assholes that did. Why? 'Cause they told us we should fight. They told us we was fightn' to keep y'all outta the white woman's pussy. What we was really fightn' for was to pre- serve them s.o.b's right to keep black slaves, so they wouldn't have to pay you or us a fair wage for our work. They still tellin' us we oughtta fight; not for us, but for them, their money, their property, and their power ovah you niggers and us. And for some reason, we keep on fightin', burnin', and killin' to preserve somebody else's crystal castle high up on the hill with fancy dinner tables I can't even sit at and daughters my son can no mo' fuck' than yours. Now, you figgah that out, boy?

"They need us to hate ya'll, boy. 'Cause if'n we didn't hate ya'll, then we all might start gittin' together. If we gits together, I might find out that you ain't the reason I ain't got a pot to piss in, and y'all 'ill find out that the grass ain't all that green on the white side of the color line. Then we might look up together on the high hill at those crystal castles and hurl stones at the motherfucker's stirring the pot. We might just realize that them folks up there who's been ah stirring the pot is got all the good meat from the soup to themselves."

I heard dozens of similar monologues. The funny thing is that to a man they explained their plight to me for the purpose of discouraging my presumed desire for whiteness. They believed to a man that I'd jump at the chance to switch races if I could. They harbored so much bourbon-induced compassion for me that they wanted me to know that they, who were born white men, had a difficult time meeting the qualifications to remain white. So I, being born a colored man, surely couldn't handle the pressures of being a white man if so blessed. The truth is I never thought much about being a member of any race at that time. It was always other folks who reminded me I was one color and not the other.

I still wasn't convinced that they suffered what colored folks did, but I did think more about who those folks were sitting up high in their crystal castles stirring the pot of racial hatred.

Whorehouses, though, were still about sex. Everything else was gaudy window dressing. I still loved Marie, so I couldn't help wondering how the men and girls in these places hooked up so quickly, stayed together so briefly, and parted so completely at the buzz of a time clock. Admittedly, these thoughts were rare, and I kept them to myself. Frankly, I was so disconnected from other people that I didn't have the capacity to moralize, judge, or rightly divide the sinner from the saint. Looking up from the viewpoint of a hobo--pious saints and moneyed sinners looked down on me pretty much the same.

So I didn't see much of a difference between saints and sinners. Most on both sides seemed to live life on autopilot, their bodies touching while their hearts shut down and minds checked out.

I'd slap the bones when the regular piano player was off, in jail, or too high to keep his fingers on the keys. Sometimes, I'd just hire on to clean up the place. The male guests never did and weren't expected to clean up after themselves, and the girl hostesses slept during cleaning hours. A detached man was a good domestic servant since most of the cleaning folks back then were colored women, and no "decent women" would take any amount of money to clean a den of lasciviousness. A male eunuch would have been the perfect choice. Indecent women, though generally better cleaners than most men, could make more money hosting than cleaning.

As you can imagine, the boss women offered to pay me cash money sometimes and alternatively, "the services" of the girls all the time. The madam would willingly give up a little something from the girls in barter if it meant that cash stayed stuffed in her brassiere. The girls were salaried--not paid piecemeal. The madam paid them more money than they could ever make in more respectable jobs since most of the girls were either poor young widows or poorer old orphans. I wasn't too interested in either money or raw carnality. I wanted only a place to rest, food to eat, and information on the whereabouts of the next whorehouse in my path over the narrow, dark backwoods of America.

Believe it or not, love would actually stumble into a brothel every now and then. I personally witnessed genuine love poke its big toe in whorehouses throughout the South. It wasn't in the girls that I found this love. The girls were all cut from the same bitter tree and were even more disconnected from society than I was. What a contradiction: they shared the most intimate aspects of their persons with strangers, but were more disconnected from the world than the man in the moon.

It was in a few of the male patrons that true love tagged along in a loose pocket or on a liquor-lubed tongue. There were four kinds of men who frequented brothels. I'll call them John, Harry, Bob, and Pete. John gave no love, brought no evidence of love with him, and did not seek love. John comprised 90% of the clientele. He was interested in pure, raw, and uncluttered sexual gratification. His visits were no more meaningful to his person than a trip to the bathroom. Sex was merely a bodily function that he willingly paid prostitutes to satisfy. There was no love offered or received by John. Harry, Bob, and Pete were a different story.

Someone at home loved Harry very much. Harry's problem

was that he didn't know how to return that love. Harry confused sex with love and boredom with falling out of love. I'd find letters from Harry's wife under beds in the cribs and in the wastebaskets in the lobby.

Harry,

Please stay home with me tonight. Please, dear, whatever it is that's pulling you away from our marriage, know that I'm willing to do whatever it takes to hold onto to you. You are everything to me, my love. Remember when we first met. I do! You were the most handsome man in the world. My heart melted the first time we touched. I need your touch now, my love. I need you to warm my heart again. Please...please don't go away tonight.

Janice

Harry married Janice, they built a home together, and he made babies with her. But when the wedding was over, the home built, and the babies near grown, Harry felt he offered Janice nothing else. Some tragedy long ago caused Harry to lock his love in an iron safe and shove it far back in a seldom-used corner of his heart. Even though he was very fond of Janice, he had long since forgotten the combination to the safe. Harry spent most of his time away from her searching for a competent safe cracker. He looked for someone or some experience to break it open and release the love experience he vaguely recalled from the past. Harry didn't understand, though, that the girls working in brothels weren't safe crackers, and they didn't care that someone waited for Harry at home who really loved him.

Bob loved a woman who cared nothing for him. She was his wife of many years, but never his lover. Bob would call home from the pay telephone in the back of the bar and hope and pray that Jane would pick up, tell him she loved him, and ask him to rush home to her. Nobody answered Bob's call, though. He wondered if Jane was with Phil from down the street or Jack from the meat market. Bob needed a hidden place to let his manhood slip away in private. He needed a place to curl up in a fetal position on the floor and cry. He needed an ear to listen to him pour out the torment in his heart without judging him. Unrequited love brought Bob to whorehouses, but the freedom to talk himself back into sanity kept him there.

Bob made me realize that the girls had some genuine feelings. When Bob walked through the door, they'd rush to him like stampeding cattle, pushing and shoving their way into his attention for a night in his company. They knew instinctively that all Bob wanted was someone with whom he could talk. He needed to talk to someone with a keen ear to listen but without credibility if they gossiped. With Bob, the girls could keep their clothes on, still get paid, and maybe even cry along with him. They were always willing to discuss Bob's plight among themselves in the break room. Bob made them feel good about the service they provided.

"Girl, he cried like a baby."

"Well, what did he say?"

"He said, 'You know what it's like being so hungry that your belly hurts and your eyes feel like they gonna bust out o' they sockets? The food you need to fill you up and make you feel good and satisfied is right there in front o' you. But you cain't reach it. You try everythang to reach for it, you stretch your arms, and you dig your fingers in clawing at the dirt till they bleed trying to pull yourself to it. You cry out in your loudest voice and command it to come to you. You fall down on your knees and plead with God in heaven to lay it at your feet, if, but for a moment, you may eat of it.

"'It just teases you. You see it in all of its beauty. You smell its sweet scent on the air, and yet, it don't come to you. Before long, alls you think about is eating that food. All you wants to do is to eat that food. All that matters is that food.

"'The food takes no mind of you. It would rather rot and be consumed by maggots than let you feast upon it. It mocks you with its rich colors, aroma, and shapes. You cry because the pangs in your belly become your constant companion, a companion that never leaves you yet reminds you unceasingly of what you can never have. I know what it's like to hurt like that.

"'You hate it as much as you want it. You think that if you cain't have it, then you'll smash it so nobody can have it. You forget who you are....'

"Girl, I tried to git his min' off that shit. I couldn't do it, though. He talked and cried, cried and talked, till he fell off to sleep in my arms. He was callin' his wife's name in his sleep and beggin' like a pussy for her to love him back. I wish some man would beg me like a pussy to love him."

That last idle, almost throwaway comment would break up the

little gossip session instantly. Each girl retreated to her room with a box of tissue and some frayed letters from her past. Some would pull out phone numbers of old boyfriends, lovers, and admirers and search diligently for their own Bob.

Pete was deeply in love with one of the girls. Pete was always *too* something, though, for the girl to love him back; *too* short, *too* fat, *too* dirty, *too* dumb, *too* ugly, or *too* country. Pete knew that he was *too* something. He believed that no woman of any decent standing in the community would give him a chance to love her. But there was that pretty girl at the whorehouse that he thought didn't mind being with him and his *too* somethings. She never mentioned or seemed to notice that he was *too* anything. She was nice to him and loved him when they were together.

Pete never understood the relationship between the money he paid at the door and the girl who treated him so nicely. Pete was there when the doors opened and paid extra to stay until they closed. For all of Pete's *toos,* he was the happiest person to ever enter the front door of a whorehouse and the saddest person to ever leave a whorehouse voluntarily or involuntarily. Pete brought flowers and chocolates when he came and was usually escorted out of the house at the working end of a .45.

Pete would wait for me to leave the premises and beg to talk to me about the girl he loved. He wanted to know her telephone number or to send her a message or some money. Our conversation was always similar:

"Man, I love that girl. I been waitin' for somebody like her all my life," he'd say.

"Pete, she's a prostitute. She sells her body for a living," I'd respond.

"I know that, man, and I don't care 'bout that. Ain't nobody perfect in the eyes of God or man. I kin take her away from all that, and she'd never have to do any kind o' work again."

"Yeah, Pete, I know you kin."

"Do she talk about me when I ain't there? Is she ready to leave yet?"

"I don't know nothin' about that, Pete. You have to talk to her about that."

"I talk to her 'bout it eve'y time I sees her. But she just keep saying, it ain't time yet. She gots to get enough money together to stand on her own two feet first. You ever heard anything so crazy?

A grown woman on her own?"

"Naw, Pete, I ain't heard nothin' like that befo'."

"Roy, I know you think I'm crazy, but I loves that girl. She the first person I been with that accepts me for who I am. I kin make her happy out here in the real world. When we is together, it seems like there's nobody else in the world but us. Folks used to say I could nevah git a pretty girl like her with a good head on her shoulders. Well, they is wrong. I loves her, and I knows she loves me too. It's just that that place got a hold on her, and I gots to break it. Kin yah talk to her for me, Roy? Tell her how I really feels about her."

"I ain't allowed to take no messages to them girls, Pete. You know that."

"Listen, Roy, I got a house full of furniture with an inside bathroom and a nice car--tell her that, please. I gots money in the colored bank in town and the white bank. She wouldn't nevah wants for nothing, nevah have to work, and I don't bleve in hittin' no woman. I know that the fellas that comes to them places puts on airs and ain't thinkin' 'bout finding no wife there. I ain't like that. Lawd knows, I didn't start out looking for no wife, but now I cain't help but want to marry her now."

"I cain't do that, Pete. You gots to do it yahself."

Pete would transform instantly before my eyes from a love struck suitor, to angry jilted lover. Having long been on the receiving end of people reminding him of his shortcomings, he was very adept at assessing and articulating the shortcomings of others. I would often be at the receiving end of one of his verbal onslaughts.

"You dumb, stupid Nigger! You ain't nothing but a shitty, homeless hobo. I kin buy and sell yo' ass a hundred times over and you couldn't do a damn thang about it. You ain't got shit, and you ain't worth shit. Who are you to tell me what I oughtta do, don't nobody want you. Gits the hell outta my face befo' I break my foot off in yah ass."

I met five or six Petes over the course of my travels, but I never got used to the anger. It was genuine anger and almost instant hatred. Pete wasn't being macho or covering shame or embarrassment. He was genuinely angry because in his eyes I stood between him and utter happiness for the rest of his life. He thought it was safe to unleash his pent up anger and hatred on me. Pete always carried brass knuckles, a switchblade, or a gun. If he carried a gun, he'd pull the gun out and press the barrel hard against my fore-head.

"You think you better that me, Niggah?"

"Naw, Pete, I don't think that."

"Then say it! Say you ain't better than me!"

"First put the gun away, man."

"How 'bout I plant a bullet in yah head 'cause you ain't saying it?"

"Alright, man, alright. I ain't better than you, Pete. I ain't better than you," I'd say barely able to form the words in my mouth.

"You right, not you or any other niggah is better than Pete Thigpen. I got a house with furniture, and I got an indoor bath-room. I got a nice car. I got money in the niggah bank and the cracker bank. I'm somebody. I am somebody, God damn it!"

Pete would walk away from me and wander off to his house, car, and bank accounts muttering to himself that he was some-body. I'd drop to my knees and try and collect myself.

I lacked the strength of heart and courage to tell Pete that his girl was just doing her job. He paid for her to love him, and she loved him for the moment because he paid. And when his time was up, she was paid to love somebody else, and she treated the next one to the same love she gave him. When the brothel bounc-er escorted Pete off the premises, she made fun of his *toos* like the rest of them. She did, however, appreciate the extra money, flowers, and chocolates he brought to the transaction. That bit of appreciation was the only unique and genuine emotion that she experienced for Pete.

I know it sounds crazy, but I was always thankful to the Petes I met. The Petes made me feel again. That gun pressing against my forehead or switchblade at my jugular brought overwhelming fear in me to the surface. The fear radiated throughout my mind, body, and spirit, bringing to life places long dormant in my being. I felt something. Feeling something, even fear, charged my batter-ies since so much time passed without me feeling anything at all. I soon discovered that it is easier to find fear in this world than peace. And I would stalk fear every now and then just to make sure I still lived.

I realized after staying at the first few brothels that I could not stay more than a couple of weeks in any one before the madam showed me to the door. First of all, I refused sex, and refusing sex in a whorehouse is akin to refusing to pray in church. Celibacy is a damned disturbing state of being in a whorehouse, kind of a carnal blasphemy.

Madams often offered me a man. "If that's what you like," they'd say. One or two men often work quietly in one of the cribs in the back of the place. Also, if I *was* a "bent boy" and so inclined, they said they could find me plenty good paying work in their establishment if I didn't mind wearing a blonde wig, gown and light make up. (The light referred to the color of the make up, not the application of the make up.) I learned quickly that if a normal functioning heterosexual male refuses sex with the girls, the madam and the few men working whorehouses, then the girls selling their bodies for a living there began to *think* about selling their bodies. That kind of thinking stirs up strife in a brothel.

At first, hiring me seemed like a bargain because I accepted low wages, no gratuitous sex, and gave them a good hard day's work. I was cheap to keep. But then it would start, usually with the fresh-faced new girl not yet hardened by business.

"Why don't you look at us like the udda mens do?" she'd ask.

"I don't know what you means, ma'am."

"You knows how they look--like they plannin' where they gonna stick it in us and wondering how much it gone cost. And why you calls me 'ma'am?' I'm a whore...I sells ass for a living. I ain't no 'ma'am.'"

"I just cleans 'round here for a place to sleep and somethin' to eat. That's all I do 'round here."

"That ain't all no man do. If'n it is, that damn sho' ain't all he wanna do. If he ain't fuckin'something, then he ain't no goddamn man. Even cats and dogs fucks when the urge come on 'em. What you wanna do when the urge comes on you? Or what is you if you don't wanna do it?"

And then the newest girl would start to "sho' her stuff." The ones who thought they were better than me would do it in the presence of the other girls to embarrass and humiliate me. Those who wanted an answer from me would find me alone, in private and offer what they thought no man could refuse in secret, especially in the secret of a whorehouse. For them, it was war. If I took what they offered, then they won. They proved that "the pussy was more powerful than any man," especially one who claims to love another woman. If I didn't take it, I wasn't playing by the rules most of them learned as children. That meant something was wrong in my head or, perhaps, maybe something was right in my heart.

"You know why I do this in this place? 'Cause, there ain't no shame in here. If I was on the street or in my own house, I'd have all kinda church folks and super-saved sistahs all over me 'cause I'm fuckin' their pastors, husbands, sons, and brothers. But here, I kin fuck...a hundred mens in an hour and ain't nobody gon' say nothin' bad 'bout it. There ain't no shame here 'cause we all doin' and wantin' the same thangs. But you, mistah, you ain't doin' and wantin' it, is yah? Why? Huh?"

"Ma'am, I jus' cleans 'round here. What you do is yah business, nobody but yours...."

"That jus' it. Ain't nobody got no business o' their own. We is everybody's business and they is our business. Look here, mistah, look at my shit. You know you wants it. My daddy wanted it. Every man with a dick that come up in here wants some o' this here. These and this here is who I am--it what I got to offer--look at it, I carry my business every day right here between my legs. It pays my bills and gits me what I wants till it wear out," she'd say while holding open her gown.

All they wanted to do was say their piece. I'd just listen numbly. Part of me knew some of what they said was not just true but also right. I was a man in the midst of a carnal paradise, but I didn't feel a thing. What was wrong with me? Couldn't I just imagine Marie's face on that body? No one, not even Marie would blame me for acting like a man! I'd drift off into thought after thought justifying adultery more driven by reason than lust. Where there is no lust, though, no amount of reason brings on desire. I remained numb.

When she finished tempting me, the new girl's face would wrinkle up and a hundred year cry would trickle down her painted cheeks. The woman inside the girl, long hidden behind cheap make up, scanty clothes, and an over-used body, would peek out from behind the heavy curtain of fear and shame. She'd absorb the morning sunlight and crisp fresh air for a quick minute, and then get slapped back down by the overprotective she-warrior from within. This warrior succubus, enraged at my chastity, would then set upon me with fists, nails, spiked heels, and whatever else there was within her reach. She wanted me to suffer, even to die if that was what needed to protect her fragile humanity, which I inadvertently exposed by celibacy, disinterest, and silence.

"What in the hell is wrong with you, you stupid fool?" she'd scream and follow with blows to my head, scratches to my face, and kicks to my shins. I'd curl up in a ball on the floor the way I saw them Civil Rights folks do on TV and just take it until she got tired.

And then she'd change before my eyes from vengeful rage, to sorrowful tears, to bitter anger, self-awareness, more anger, and then utter exhaustion. Years of exhaustion buried deep under mounds of hurt, disgrace, shame, and pain would fall away from her body like the weight of the world slipping from the shoulders of Atlas. More tears followed, and then peace, and then a gentle calmness devoid of any emotion. Well, really more than just calmness, I'd say then came tranquility. Only then would she ask the question.

"Why are you different?"

I knew it was time for me to give an answer.

"I know what true love is," I'd answer. "I have given myself to a woman without condition or reserve. She has given herself to me, likewise, without condition or reserve. There is no one else in the world between us."

"I cain't 'cept that, that's too easy, Mr. Roy. All I got is what I sits on. You ain't got to love me or not love your woman to play with what I got. This is alls I got, Mr. Roy, and I wanted you to have it for nothin' 'cause you treat me nice...you look at me like I'm a real person--a person with feelings. This is all I gots to give you. You thinks I give it to these mens that come in here? Naw, they sho' 'nough takes something, but it jus' them takin', it ain't me givin'. I don't have nothing to do with what they gits or how they gits it. I ain't nevah give no man like that nothing. I still got me right in here, and I wanted to give me to you."

They would all seem to arrive at that point. They were telling me that they were still virgins just waiting for the right man to love them. I'd find myself in the dark of unabashed whorehouses, talking to working prostitutes and wondering too if they were still virgins. Stuff had been taken from them all their lives. Yet, no one ever asked their permission. Their bodies were taken, and they didn't know how to get them back. So they hid themselves under the layers of flesh and pulled the plug on their feelings. After a time, I began to truly believe that they were still virgins. They were virgins buried under mounds of shame, fear, and guilt, but virgins nonetheless. They were virgins because their hearts were truly unbroken earth never plowed, tilled, and planted by men. Their youth was taken away prematurely and not allowed to fade away on the heels of time and life experience.

I was a man. Men were the very instruments of their oppression. The one thing that they were certain about was that all men were takers. But I wasn't taking. I was disrupting the natural order of their lives. They needed to know why.

"I want you to know this then," I'd add. "I believe there is more to you than them fellas and that woman upstairs think you got to offer. But me telling you that ain't gone make you know that. There is someone out there for you, somebody who was born to love just you. He don't know you yet, and Lord knows you don't know him. There's a whole world of demons, imps, and well-meaning good folks out there tryin' to keep y'all apart. But you listen close, child. Once y'all find each other, nothing else in the world will matter. He may be in the next county or halfway across the world, but wherever he is, he was born to love you and you were born to love him. When you two meet, and you will if you will yourselves to meet, no other man or woman, real or imagined, will come between you. And if you are ever separated, everything inside of you will die except the desire to reunite. Nothing else matters, but to see again, touch again, be again. Your heart will ache for even one day together. One day would be worth more than all the days of your life before. There is a man out there, somewhere, who will know until the day he dies that you are far more than you think you are here today."

She'd wrap up her exposed body and decide to find and display that person inside so long buried. She would leave me wherever I stood without a goodbye or any word. This new person would have a deeply personal talk with her coworkers while hastily packing her bags. She'd walk out the door in silence and never return.

The other girls would find me. They wouldn't ask questions. They'd just stare at me while I worked, looking for evidence of the juju I sprinkled on their co-worker or perhaps some demon reflecting off my plane of existence. Some feared me. They thought I possessed the power to condemn them to eternal damnation in hell. Others turned their faces away from me in shame. Two, three, or four others would pack their bags, hit the door, and never be seen in those parts again. I knew then that it was time for me to pack up my rags and hit the road. I learned from experience that the women bosses of those houses would come looking for me after the girls slowly trickle out the door. Some would ask politely that I leave, while others would order me out at the end of a .45, a butcher's knife, or the fists of a local brute.

I'd go before it got to that point when I could--if I knew it was time. I'd go quickly and under the cover of darkness. I'd walk, hitch rides, and offer my piano playing and cleaning services at the next brothel when my feet were too tired to hit the pavement again.

I have enclosed a handkerchief in this envelope that I want you to keep, Sis. Honey Devine Breedlove gave it to me. She stitched these words around the border.

"Blessed be the man who has compassion for the whore. Blessed be the man who finds the heart of a woman. Blessed be the man that walks not in the counsel of the judges, but spreads seeds of hope in fields of despair. For of such is the Kingdom of Heaven made."

Chapter Twenty-Two

Signs and Wonders

Dear Lil Sis, I stayed in places other than brothels on a few occasions. The one that most comes to mind was in the backwoods of Tennessee with The Church of the Savior with Signs Following. They and the prostitutes both lived on the fringes of society, but these people possessed undeniable assurance of the rightness of their faith.

I was somewhere in eastern Tennessee walking along a two-lane highway at about one o'clock in the afternoon. An old, but well-kept wood-paneled station wagon blew past me at about 75 mph. The wagon suddenly screeched to a rubber-burning stop a few hundred yards up the road. The driver pulled over on the shoulder, shifted it in reverse, and burned rubber backwards on his way to me. Even from a hundred yards away, I could see that the stowage compartment of the wagon was packed from floor to roof. There were also boxes tied down four feet high on top of the vehicle bundled under a surplus army flap tent. The load was so heavy that the rear of the wagon was almost dragging on the ground, and when the car hit a pothole, it left a trail of sparks, smoke, and bumper fragments in its wake.

The driver was a red-faced man with a full head of hair badly in need of a trim and shampoo. He maneuvered his long body out of the car and headed my way. His charcoal gray suit, matching tie, white shirt, and black work shoes unfolded along with his body. He stretched his body to its limits with each brisk stride he took toward me. He appeared determined to get to me before some great calamity struck. He was in his mid-50s, I'd guess, with a slender 6'3" frame and a mustache-free beard covering his cheeks and chin.

I didn't know what to make of him at first. He didn't have any of the trappings of the men I learned to avoid other than being a southern white male. He wasn't a policeman; he wasn't part of a group of doped up teenage boys or middle-aged men soaked in alcohol and marinated in low self-esteem. As he came closer, I noticed that he clutched a black, leather-bound, gold embossed KJV Bible in his right hand.

"A Holy Roller," I thought to myself while breathing a sigh of relief. He must have caught a whiff of the Pink Pony Playhouse on me when he passed and decided that I desperately needed saving. Holy Rollers I could deal with; they weren't dangerous. Those who genuinely cared enough to pullover and save me from my sins were especially not dangerous. I'd just say *yes* to whatever he asked me about the Lord, pray with him, and then I'd be free to continue my journey. I practiced in my head how I'd answer his questions before he got in speaking distance:

Do you know the Lord, boy?

Yes, sir, I knows the Lawd. Yeees, sir.

Is Jesus the Christ your personal savior?

Yes, sir, he sho' 'nough is.

Did He die on the cross for your sins and rise from the dead in triumph over sin, the devil, and the forces of darkness on the third day?

Yes, sir, He did sho' as the sun is in the sky.

Then I declare here in the presence of God, the angels and all of creation that you, boy, shall be saved.

Amen, amen, and amen, thank yah, sir.

Now you listen to me, boy. Find yahself a nice, non-agitating, colored church and join it, yah hear? The Lord will not forsake the coming together of the saints.

Naw, sir, the Lawd ain't neve' gone forsakes his people a-comin' together.

How ironic. The Lord surely wouldn't forsake his people coming together, but men like this one certainly would.

I was ready for the red-faced man in the plain gray suit.

"Greetings in the Name of the Lord, brother," he said. The "brother" reference threw me off from the beginning. I opened my mouth to say yes, but closed it, speechless.

"As I drove by you, the Holy Ghost himself spoke to me in a wee audible voice right here in my good ear. He said, 'Walloon, that is a brother who can play the piano for God's glory.' I tell yah, brother, that God is always on time. Amen? Cause as fate--the F-A-T-E kind, would have it, I am in need of a sanctified, righteous, and God-inspired Brother in Christ to play the church's e-lectric piano. Come on and git in our mo-bile house of the Lord, brother." He said this in a fire and brimstone preacher's cadence while taking me by the arm and escorting me to the station wagon.

"I--I--" I tried to say no, but I hadn't practiced saying it and couldn't get it out before he continued.

"You don't have to thank me, brother. Just give all the glory, honor, and praise to the Lord. When you git settled in, we'll see what we kin do about blessing you with some clean clothes, plenty o' good ol' home cooking, a warm, soft place to lay your head at night, and some walking around change."

"I...."

"It's a deal then. The Lord *told* me that you were the brother for me. You must be a mighty blessed piano player, 'cause the Lord don't neva' steer his disciple wrong. By the way, I am Brother Josiah Zachius Walloon--pastor, teacher, prophet and evangelist of the Church of the Savior with Signs Following. I have been in the service of the Lord for thirty-five years. I'm living testimony that the divinely inspired word of God is the truth, the whole truth and nothing but the truth from Genesis to Revelations. Amen?"

Brother Walloon never allowed me an opportunity to protest, politely decline, or walk away. Normally, I would have done one of the aforementioned, but he seemed harmless enough and getting out of the blistering hot Tennessee sun seemed like a good idea at the time.

"I'm Roy."

"Well, Brother Roy, welcome to my vineyard--the harvest is plentiful, but the workers is few. But like Brother George Went Hensley used to say, 'If the Lawd is with yah, who kin be agin yah?'"

Before I could speak again, or even ask who Brother George Went Hensley was, I found myself packed in the backseat of Pastor Walloon's station wagon headed down a heavily wooded stretch of dirt road toward his church. The old Ford wagon was indeed a mo-bile church. Rev. Walloon packed it tight with Bibles, songbooks, tambourines, folding chairs, hand fans, and several bottles of Crisco oil, among other assorted church paraphernalia. Oddly, there were a dozen or so live lab mice packed in cages and two tightly sealed and unmarked wooden crates with pea-sized air holes.

Sitting next to him in the front seat was his teenage son, David Paul Walloon, and his wife, Sister Ruth Ester Walloon. Tall and slender like his father, but without the Amish beard and apparent enthusiasm for the Lord, David slid slowly down in the seat in shame when I crawled into the backseat. I could tell that he'd rather be in school or batting around a baseball in a Levittown somewhere rather than be part of his father's traveling freak show. Ruth Ester stood about 4'9" and could not have weighed more than 100 pounds. Her long brown, never-cut hair reached to her lower back. She sat comfortably in a simple long-sleeved print top, a black skirt to her ankles, and sturdy black shoes. She bore an expression of undying devotion to her husband on her makeup-free face.

Sitting next to me in the backseat was a fellow who called himself Moonstone. Like me, he didn't seem to fit into the Walloon clan. When he used the words 'peace' and 'brother', I sensed that he didn't mean the same kind of 'peace' and 'brotherhood' to which Brother Walloon referred. His hair fell a quarter-inch shy of Ruth Esters'. He bunched it together on the top of his head with a purple headband. He sported a patchy red beard with a Genghis Kahn mustache, a psychedelic Nehru jacket and the hint of recently smoked dope about him. He was probably in his early twenties and either looking for or running away from something. We shared that much in common.

Moonstone was a drummer. Brother Walloon, though not certain about the state of Moonstone's soul, needed a drummer for his services--saint or sinner. Moonstone, on the other hand, needed company, some good food, and a little walking around change, so he didn't mind beating the skins for a few days for some slightly off-center Holy Rollers.

We drove ten or fifteen miles into the pine-covered mountains. The back woods of Tennessee rank among the most beautiful places I have ever seen. The hills and mountains rose above the Earth dwarfing our merry little band of travelers. The pine trees cooled the ground level to moderate temperatures and filtered out much of the ultra-bright light from the hot sun. The tall, green trees spread their heavy scent on the air. We drove miles past civilization, it seemed, but every now and then a friendly hand would wave from a roadside mailbox, or I'd smell the hickory-tinged smoke of a wood burning stove. Pine needles, pinecones, broken branches, and moss-covered boulders formed a carpet on the forest floor far off into the horizon. Squirrels, chipmunks, various and sundry kinds of birds and deer jetted in and out of the trees.

We arrived at our destination at a dirt and gravel crossroads deep in the woods. Two crudely built and understandably dilapidated, wood-framed buildings sat about 100 yards back from the road. The larger of the two structures was a church, though one not used for several years. Exterior spots here and there held on tightly to leftover splatters of white paint. But mostly, the exterior was exposed, wooden planks covered in green mold. If this wasn't our destination, I'm sure I would have walked by these buildings and never even discerned them from the rest of the forest.

A purple Dodge Dart with a hand-sprayed yellow roof and New Hampshire plates was parked to the side of the smaller building, a vehicle that no doubt belonged to Moonstone. The smaller building was either a parsonage or storage shed. I decided it was a parsonage when I noticed the chimney sticking out of the roof.

A hand-painted wooden sign in front of the church read Bethel Memorial AME Church. I did a double take, looked at the sign again, and then looked closely at the Walloons.

Could there be more to them than was visible to the eye? Could they be colored? I thought to myself. After all, AME or African Methodist Episcopal is a colored denomination.

Maybe they been passing? That would explain all that 'brother' stuff and why they seem to cotton to me so easily. But didn't he tell me his church was called Church of the Savior with Signs Following? I wondered.

Brother Walloon picked up on my confused pensiveness and gestured to me that we would talk about it later. One of the first things he did was to tie a hand-painted sheet sign over the wooden Bethel Memorial AME sign. Sure enough it read, in all capital letters:

CHURCH OF THE SAVIOR WITH SIGNS FOLLOW-ING   BROTHER J. Z. WALLOON, APOSTLE

He folded the sheet in such a way that when unfolded the creases formed a perfect cross right up the middle.

"Hurry up, y'all. We cain't keep the Lord waitin', and I done already made the call. We gonna have our first service here tonight. We gottah unpack the Mo-bile House of the Lord, clean up the sanctuary and git ready to greet the saints," said Brother Walloon.

I supposed I would have to wait for my explanation until after the work was done.

Brother Walloon assigned Moonstone and me to clean up the

church. He and his family pulled brooms, mops, buckets, cleansers, and furniture polish out of the station wagon. We cleaned every corner of that building. The place went from dusty to dull, to somewhat livable in no time. We used burlap sacks to fill holes in the walls and sheets of used plywood to patch soft spots in the floor.

"We got to have a sturdy floor 'cause we believes in dancing to the glory of the Lord," Brother Walloon told us.

Moonstone was a little squeamish around the mice in the car, so he left it to me to remove the rats' nests, beehives, and spider webs in the building. Brother Walloon asked jokingly that we catch any small rodents we could. At least I *thought* he was joking.

Brother Walloon set up a portable generator outside the window nearest the pulpit and ran electric cables into the building. He strung droplights from the ceiling rafters and connected and tested an electric piano, slide guitar, and the sound system. I was very impressed with the skill and efficiency with which he worked. The place looked as if it were a church again by 6:30 p.m. Brother Walloon told us that the service would begin at 9:00 p.m.

An elderly colored man in a broken down pickup drove up shortly after we completed our tasks. He pulled the truck right up to the door and asked for Mr. Walloon.

"Is Mr. Walloon in? Tell him that Billy Gallimore is here to see 'im," he said.

Walloon came from around the corner. "Brother Gallimore, glad you could make it so soon. Come on over to my wagon, and we can git all squared away."

I saw Walloon pull a gold-painted King Edward cigar box from under the driver's seat. He opened the box and pulled out a palm full of cash. He carefully counted a portion out to Mr. Gallimore and the two shook hands.

"That should keep us for thirty days, Brother Gallimore?" Brother Walloon said.

"Yes, sir. And if'n you wants to stay longer, just let me know," he responded.

Now I understood. Walloon rented the vacant Bethel Memorial AME church for thirty days.

We washed up and sat down to a home cooked meal of cornbread, fried chicken, tossed salad, string beans, and fresh squeezed lemonade. We were very hungry by then, having worked non-stop since arriving, so there wasn't much talking between bites. We each found a corner and ate by ourselves after Brother Walloon said grace. Brother Walloon excused himself early to work on his sermon. I noticed David carrying the mice toward the station wagon parked out front. I fell asleep in my little corner after cleaning my plate. I was exhausted from a long and hard day's work. From what I knew about the Walloons and other holiness types, I expected that their service would go far into the night. I needed some sleep if I was going to make it through the service.

Car doors slamming and happy people chattering woke me up at about 8:45 p.m. David finished setting up a podium and all the musical instruments while Moonstone, and I napped. The two wooden crates from the back of the wagon were prominently displayed on a table right in front of the pulpit. I walked over to the electric piano when I was awake enough to stand and tried to figure out how it worked. David helped and gave us both hymnals with certain numbers already marked. Moonstone warmed up on the drums.

"I'm gonna be playing the slide guitar; y'all just follow me," David said. "We gonna play the old timey hymns I marked to warm up the congregation befo' Daddy comes out to preach, then it will all be instrumental after that. Near the end of his sermon, we will start out slow, and then speed it up. We won't stop playing for 30-40 minutes after that. I do a lot of improvising, so y'all just have to keep up. Whatever happens, y'all just keep playing."

"What do you mean, 'whatever happens'?" I asked.

"Just whatever happens," David replied.

The members were punctual; all thirty or so of them were in the church and seated at the stroke of 9:00 P.M. They all looked the same. You know how when you go in the Army and they shave off all of your hair, change all your names to 'private,' and dress you in the same clothes? That's how they looked alike, not exactly twins, but alike like people who are part of the same cause.

The men were plain, and the women were plainer. The women were all dressed in solid colors, in black, white, or gray. Their hair was unstyled and uncut, and they refused to decorate their bodies with jewelry or make up. The men dressed in white shirts, gray or black slacks, and dark plain shoes. Not one of them had a watch buckled around their wrist or any other jewelry. I could tell by their rough hands and weather-beaten faces that they were all working people. Oddly, the men greeted one another with a kiss on the mouth. Not a full-blown kiss, but more of a full lip-on-lip peck. I was told that the Bible commands that the saints greet each other with a kiss.

If I guessed, I would say that worshipping in Brother Walloon's church was the only free choice most of them made in life. Further, there was something secretive and mischievous about the whole enterprise that I just couldn't put my finger on.

The service began when David gave the word. Sister Walloon led the congregation in three hymns. They sang, and we played them just as they were written in the hymnal. Brother Walloon came out of the back for his sermon at precisely 9:30. He behaved differently--almost in a trance. His eyes were fixed and unemotional. He seemed to float into the pulpit. Before he spoke a word, he got down on his knees, bowed his head, and prayed silently to God. He stood from the prayer and began his sermon or his extended testimony.

"I was born in Kingsport, Tennessee. My daddy was a pig farmer and my mama the daughter of a moonshiner. There wuz five of us kids, all boys; Jimmy, James, Jonathan, Jeffrey and me, Josiah. My daddy was a mean man. He drank white lightnin', and he beat mama and us kids regularly to within an inch of our lives. Now the Lord says you must honor your mother *and* your father, so that your days may be long. I'm not tellin' you that my daddy was mean to dishonor him. I'm tellin' you he was mean cause that was how it was and so you kin understand how I come to stand befo' you today.

"He beat us with his fists, whipped us with studded straps, paddled us with splintered boards, and went across our heads with wet riding crops. I was the oldest, so whenever I could, I'd try to take a beatin' for Mama and the other boys. But when I turned 17, I made up my mind that the beatin's was gonna stop. By then Jeff and me was tall enough to look Daddy in the eye, and we hauled enough pig slop to make us strong enough to rassle a grizzly bear to the ground. Jeff and me brought John, James, and Jimmy together while Daddy was out gettin' liquored up. We tol' 'em that we ain't gonna let Daddy beat Mama or us no mo', and we ain't gonna let him beat them no mo', but we needed they help. We tol' 'em just to follow our lead.

"Sho' 'nough, Daddy come bustin' in the house not an hour

later a screaming and cussing to beat the band.

"'Daddy,' I says, looking him straight in the eye, 'we gottah talk to yah 'bout something.' Befo' I could speak another word his right fist smashed into my mouth and crushed my bottom lip. Blood poured out on my shirt like a fountain and dripped on the floor. I backed up, and he came at me again.

"'Now, Jeff! Now!'" I shouted.

"Jeff and I tackled Daddy, I hit him high and Jeff hit 'im low. We held him to the floor. It seemed easy; evidently he could hit a lot harder than he could fight back when we took him down. We held him down 'til John came with the 12-guage. John, the third oldest, took my place holding Daddy, and I took hold o' the shot-gun. I was shaking from head to toe, and sweat poured down my brow. I stuck the barrel of that gun in Daddy's mouth. He sobered up quick. I told him in a serious manner that only God in Heaven was keepin' me from pulling this trigger.

"Thank God I didn't shoot 'im, but I said to 'im, 'Right now I wanna blow your head to kingdom come. Somethin' bigger than me, though, is holding me back from doin' such a thang. But if you so much as blink an eye, won't nothing hold me back from pullin' this trigger. We boys want you on notice that from this day hence you ain't never to put your hands on or raise yah fists to us or our Mama agin. You do, and we will guarantee that you will neve' raise up against nobody else. You is still our daddy, but you gonna be our daddy without all the cussing, all the beatin', all the drankin', and all the threatenin'.'

"I saw fear in my daddy's eyes for the first time in my life. Tears ran out of the corner of his eyes, and his pants bled with fresh urine. He didn't answer--he couldn't answer--but he got the message. We let him up and tol' him to go sleep off the liquor in the shed. We locked the doors to the house, hid the bullets for the guns, and took turns standing guard all night.

"We all went off to school together the next morning after telling Mama what we did to Daddy the night befo'. Mama asked if we hurt 'im.

"'I don't know what I would do without him,' she cried. 'Y'all oughtta know better than to do that. Yah daddy don't really mean nothin' when he hits us; it be the corn whiskey, that's all, jus' the corn whiskey.'

"When we got home that same day, Daddy, the truck, all his

stuff, and Mama wuz gone. We wuz all by ourselves with nobody but God to make a way for us. I quit school and got a job in town to keep us in groceries. I made my brothers stay in school even though they wanted to quit. I jus' tol' em to do good in school and help me run the farm. Three years went by befo' we heard from Mama or Daddy again. In that time, I worked in the town, we worked the farm, and Jeff and John were ready to go off to college.

"Mama called the farm one day, and she was crying. She said she missed all us boys and really wanted to see us. She asked if I could come get her just two counties over and brang her home for a visit. I asked her where Daddy wuz, and she said that he'd be at work--he worked a regular job for six or mo' months. They wuz just gittin settled in, and since he been working, she wuz alone more and thinkin' an awful lot 'bout her boys. I told Mama that I'd come for her.

"An hour and a half later, I drove into the First National Bank parking lot in La Follette. I wuz a few minutes early, so I got out of the car and walked over to the soda pop machine and got me a drank and a Lafollette Press from the paper box. When I turned around to walk back to my car, there, looking me dead in the eyes, wuz my daddy. He looked older and smaller than I recalled, but it was him.

"'Hey, Daddy,' I said with some hesitation. Lord knows I didn't hate 'im. We just didn't wanna be beat no more. Daddy didn't say hey back. He didn't grab me and hug me or say how much he missed me. He didn't say that he loved his other sons and me. No, instead Daddy pulled a copper pipe from behind his back and commenced to hittin' me. He pounded me in my rib cage, cracked my skull, and kicked me while I writhed in pain, coughing up blood on the steaming concrete. When the pipe bent too far back, and he couldn't connect with it, he hit me with his fists. In no time, I couldn't fight back or even protect myself from his blows. Women coming out of the bank were screaming for him to stop and leave me alone. I never saw Mama or heard her voice. All I could think was that those women didn't know my daddy. He wouldn't stop until he was satisfied I paid enough for driving him from his own home.

"Then a man's voice cried out above all the others.

"'Satan, in the name of Jesus, I command you to flee from this place! Satan, in the name of Jesus, I command you to flee from this place!'

"Then as quickly as Daddy started beating me, he stopped. He seemed to come to his senses for a moment. He looked at me nearly lifeless on the ground and seemed to recognize that I was a human being and his own flesh and blood. For a moment, his compassion seemed to peek through his barricade of revenge. He ran away afraid at the command of that man's voice in the crowd while I lay on the ground, ready to die.

"That voice in the crowd came to me in the flesh, though.

"'Brother, it is not your time to die,' he proclaimed with authority while lifting my head from the pavement and placing it gently on his lap. 'The Lord has mighty work for you to do yet. Open your eyes, brother, and look at me. I am Brother George Went Hensley. I am a true disciple of our Lord and Savior, Jesus Christ. The Holy Ghost sent me here just for you. He said to me, "George, there will be a brother that will need a healing of the mind, body, and spirit--go to him." Open your eyes and look at me brother! The Lord ain't done with you yet, and he needs you strong and healthy.'

"I opened my eyes and looked into Brother Hensley's eyes. He began to quote the Holy Word of God.

"'And Jesus said to them, Go ye into all the world, and preach the gospel to every creature. He that believeth and is baptized shall be saved; but he that believeth not shall be damned. And these signs shall follow them that believe: in my name they shall cast out devils; they shall speak with new tongues. They shall take up serpents; and if they drink any deadly thing, it shall not hurt them; they shall lay hands on the sick, and they shall recover.

"'Brother, the Devil wants to sift you like wheat, but the Lord wants to use you as his vessel of faith. I need you to squeeze my hand tight, believe and your faith will make you whole.'

"I squeezed Brother George's hand and called on the name of Jesus. Brother Hensley stretched out my body in the shape of a cross and locked his hands into mine and lay atop of me praying in unknown tongues. I could feel my body warming up and mending. The warmer it got, the more the pain faded away. I could feel the power of God passing from his body into mine! I could feel the strength returning to my limbs and clarity returning to my thoughts! Some of the people who witnessed what I'm talking about say that Brother Hensley glowed bright as a star in heaven.

"Before the ambulance rounded the corner, I was on my feet!

Before the paramedics opened the door, I was shouting the victory to the Lord! Before they asked who called an ambulance, I danced unto the Lord of Heaven, Earth and all of creation!"

I sensed that Brother Walloon was wrapping up his sermon because David began playing on the slide guitar and the people were whipped up into fervor. Moonstone and I followed his lead on the drums and electric piano. Brother Walloon began to dance in the pulpit, and the congregation danced in the aisle. The women danced differently from the men. They bent at the waist, cocked their heads to one side, and jumped up and down to the rhythm of the music. A guest walking in late might have thought they were swimmers trying to get pool water out of their ears. The men locked their hands behind their backs, moved their feet up and down, and turned in tight circles. They seemed to bow at the waist on every full turn. Those that didn't dance spoke in tongues, and those that did neither were slain in the spirit and passed out on the floor. It all appeared rather chaotic to me--*sincere,* yes--but still chaotic.

I even got caught up in the excitement of the moment. The excitement built up in me into an erupting volcano. My fingers moved across the keyboard faster than I could think. I wanted to dance, shout, and pass out, too. I don't know that I believed any of the stuff Brother Walloon testified about, but it had been so long since I was excited about something, *anything,* that I wanted to cut loose. I kept playing and swaying--I supposed my time to dance, shout, and pass-out would come later.

Brother Walloon gestured for us to lower the volume and slow the music after several minutes of dancing, speaking in tongues, passing out, and shouting. And then he stepped forward to finish his testimony.

"Brother Hensley taught me something that day and for many more thereafter. He taught me that Jesus is real. He taught me that even in our wicked modern world Jesus' disciples still walk upon the face of the Earth. He said what Jesus said, '*And these signs shall follow them that believe....*' He told me that one day he preached from Mark 16, when some unbelievers tested his resolve. '*Jesus said that those who follow him shall take up serpents and it shall not hurt them.*' These unbelievers loosed a poisonous serpent at Brother Hensley's feet whilst he preached. Brother Hensley reached down and took up the serpent and continued to preach the word without hurt, harm or danger! These are the signs that follow them! These are the signs that follow them!"

David picked up the tempo and played more loudly again. I sensed we were building to a crescendo. The congregation was worked up, and the chapel was hot and humid from their over-heated bodies. Brother Walloon left his microphone and stepped down from the pulpit. He went to one of the wooden crates and opened a small door in the crate. He quickly shoved a curved stick inside the box and pulled out a scaly, five-foot long rattlesnake. I pulled my hands away from the piano and backed away from the pulpit. Moonstone dropped his drumsticks and stared in terror at the snake. David gestured feverishly to both of us to keep playing.

I looked over at Moonstone, and he sat board stiff with his eye-lids pulled so far back in his head I couldn't see them. I knew he would bolt for the door at the first clear opportunity. But Brother Walloon took the snake in his hands and danced with it across the front of the church, cutting off Moonstone's exit. He held it inches from his face, thumping its head, yet the snake made no sound and didn't strike. The serpent turned its head away from Brother Walloon's taunts.

Moonstone soon saw an opening through which he could run. He was up from his stool in the middle of a downbeat and fall-ing over the drums to the base of the pulpit after his first step. The rattlesnake was the only obstacle he paid attention to on his way toward the door. His body collapsed and crumpled with every fall, trip, and stumble, but his head remained fixed and his gaze focused on the snake. David and I were the only ones to realize that Moonstone was running for the exit. He picked himself up, moved two steps, and fell again over the railing separating the pul-pit from the congregation. He got to his feet a second time and charged at top speed up the center aisle. He bolted passed Brother Walloon and the crates, screaming profanities at the top of his lungs. He ran up the aisle, tripping over a few folks still slain in the spirit, and nearly tore the door off its hinges getting outside. A few people in the congregation shouted "Amen" when Moonstone blew by; they thought he was running and shouting for the Lord, not from the Lord.

David got my attention again and gestured for me to keep playing. He moved over to the drums, and Sister Walloon came up to play the slide guitar. Brother Walloon never missed a beat and kept dancing with the snake. Two other men soon joined him after fishing two snakes of their own out of the box. Years of accumulated dust fell from the rafters and filled the air with a dusty fog. The burlap sack filled walls vibrated, and the plain people rocked. I was genuinely excited by it all. If I didn't have a smile on my face, my spirit was certainly grinning on the inside from ear to ear.

The grinning came to an abrupt end when Brother Walloon and his snake danced over to me. Brother Walloon danced around the front of the church in an improvised, unscripted way up to that point. But now he moved very deliberately in my direction. The more deliberate he became, the more irritated the snake appeared. I could hear Brother Walloon speaking clearly to me in the midst of all the other noise and confusion.

"The Devil is snapping at your heels, Brother Roy. He has come to steal, kill, and destroy all that you value in this world. You are a man who's communed with the Father. Satan don't like that one bit, and he wants your life. Only your faith will save you--take up this serpent, be free, and prove the truth of the Word of God."

Maybe it was the combination of the pulsating music, sanctified dancing, righteous shouting, and passing out that made me feel that anything was doable. A man I barely knew held a live rattlesnake in his hands not ten inches from my face, and I wasn't running away. I wasn't even the least bit apprehensive. He asked me to take the creature from him and handle it. I should've berated the lunacy of his offer, but I did not. I was actually thinking about doing it. I was thinking that I could do it. I was reaching for the black-eyed, timber rattler before reason could take hold of my thoughts. As I reached for it, the snake opened its mouth wide displaying its deadly fangs. I drew my hand back. I heard a choir speaking in unison and repeating rhythmically, "These signs shall follow them, they shall take up serpents, these signs shall follow them, they shall take up serpents." I decided that the creature was simply yawning and again moved my hands out for its scaly body and grabbed it. I could feel the muscular body rippling in the palm of my hand. Its black eyes met mine, and its dry scaly skin absorbed the warmth of my hand.

Before I knew it, I was shouting and dancing with a rattlesnake body pulsating in my hand. I lost control over my mind and body. In fact, I seemed to float outside of my body, watching intently the insane events unfolding before me from a safe distance. The snake wrapped its lower three feet around my forearm and stared at me contentedly as I danced in the spirit. Things started going wrong when the shooting started.

I learned later that Tennessee outlawed snake handling in 1947. That's when it all made sense: Brother Walloon's church was "mo-bile" so he could stay one step ahead of the law. Moonstone apparently was not just frightened for himself, but he thought the Walloons were dangerous. He notified the police of their snake handling service from the first telephone he came across.

The county sheriff and three deputies burst through the main doors of the church not a half-hour later in full riot gear. The music, dancing, shouting, and passing-out ceased when they filled the room with threats and commands. In that moment of silence between the shock of the raid and the chaos of people scrambling to get away, the timber rattlesnake I was handling shook off the aura of docility. It coiled the two feet of its body I did not have a hold on into striking position, and, in the span of a fleeting second, sank its fangs into my upper arm, and then withdrew before I felt the piercing pain. The rattler struck again in my right bicep before the "let go" message from my brain reached my hand. I dropped it with a yelp, and it slither across my feet and into a crack at the base of the pulpit.

I lost control of my right arm just about the time the shooting started. I wasn't the only participant to drop a snake. Three or four of them slithered around the sanctuary to the dismay of the sheriff whose recklessness replaced chaotic euphoria with confused hysteria. The sheriff and his deputies flatly refused to handle the reptiles or even to preserve them as live evidence. They pulled their service issued revolvers from their holsters with little hesitation and shot at any snake in their line of sight.

Brother Walloon's flock screamed out of fear for the first time that night at the actions of the police, rather than the snakes. He tried to take control of the situation and calm everyone down, including the police, but the people ignored him, and a deputy tackled and handcuffed him. I fell to the floor on the fat of my butt when my non-responsive knees collapsed. I tipped over from my butt onto my aching side like a late falling bowling pin a few seconds later. Everything that happened after that was a blur.

I vaguely recall one of the deputies talking to me. "We gonna comeback and git you, boy, after we takes care of these white folks."

He shook me. "You hear me, boy? Now don't this beat all! Why in the world they let a drunk-ass nigger in they church? They *are* crazy."

I thought I was going to die for sure. My body shook violently as a creeping paralysis migrated from the site of the bite. I didn't expect the deputy to come back for me, but the snake lurking under the pulpit might want to finish what it started. I passed out when my brain lost contact with the rest of my body and slipped into shock.

I awoke the next morning in the small parsonage snuggled in a cozy sleeping bag. The aroma of fresh bacon cooking outside greeted my first deep inhale. The events of the day before meshed with and faded away into my nighttime dreams. I realized that it was not a dream when I tried to get out of the bag and stand. I fell to the floor like a sack of potatoes and landed hard on my right arm. Pain shot through the arm in every direction with the discomfort of pricking needles driven deep into the muscle. Whoever brought me from the chapel and dragged me to bed heard the thud, and I could hear footsteps running into the parsonage. It was David.

"Don't try to get up yet, Mr. Roy. You ain't ready. Stay in that bed for a couple o' more hours, and you should at least be well enough to eat something then."

"What happened to me?"

"Don't you remember?"

"I remembers bits and pieces, that's all."

"Well, ol' Cuba took a couple o' bites outtah you."

"Cuba?"

"Cuba is the timber rattler you wuz handling. I don't know why Dad let you handle Cuba. Jezzi or Saul are a lot easier to handle. Cuba done bit Dad three times. I tries to feed 'em an hour before the service so there ain't so much venom in the fangs, and they ain't so mean after being fed. I even milks 'em sometimes, if necessary. I trades raw venom for snakebite antidote with the hospitals around here. Feedin' em and keepin' the music going seems to sooth most o' the wildness in 'em. But when the sheriff and his posse busted in shootin' and disrupted the music, there weren't enough charmin' in the world to keep ol' Cuba from bitin' yah. He got yah twice on your right arm befo' yah let him go."

"What was I doing thinking I kin handle a rattlesnake?"

"You did jus' fine. The faith ain't in the handling o' the snake without being bitten. That's what carnival folks do. The faith is evident in not dying if yah are bitten. And yah ain't dead, so I'd say that yah have some pretty powerful faith."

"Well, either I have pretty powerful faith or you know enough about rattlesnakes to keep your folks, me, and a whole lottah other folks, alive."

"I don't know about all that; I'm just a kid."

"You're a kid that's not anxious for orphanhood anytime soon, from what I can tell."

"Maybe not. Well, look, Mr. Roy, you git some rest 'cause you gottah drive me to town to bail out my folks. The sheriffs always lets the others go, but keeps my folks overnight just to make an example of 'em. Dad always leaves a full cash box in the wagon just for times like these."

"I ain't drove a car in over twenty years, son. You might be better off driving yourself."

"I don't have a driver's license yet, and Daddy won't let me drive 'til I gets one 'cause it's against the law."

"Well, ain't snake handling against the law too?"

"That's against man's law, not God's. From what I know, the Bible don't say nothin' one way or the other about driving automobiles."

I took David's suggestion and slept for a few more hours. I could not have been in better hands. He knew as much about snakes and treating snakebites as anybody. I wondered if his father knew how fortunate he was to have David.

David packed up the entire mo-bile church before I awoke. He only needed help tying down the load on the roof of the wagon. He even packed the mice and the wooden crates with the air holes.

"How many snakes did you lose?"

"Four. Just the ones the police shot. But I kin git three or four more in an afternoon 'round here."

"Well, I for one won't miss Cuba."

"'Oh, they didn't git Cuba. He was safe under the pulpit where I was hiding. I got him right there in the box."

Knowing that Cuba was still alive and less than three feet away certainly made me uneasy, but I was confident that David knew how to handle Cuba and any other belly crawlers that might cross our path. So I got behind the driver's wheel and, after a rough start, drove toward the county seat where the courthouse and jail were located. David pulled out the exact amount of cash he needed when we arrived. I followed him into the county clerk's office where he paid his parents' fine and got a receipt. He proceeded with the receipt to the county lock up on the third floor and presented it to the deputy in charge.

"Bring up the snake handlers. They fine done been paid," the deputy yelled down the cellblock.

"Amen, thank the Lord, salvation is at hand," Brother Walloon's voice echoed off the bare concrete block walls.

The Walloons dropped me off the next day at the Tennessee and Virginia border. They were careful not to take their 'mo-bile' church out of Tennessee. Crossing state lines might bring the unwanted attention of the federal government. The Tennessee legislature outlawed snake handling, but it's still a fairly minor crime and not every county sheriff enforced the law. Furthermore, the Walloon's needed to stay within driving distance of their small but faithful congregation.

"Brother Roy, you done had an adventure with us. I believe this shows that your faith is great, and you have a good heart. I will pray a fervent prayer that you find whatever it is you are looking for. But I want you to know that if you don't find it, you always got a home with me and my family."

"Thank you, Brother Walloon. I will never forget you and your family. God bless you."

The Walloons piled into their wood-paneled Ford wagon, made a wide u-turn, taking in gravel from the road's shoulder, and sputtered their way back south. They drove a few yards down the road and stopped.

David came running after me when I got about fifty yards down the road.

"Mr. Roy! Mr. Roy! Wait a minute!"

"Okay. What's up?"

"Mama made a little something for you to eat. She said you kin eat on this for a day or two without puttin' it in an icebox. You gottah throw it away after that."

"Tell your mama I said thanks, David. I want to thank you, too, for saving my life. You have more strength, faith, and courage than anyone I know. You keep takin' care o' your folks; they are good people. I wish more folks was like them."

"I will, Mr. Roy, I will."

David gave me a post office box number where I could reach them if I ever needed to. I used it over the years to correspond with David and send him books that he could learn from on the road. The last time I heard from him he told me that his parents retired from the snake-handling ministry, and he was now Dr. David Walloon, Director of Reptiles at the San Diego Zoo.

Chapter Twenty-Three

A Short Flight

Someday, Sis, I'll tell you in more detail about the P-51 Mustang I "borrowed" from a rural eastern Pennsylvania air show. I'm writing just a short note now because we have to bike to town this morning. Anyway, I flew that baby all the way to Queens, NY, before they got me. I could not remember a time when I felt the kind of high I did sitting in the cockpit of that plane. I felt free for the first time in a long time. The gist of the story follows.

I walked onto the tarmac right through security and out onto the runway with a bucket of soapy water in my left hand, a swish broom in my right hand, and dirty rags hanging from my back pocket. I was as conspicuous as wallpaper. They knew I was there, but a man carrying dusty rags and a bucket of soapy water was of no significant consequence at an air show. They expected me to do exactly what I was doing...no more or less.

The first pilot I came across noticed my get up, but still he did not notice me. He gave me specific directions regarding where he spilled his pop in the cockpit and precisely how he wanted me to clean it. He told me that he was headed to the snack bar and bathroom and exactly when he would be back and what I should do in his absence. He went for a salami hoagie, the ground crew gassed her up, and I took her airborne before the pilot could zip his fly.

I couldn't just fly off into the clear blue skies and disappoint the crowd, though. They paid good money to see that Mustang run the tables in the hands of a hot dog pilot. I aimed to please. So I made a couple of quick passes over the bleachers and did a dead drop from 1500 feet, pulling out a mere 250 feet from the ground. I did a 360 in midair and came close enough to the honorary grandstand to inhale the pleasing aroma of the important ladies' perfume. The crowd jumped to its feet, cheered wildly, and waved their pennants in approval while the air marshal waived his warning flags. I saluted them on a final buzz cut pass by the press box, which blew the corrugated tin roof off the structure.

The pilot heard his name announced glowingly over the public address system buttressed by the roar of the crowd when he emerged from the bathroom. It wasn't until he looked up into the eastern sky that he knew that I, the rag man, was flying the wings off his vintage P-51C Mustang. He ran after me, yelling something I couldn't discern from the distance between us and the rush of wind noise, in a fruitless attempt to order me down. I was a half-mile away before he pulled his pants up from around his ankles and wiped the black exhaust from the bridge of his nose.

I was tempted to fly her out over the Atlantic Ocean until she sputtered out, and then walk the rest of the way back to my beloved in France. I convinced myself during the months of preparation that I could walk across the ocean to France if I was very careful. But being in the cockpit of that plane, hundreds of feet above the noise and confusion of everyday life, afforded me a moment of rational clarity unlike any I experienced in the previous decade. Life itself seemed to slow to a comprehensible snail's pace. In the added time, I contemplated matters as minute as the moisture ratio of my next breath and as large as the worth of continuing to live in the depths of despair. Ideas, notions, passions, and emotions all played out on a blank slate of sky blue heaven.

I wanted to stay in that cockpit above it all forever and extend the peace of mind that the clarity brought me. But I thought about Marie. I think I always knew how deeply I loved Marie, but I didn't know it from the vantage point of self-sacrifice. We were apart because the universe conspired to keep us apart. We weren't apart for reasons of willful self-sacrifice or selfish indignation. That day, however, I had a choice whether to sacrifice: I could land the plane and descend back into the chaos in my continued search for Marie, or I could continue the high being airborne gave me from emotional purgatory and plunge into the Atlantic Ocean to freedom in death. I decided that I loved Marie more than I despised the emotional impotence of the last three decades of my miserable life.

I carried neither a navigator nor air maps to guide me through the endless skies. So I flew due east toward the Atlantic Ocean, and then up the New Jersey coastline. I flew so close to the Statute of Liberty I could've puckered my Yoruba lips and kissed her on her massive green cheek. I landed a short time later in Queens, New York, between a Pan-Am flight from Baltimore and a Continental flight from Chicago. I taxied the plane to the terminal, climbed out of the cockpit, saluted airport security, and bolted for the luggage dock. I was almost through baggage claim before they pulled me off the conveyor belt. A cranky New York judge committed me to

Bellevue for psychological evaluation by sunset.

Charles Trotter visited me in Bellevue a couple of days before y'all came to get me. He owned the Mustang I borrowed, and the FAA called him the next day to pick up his plane.

"Mister, I want you to know that I ain't never seen no man fly a plane like you did. You done made me a rich man. I got offers from all over the country to fly in air shows. I want you to join me. We kin be partners and split things right down the middle, 50/50."

"Roy, my name is Roy," I said, holding out my hand for a shake.

"I was thinking we could call you something more like the 'Zulu Ace' or the 'Black Hawk?'"

"No, it's just Roy."

"Well, Roy, what do you say? Are you gonna take me up on my offer? I think it's mighty generous because you only got to bring whatever magic you possess when you crawl into the cockpit. I'll do everything else."

"Not now, Mr. Trotter, I got somethin' to do 'foes I kin think about barnstorming around the country."

We talked for hours before Trotter accepted "no" for an answer. Nevertheless, he told me that he owed me a lot, and he'd be forever grateful. He decided before that show to cash in his chips and spend the rest of his life working in his father's hardware store in Ithaca, NY. He also told me that he got the government to drop the theft charges against me, but I may still have some probation for the illegal landing. They ended up giving me eight years, which meant monthly trips to a federal probation officer in Manhattan.

"You know something, Roy? I wasn't planning on telling you that the charges were dropped until I was sure you weren't gonna be my partner. I was gonna hold the prospect of ten years in the federal pen over your head. I changed my mind an hour ago. I kin see all over your face that you are a man on a mission. You are a man determined to see through whatever it is that's driving you. I can respect that. I just hope you are really sure that what you are pursuing is worth the sacrifice."

"There is not enough of me to sacrifice to be worthy of Marie," I said.

Charles departed with a firm handshake and a thankful bear hug. We have written each other over the years, but we never met face-to-face again.

Chapter Twenty-Four

The Yin And The Yang

As you know, Sis, I spent many years churning, molding, and aging cheese in that basement apartment in Hartford after y'all rescued me from Bellevue Hospital. You probably don't know, though, that I only made one kind of cheese that entire time. Marie's father shared a 150-year-old family recipe for Carré de Roucq with me and walked me through its preparation step by step until I learned to prepare it perfectly. I repeated those steps hundreds of times in your basement and made a good living selling the cheese to fancy New York City restaurants. In fact, that cheese paid for Chris' college and law school. That cheese also drew Mancel Marchant into my solitary life.

It took me six years to find the right suppliers and prepare a decent batch for sale. When I finally got it right, I took the Amtrak Noreaster to New York City's Grand Central Station about once every month to sell it to a select handful of chefs and check-in with my probation officer. I charged $200-300 a batch when that was still a lot of money. There was something about the salty sea air the chefs told me that changed the taste of certain cheeses coming directly from France. My cheeses, however, were fresh and unspoiled to their fine-tuned palates.

They always wanted more than I could supply, but I told them it takes time to do it right, and do it right I always would. The Carré de Roucq reminded me of the farm in Giverny and, by relation, of Marie. The flavor was slightly different from the cheese I made on the farm because the smells, the woods, and animals of Connecticut weren't the same. But they were close enough to inspire dreams. It was close enough also for anyone with a well-developed taste for my father-in-law's cheese to recognize it.

It was the first Thursday of an odd month. I was on the Amtrak Noreaster headed to Grand Central Station in New York City. We stopped in New Haven to change from a diesel engine to an electric engine. I stared out the window counting the empty cars in the yard and thinking about Marie. Wouldn't she be proud of my cheese? Wouldn't it be nice to hold her in my arms? Wouldn't it be wonderful to kiss her again?

The electric engine bumped into the coupling, jolted all the cars behind it including mine, latched on and jerked forward pulling us toward Manhattan. We pulled out of New Haven at 6:00 a.m. I sat in the seat I always occupied. The businessmen were in their usual seats. The porter did what he always did; punched tickets from front of the train to back.

By 8:00 a.m., I was in a yellow taxi headed toward the De Jour Restaurante on Fifth Avenue. I liked Chef Pierre there because he always took time to talk to me. He was also a true cheese lover. He prepared exquisite seven course meals around my Carré De Roucq. Very few people who ate in his restaurant realized that, and many left less than fully satisfied because they didn't start or chase their meal with cheese. He never haggled about price either. On several occasions, he actually paid more for a batch he found particularly satisfying.

I never actually told him that I made the cheese. He just assumed I did not, presumably because I was an American. Some of the best French cheese recipes are family recipes passed down the generations and are closely held secrets kept within the family. He couldn't imagine that I was part of such a French family, though we often conversed in French. He begged me to tell my "employer" to come to his restaurant on the house. It would be a long overdue thank you. I said I would.

* * * *

The cleaning staff let me in as usual that day, and I sat in the cramped back office just off the kitchen. Chef Pierre stuck his head in and said there was another customer in the dining room that wanted to meet me. This happened a few times before, so I wasn't surprised. Sometimes they wanted my boss' name or telephone number; others offered me generous bribes if I could get them his recipe. Not once did any one of them ever consider the possibility that I made the cheese.

I entered the dining hall and spotted the back of a man in the middle of the room. He was so large that parts of him hung over the chair, and his clothes seemed more like an elaborate costume than everyday wear. He didn't bother to turn and acknowledge me when I entered the room, but just sat there. His greater than thou demeanor reminded me of a spoiled king sitting statue like on a throne waiting for his subjects to come into his line of vision. He dare not shift his body or strain his royal neck by turning the divine head to meet his subjects' gaze. I accommodated by walking around the table and greeting the man I would come to know as Mancel Marchant with a smile and outstretched hand.

Marchant›s eyelids jerked back into their sockets with what I thought was surprise when I came into his line of vision. He pushed his body away from the table before his legs posted under him. Instead of standing and running away as he intended, he crashed to the floor with a thud and pulled the table down with him.

"Whoa, whoa, be careful there, fella," I said reaching out a helping hand. I could have saved him if he'd only reached back for my hand. He pulled away from me instead, accelerating his unobstructed butt-busting descent to the floor. He didn't stop when he hit the floor, but he dragged his massive body across the carpet, putting all the distance the room would allow between us. He breathed heavily and sweated profusely within the brief fifteen or so seconds I'd been in the room. Again, I focused on his eyes, and I think I saw surprise but...also fear. I couldn't think of a reason the man feared me, so I concluded that I saw only surprise in his face. Maybe he wasn't a king on his throne waiting for me to come into his view after all.

"Whoa, whoa, stop. I'm not going to hurt you. Come on now, get up off the floor," I said, reaching out a helping hand.

By this time, half the cleaning staff and Chef Pierre were in the dining hall wondering what all the commotion was about. I said that he fell off the chair, but I thought he'd be okay.

"Come on, man, let me help you up. You have to be more careful. I certainly apologize if I startled you, but I thought you were expecting me," I explained.

He looked at me this time with an expression I was sure was surprise. He even smiled and stretched forth his hand for me to help him to his feet. After I helped him up, he straightened his jumbled clothes and sat down cautiously. I sat across from him, and we talked about cheese. I didn't realize until later, but we conversed in French without him asking if I even spoke French, and, unlike the others, he never questioned whether I made the cheese. He asked me about *how* the cheese was made, not *who* made it. I instantly trusted Mancel Marchant because he seemed to believe in the me inside.

Mancel Marchant became my business partner and best friend from that day forward. I made the cheese, and he sold it to some of America's finest restaurants. He was my confidante and often my only contact with the outside world for months at a time. When I spoke of returning to France, *he* told me the government men wouldn't approve my passport. I believed him. *He* told me that there was no record of Marie Renoir ever living in Giverny and part of me believed that too. He brought me the farmer Renoir's obituary from the local paper, and the article didn't mention a daughter. He was the one who suggested that maybe Marie was not real.

Chapter Twenty-Five

Friend No More

Dear Lil Sis, I kept the farmer's obituary for reasons I don't fully understand. I'd take it out periodically and read it over again in hopes that I missed some small reference to Marie. I lost it forever eight months before Chris asked me to go to France. It blew out of my hands and drifted into the small brick fireplace in my living area. I tried to save it, but what remained was so charred that I couldn't make out the words. I thought about just letting it be gone forever, but it became part of my life now on par with his recipe. It helped to anchor me solidly in the world of the living when not chasing my fantasies. It was an anchor I sorely needed because Marie, real or imagined, stayed on my mind. So I called a long lost friend in Paris, and he promised to drive to the newspaper office in Giverny and get me another copy.

A microfiche copy of the entire paper arrived six months later by international airmail. I knew what was in the envelope, so I didn't open it right away. I decided to wait until the urge hit me again. Well, it hit a few days later, and I opened the envelope, held it up to the light and again read of my friend's passing. I took it to the Albany Avenue branch of the Hartford Public Library and read about his simple life on the farm, his skill at crafting great cheeses, and his service to the Résistance during WWII. I read about the son who was lost during the allied bombing campaign bringing an end to the ancient family name. But there was more; the obituary was continued on the next page of the paper. There were columns I hadn't seen before. There were columns Marchant hadn't shared with me.

Buried in those columns was exactly what I hoped for: "His daughter has arranged services for next week at Saint Radegonde. All are welcome to attend."

It seemed so obvious, then, that there was more to the obituary; all obituaries need to mention a place and a time for services. I rejoiced, and yet I was angry. I ran around the room with the excitement of a child planning my return to France, and then I'd fly into rages and destroy anything in my path. There was the self I wanted to be and the self I couldn't control on display that day.

That twenty-odd-year-old article gave me hope that Marie was still alive. Those words where sweet pleasure to my ears. But how could I reconcile the fact that my friend Marchant withheld this news from me? *Why? What else? It must be the money*, I thought. I made the cheese that sustained his lifestyle. He needed me to stay exactly where I was. Mancel Marchant was a friend no more. It would be many more months before I discovered that something graver than profit drove him to deceive me.

Chapter Twenty-Six

Search For Marie

I never thought much about what Uncle Roy did while I was at school during the day. I hadn't really thought much about it until I read the series of letters I have summarized below. Just a brief observation before we start, though. Uncle Roy's life had always experienced the strangest sort of balance. Some incredibly good experience was always followed by one equally as bad. The balance ended shortly after the events told below:

Dear Lil Sis, every morning after seeing Chris off to school, I took a twenty-minute train ride to Paris' Central Hall of Records. I learned that Marie left the farm shortly after the war. I searched through reams and reams of dusty official records looking for any trace of her. It was there that I discovered that the French authorities wanted her brother for collaborating with the Nazis. He was a vile sort, if the records were accurate. The French authorities believed that the retreating Germans murdered him or that he received refuge with the advancing Americans in return for information. Though his crimes were serious, others committed greater atrocities and were more of a priority to find. So his escape or demise had never actually been confirmed.

Marie heavily mortgaged the farm to pay reparations for her brother's crimes. The records indicated that Marie left the farm shortly after the war and moved to the small city of Rouen. The English burned Joan of Arc at the stake in Rouen. Marie lived in a modest country cottage right on the edge of town. There was little else said about her, except that she served as a true French patriot during the war. There was nothing in her file regarding a family or me.

When I first arrived in Rouen, it was a very simple matter to find Marie. She rode her bicycle into town everyday to collect her mail and buy fresh vegetables. She was more beautiful than I remembered. What she and I had was more than physical; it transcended even our ability to understand. We just knew our love was intimate and timeless, yet indescribable. It was that something that compelled me to wait for her all these years and to one day find my way back to France.

Watching her for the first time in thirty years peddling her bicycle through the town center caused the years to catch up with me. Fear of rejection suddenly became the foremost emotion in my mind, displacing even love. The fear manifested itself in the form of questions that couldn't be answered without confrontation. And confrontation couldn't come without the risk of receiving the wrong answers. I wondered for the first time if she waited for me and if she felt what I still felt. Could I blame her if she moved on with her life?

I sat on the edge of a 17th century fountain with streams of water flowing from the genitals of well-eroded cherubim. I stared at my face in the still waters at the base of the small pool. I was an old man. When did that happen? Where had I been when it happened? In those few seconds, I woke up from a thirty-year nap. I wondered if it was the pursuit of love that sustained me and not the attainment of the love I pursued. What I had missed in pursuit of a love I wasn't even sure would or could be returned. *Will she see this wrinkled, rusted-out, old body and turn away in disgust, or will she see me, the ageless me inside that has on some incomprehensible level always loved her? Will she recognize me as the brown man she brought back to life?*

Doubt brought on by fear is a mean son-of-a-bitch. It whipped my ass in that square on the first day she caught my eye. Only forty-five minutes remained before the last train that would get me home to Chris in time. The person I wanted more than any other in the world was before me, and I couldn't move. I couldn't even bring myself to call her name. I couldn't grab the brass ring that eluded me for so long, that stood unobstructed only a few feet away.

I took the long train ride home and returned to the fountain for twelve straight days. Every one of those chilly mornings, I left our flat, having made up my mind that I would reclaim my true love that day. These were mornings following close on the tail of sleepless nights spent wallowing in self-pity and shame. Then every afternoon, just when she came into view, I'd decide not to complicate her life by reentering it. Her rides seemed so simple and pleasurable, her days organized and predictable. No just man, I convinced myself, could take that from her.

On day thirteen, my world seemed to collapse in on itself. I arrived at the square with Chris in tow and every shred of courage left in my body stuffed tightly into my puffed out chest. *This is the day I will make myself known to Marie,* I repeated to myself all the way to Rouen. I decided to sit on the bench outside the post office this time, too near to run away and too close to hide. I decided to sit directly in her line of vision, thinking that if she felt even an ounce of what I did for her, we wouldn't need to exchange words. She peddled around the bakery and onto the main road near city hall. She was still beautiful. I removed my brown fedora and sat as erect as my aged bones allowed. When she passed the bakery, barely a block away, a voice called out to her, "Mama." She stopped her bicycle, laid it against a lamppost, and greeted her son.

Time stopped for me. The man calling her name was mixed, I could tell from where I sat. He was in his thirties with jet-black, wavy hair, and yellow skin. Could he be *our* son? No, the answer came soon when another called, "Mama." He was mixed too. His hair was tighter and brown. His skin was browner. I overheard them discuss dinner at her house for that night with their other three brothers and their families.

"Do you know those people, Uncle Roy?" Chris asked.

"Maybe. I don't know yet," I answered.

So, she has moved on, I thought. My answer stood before me. She didn't feel what I felt. The cables holding my elevator snapped and sent me plunging to the ground floor twenty flights below. Every emotion, dream, and hope that formed the foundation of my life up to that point suddenly receded into darkness. I was free falling into the hell of despair with no reason, desire or way to stop. From one minute to the next, my life lost purpose.

I remember being silent, imploding into myself and breaking down. Everything that was wrong with that quaint French city-- the screeching train wheels, screaming babies, and haggling marketers--was suddenly pounding relentlessly on my head trying to get in and cause havoc.

I was up from the bench and dragging Chris behind me before I thought about fleeing. I was walking toward the train station before I thought about leaving. I remember wanting to hit something, anything. I wanted to hear the sound of splitting wood, breaking glass, or even crushing human bone. I wanted a reason to explode, to destroy and decimate order. I wanted to kick myself in the ass until I couldn't walk any more. I wanted to curl up in the middle of the street and waste away to nothing bearing the entire pain and disfigurement attendant thereto. The next train would leave in less than thirty minutes, and I wanted more to throw myself under it than ride in it. I remember wondering whether I would feel any pain when it tore across my body, or whether I was now beyond physical pain and suffering.

As I walked away, it was then that I drew her attention. Marie told me later that I cried out her name like a drowning man exhaling his last breath. I don't remember that. She said my cry jolted her, almost knocking her off her feet. It was then that she answered and called out to me. Her familiar voice drowned out the noise and destruction pounding inside my head.

"Roy! Please, my God, let it be you."

I turned to find Marie suddenly in my arms. She was warm, frail, and her mostly gray hair still smelled of honeysuckle. Tears streamed down her reddened cheeks, and she could barely take in air. When she touched me, we dropped to our knees, finally succumbing to the burdens of thirty-five years apart.

"Why so long?" she asked. Before I could answer, she placed two fingers across my lips gently and said, "Never mind why; today is yesterday; today is tomorrow; today is forever."

Marie's *adopted* sons stood in front of the bakery, looking very serious, not moving or speaking. They were clearly confused. I learned later that they were the children of Black American soldiers and European women. Marie had rescued them and seven others from French, Italian, and German orphanages after the war and raised them to adulthood. Perhaps it was a bit easier for her being told that I was dead. It created room in her heart for others. But I knew that most of her heart was still reserved for me, alive or dead.

"Why are you kissing that woman, Uncle Roy?" Chris asked.

Marie's sons must have wondered whether to rescue their mother from this dark stranger or to remember every moment of what was transpiring so they could tell the story in all its rich detail to their children one day. They could tell how I carried their beloved mother away wrapped in my arms and how she embraced me for the ages.

"I am sure, but I must be sure. It has been so long," she said.

Her soft hand loosened two buttons on my freshly pressed shirt, and her fingers searched for the scars from wounds she mended on a body she restored to life. Marie collapsed into my hands, and I held onto to her, this time forever.

"Chris, I'd like you to meet my wife and your aunt, Marie," I said through tears, smiles, and sobs.

"Boys, this is my husband, Roy," Marie said to her adopted sons.

[Something happened later that day that Uncle Roy omitted from his letters to Grandma. I was there and a witness, so I've decided to insert it here.]

Marie drove Uncle Roy and me back to our apartment at the school the next morning to pack our things. She drove around looking for a place to park while Uncle Roy and I went up. It was clear to me that we weren't just packing for a weekend, but we were preparing to move out. I was upset because I wasn't sure if I'd be able to finish the program, and the long lost love thing was more than my youth and inexperience could appreciate.

We entered the dark apartment, and I reached for the light but could not flick the switch. There was something covering it.

"I have a gun. Leave the light off and both of you come into the room and be quiet," a vaguely familiar voice calmly ordered from the darkness.

We complied.

"Let the boy go to his room; this is between us," Uncle Roy said, and he didn't wait for an answer. "Chris, go to your room and lock the door." I did, and Uncle Roy walked between the gunman and me. I pressed my ear against the door and heard a chair being jammed behind it so I couldn't get out. And then I heard the voice again.

"You are everything I am not. You have even taken possession of my inheritance. MY INHERITENCE! A man can only be expected to tolerate so much taking before he has to take back," the now angry voice said, shouting certain words and phrases.

"I didn't realize who you were until this very moment. I thought all these years that you were just a greedy son-of-a-bitch living off the fat of the land. But your voice in the darkness has the same twisted anger and desperation I heard from that barn loft thirty plus years ago. You must have thought I was a fool not catching on in all these years. I thought you just wanted to make money off me all this time when all along you were crushing my heart in a vice of fear and lies.

"You denied me Marie! *You* kept us apart and slowly drove screws of torment into my flesh. I can never forgive you for that,"

Uncle Roy warned.

"This is *my* country, *my* home. That farm should have been mine, and it was for me to give my sister's heart. And you...you fell out of the sky and took it away...took it all away. I am France, not you! The essence of Giverny runs through my veins, not yours," the voice said rambling and inconsistent.

"Why did you leave France? Did I drive you from here? Don't answer, I know of you already. You see, I understand the contempt a traitor stirs up in the hearts of his countrymen. Enemies can be forgiven and honor can be restored, but the stench of a traitor lingers forever. I am not your enemy. You are your enemy. Your arrogance is your enemy...your greed...your anger is your enemy."

"Shut up, shut up, you stupid nigger. I have the gun, not you. I have the power," the voice shouted.

"So you've learned something in America. What else should I have expected but that you live in America in the midst of her grandeur and beauty and you only pick up her bad habits."

"Shut up, shut up...you stupid... I have the gun, not you. I have the power," the voice repeated desperately.

"You may have the gun, but your sister and I have the power. I am all that she has, and she is all that I have. So what do you want to do? You want to send a bullet between my eyes? Well, do it! Do it, and you'll fire one in hers too! You want to kill me and deprive her of me? Know this before you pull the trigger: Marie may be the very last person on this planet to have a remnant of love in her heart for you. You haven't lost everything until you've lost all the love there is for you in this world. So go ahead and pull the trigger; that might be just what you deserve."

I heard the man get up from the chair and bulldoze his way across the room. I heard furniture crashing, glass shattering, and bodies falling to the floor. I heard the dull ominous thud of flesh pounding flesh. I struggled to open the door. I pounded it with my closed fists, kicked it with my shoed toe, and hacked at it with the fireplace poker, but it refused to relent. Uncle Roy was in a struggle for his life, and I believed that I could save him. After all, I took on bullies before and now somebody I cared about was being hurt. But the chair held, and the hundred-year-old solid wood door stood strong.

I learned later that the voice was Mr. Marchant, the only friend I thought Uncle Roy ever had. Again, I judged someone wrongly.

Uncle Roy was careful not to say his name for my sake. He didn't want Marchant to believe I could identify him.

I swear that I could smell the odor of freshly spilled blood seeping through the cracks in the door. I cried out in fear for Uncle Roy's life and out of anger that the door would not yield. I slid down in defeat on my butt with my back pressed against the door and buried my head in my knees.

"Shut up. Shut up. Stop talking," Marchant shouted.

And then I heard Uncle Roy's voice. It was weaker and tired but no less convicting in its tone.

"You're already dead. You've been dead for decades, and you don't even know it. You were dead when you bartered the lives of innocent men and women for your pathetic existence. You were dead when you bargained away your country for thirty pieces of silver. You're just hollowed out flesh sustaining itself by torment-ing others. You...can't...kill me...the dead have no dominion over the living," Uncle Roy declared.

I lowered my left eye to the keyhole to try and see what I could. I saw Marchant raise his large body from the floor. I could hear the soles of his feet sliding across the exposed wood. The cur-tains were ripped from the window so the sunlight lit the room. He stood between the flickering blades of sunlight and Uncle Roy with his back to the window.

"You are wrong. I can kill you," he said calmly and with cold-hearted certainty. "And I *will* be satisfied when you are dead."

The window, I thought. I decided to crawl out of the window and work my way along the ledge to the front of the apartment. I thought I could get in that way and save Uncle Roy. I sat on that ledge many times before just watching Paris go by. So I was famil-iar with it. I could traverse it without giving thought to every step and without fear hounding every move I made. I was on the ledge before I could think too deeply about stepping out over the streets of Paris. I entered the mindset of the sacrificial lamb.

I decided in the seconds it took to climb between the floor and the ledge that it was my duty to preserve Uncle Roy's life whether or not I preserved my own. My mind was clear and uncluttered for the first time in my young life. The clarity brought a liberating eu-phoria that I have never again experienced. The burdens of social conformity disappeared; I didn't care how I looked from the street or whether the law forbade me from taking such a risk or whether

I was breaking one of Mama's rules. The burdens attendant to the maintenance of life were simply gone. With the ever-present desire to live gone, my every sense was enhanced, and the feel of warm blood rushing through my veins was both discernable and pleasurable. All physical and emotional response to my environment ceased.

I enlisted every aspect of my existence for one single, solitary purpose. I rounded the ledge and stood before the front window ready to burst in.

I saw Marchant raise his pistol and aim it at Uncle Roy's heart.

"Everything that you are, I'm not...loved, *despised*; alive, *dead;* home, *homeless.* Since I am already dead, then killing you will make me no worse off. But in my heart, I will rejoice, and that's enough for me today," Marchant said.

I grabbed a shutter brace with my right hand and swung my body back from the window and prepared to launch myself shoulder first through the plate glass.

"Chris, Chris," a voice called out from behind me.

I turned my head to see Mr. Cristol on the roof of the building across the street. Somehow, in the midst of all the noise of the city, I heard his voice across the distance despite my single-minded focus. He must have yelled to me, but I heard a calm, reassuring whisper. "I'll take care of this. Don't worry. You won't have to bear this burden," was what I understood just from the way he called my name.

I stepped away from the window and turned with my back to the wall. I saw the high-powered rifle when Mr. Cristol came into clear focus. It rested on a two-legged stand and was fitted with a scope. He lay on the roof with his legs in the shape of a four and his left hand on the barrel. He fired before I could even blink once. He fired with the confidence of someone well practiced in the art of assassination. He didn't wait to see if he hit his target. I didn't see the bullet, but I heard it rush by and crash through the window. I carefully made my way back to my room. I took Mr. Cristol at his word, so I didn't bother to look through the window when I passed to confirm whether he hit his target.

There were twenty or thirty seconds of complete silence after I made it back through the window. I imagined that the two men stared at one another for one last time. I imagined that one of them saw his life pass before his eyes. I imagined that the full array of human emotions came and went in that room in those few seconds.

Minutes passed, and nothing happened. Finally, I could hear someone removing the chair from the door. The handle began to turn, and I heard Marie's gentle voice on the other side.

"Chris, are you alright?"

I didn't answer. I didn't intend to behave rudely, but Marie's was not the voice I wanted to hear at that time. And then Uncle Roy called to me. "Boy, are you okay?"

My heart skipped a beat. I opened the door and ran to Uncle Roy as fast as I could. I wrapped my arms around his waist and held onto to him tightly. I didn't know that I could be so happy. I experienced tears of joy that day, yet another first in my life.

Marchant lay flat on his face in front of the window. I confess that I was too young to see a freshly dead body, but it was too late. The impact was not immediate because my emotions were spent by then anyway. Frankly, I was more curious than horrified. I suppose underneath the events of that day I rejoiced that Uncle Roy was alive and was repulsed at the same time by Marchant's dead body. The day came two years later when his lifeless body began to haunt me.

The blood leaked slowly from a bullet hole in Marchant's back. His dead right hand still held tightly to the silver pistol I saw sticking out from the shadows when I entered the apartment. There was a perfectly round bullet hole in the window facing the boulevard. Uncle Roy was in the bathroom washing the blood from his hands he got from catching Marchant's falling body. I imagine the red blood washed away down the basin and into the city sewers.

Marie mourned the loss of her brother.

Chapter Twenty-Seven

All About The Cheese

Uncle Roy and I moved in with Marie the very next day. It was convenient for us since the police cordoned off the flat for the crime scene investigation and forbade our reentry. Of course, convenience wasn't what they had in mind. The school called me two days later at Marie's home to offer me the opportunity to board there for the rest of the academic year. The headmaster informed me that the chairman of the scholarship committee personally arranged for payment of the additional boarding fees. I had wondered shortly after arriving in France why I wasn't boarding to begin with. Several students younger than me and from farther away places than me boarded after all. I dismissed it then because I was just happy to be there.

"Your sponsors took care of the fees...you need bring nothing but yourself. We have also arranged for you to see a counselor twice a week. We understand that young minds need help processing tragedy," the headmaster said.

I spoke French fluently within three weeks of my arrival. I mastered the language within the next six. I thought the scholarship committee must've been compelled by my extraordinary effort to offer me the opportunity to board. Uncle Roy didn't object, but he did ask me several probing questions to make sure I wanted the new arrangements. We agreed not to tell Mom and Dad; we kept this a secret between us. It was one of many secrets that would remain between me and Uncle Roy for the rest of our lives.

Mom sent us an article about a week later about Marchant's killing in Paris. Her letter said the newspaper described Marchant as "some kind of war criminal," and the French authorities believed that he was murdered by partisans. She asked in the last line of the letter whether we saw him in Paris. Neither I nor Uncle Roy ever responded to her question.

I took a high-speed train to Rouen every other weekend and spent it with Uncle Roy and Marie. Strangely enough, I actually considered visiting them *every* weekend just to take care of them. They didn't seem to spend any time standing still, doing housework, or even eating right. I cleaned the house the best way that

I knew how, and I food shopped at the local market and stocked Marie's tiny cupboards. Marie's penchant for fresh vegetables picked daily from the open-air market meant that she didn't have much room in her home allotted for food storage. I made due with stacked boxes and an overstuffed tiny refrigerator.

They seemed extraordinarily happy despite their Spartan lifestyle. And I bathed in overwhelming joy every time I crossed the threshold of the cottage. I knew even at thirteen years old that those two were extraordinarily special people. They lived apart for more than thirty years and were barely together before the separation. Yet now they moved through life in perfect syncopation, dancing a sensual and flawless tango of passion and unceasing desire as if they were born in love.

I settled in my usual seat one Sunday on the commuter train back to Paris with my mind half on the weekend's homework I hadn't finished and half on Uncle Roy when a man sat next to me. It irritated me that he would choose to sit next to me when so many other rows in the car remained open and available, so I turned toward the window with my back half to him and stared out at the passing country side. The man spoke first. My name flowed from his lips close behind a well-spoken English hello.

"Hello, Chris. I trust that you are still enjoying your time in France?"

"Oh, Mr. Cristol, good morning. Please forgive my rudeness; I didn't know it was you. Yes...I am still enjoying France."

"I haven't been on a train in thirty-five years. Trains are so goddamned efficient at moving many people many miles into hidden places. Why are they so fucking efficient?" Mr. Cristol said bitterly, drifting off into deep thought for a moment.

His acerbic and distant thoughts on trains perplexed me. After all, speed and the efficient movement of large numbers of people, goods and services is the whole point of trains.

"Isn't that what trains are supposed to be...fast and efficient people movers?" I half asked and half commented.

"Yes. You are right, of course. I guess it is not the train but the conductors who make the difference. Trains are just mindless, heartless machines."

The whole conversation started off very weird from my perspective. So weird, in fact, I didn't think to question Mr. Cristol about why he was even on the train. He did not seem to be the same happy, jovial Daniel Cristol that met us at the airport or the cold, precise killer I saw on the roof of the flat across the street. The man sitting next to me that day seemed to ebb in and out of existence. Maybe he'd completed his prescribed purpose for living and was now consumed with taking an account of all things great and small in his life up to that point. Perhaps he'd calculated his life's debits and credits and hoped at the end of the spreadsheet he'd be in the black. I assumed that the conversation we were about to have would add something to the credit column.

The more I thought about Mr. Cristol's presence on my train, the more nervous and uncomfortable I became. Even had he behaved normally, I still would have been nervous because I knew that he killed Marchant. I also knew that he was sure that there was at least one eyewitness to his "crime." Me. He was the first killer of who I ever had personal knowledge. Yet, he was not what I expected of a killer. I know Uncle Roy must have killed in the war, and I heard that Barber Street Washington killed a man back home. But I saw Mr. Cristol blow a plum-sized hole in a man, pack up his high-powered rifle, and walk coldly away as if he were leaving the driving range.

That's when it hit me: He wasn't a hero to me yet because I didn't know if I was next in his crosshairs. After all, only I witnessed him kill Marchant. Not being one for surprises, I got right to the point.

"Are you going to kill me, too, Mr. Cristol?" I asked with less courage than the directness of the words denote.

"For heaven's sake no! Unless of course you've done something that I should kill you for. Have you?" he said in a very serious tone of voice.

I stared at him in terrified silence while he laughed a deep, rolling, belly laugh that seemed to fill up the vacant car of the train.

"I'm done with killing, my American friend. I just thought that I owed you an explanation. I will give it, but I ask that you please not share it with your uncle. I want him to be my friend for the rest of my life. I'm afraid that he will no longer care for me if he ever hears what I have to say. You don't have to answer; I will trust you to use your discretion.

"Your uncle and I participated in the most wretched war in human history. We've both managed to live with our role in the carnage we caused and witnessed in those days. It's enough to drive

197

ordinary men to slit their own throats. I know he knows how to cope. But I didn't know about you. I didn't know if you could cope without knowing the full truth."

"I don't need to know why. He was trying to kill Uncle Roy. If I could have killed him, I would have too. You don't have to worry about me."

"Well, Chris, you know what you know, you know what you don't know, but you don't know what you don't know. We don't have much time left; my stop is next, so I want you to listen before I change my mind about not killing anymore.

I dropped my adolescent façade of street toughness and listened to Mr. Cristol tell me what I didn't know I didn't know.

"About four years ago, I was in New York City on business. I am the Wiesenthal Professor of Ornithology at the University of Tel Aviv. Does the name Wiesenthal mean anything to you?" he asked.

"No, it doesn't," I responded.

"Well, it will someday. Nonetheless, I specialized mostly in rare German and French fowl abundant here in the 30's and 40's. Many migrated to nest in South America, Eastern Europe, and sometimes in North America. I identify, capture, and ship the birds I find to Israel for study. But the Americans would not allow me to capture birds in America and ship them to Israel.

"To any extent, while sitting in JFK on my way to Peru, I picked up a copy of the New York Times food section that someone left on the seat next to me. I read with great curiosity the story of a certain Carré de Roucq cheese made in America that rivaled that made in Northern France. It was apparently made by a recluse in Connecticut and delivered by a shaggy black man to some of the finest restaurants in New York. There was a photograph of this black man holding several blocks of cheese and standing next to a French Chef.

"That black man was your uncle. I recognized him even under all the hair from our time together in service to the Résistance."

"Uncle Roy was in the Résistance?"

"Indeed he was, and he served with great distinction. There is a French medal of honor waiting for the president to drape around his neck right now. Now that this Marchant affair has been resolved, I'll make your uncle's presence in France known to the right government officials."

"What do you mean *Marchant affair?*"

"We will get there. Be patient, my friend. I returned to France and asked my contacts in America to track down your uncle. They did, and I began to correspond with him about six months later. We both still bled from open and festering wounds from the war, and we worked them out slowly and surely in letter after letter over the next few years. I asked him repeatedly to come visit me in Paris, but he refused. He wrote something about 'government men' and France being filled with too many painful memories for him to ever return. So I stopped trying after a time to get him to come here, but I promised to break bread with him the next time I was in New York. That time came about two years ago.

"I met Roy at Chef Pierre's restaurant for lunch on a Thursday. He was delivering cheese, and I had only forty-eight hours in New York before heading on to Argentina.

"'Daniel, my friend, it is good to see you,' Roy said.

"'Likewise, it is good to finally lay eyes on you too my friend,' I responded.

"You probably know by now, Chris, that we French enjoy lunch more than any other meal of the day. We don't rush through it the way Americans tend to do. Roy and I enjoyed such a lunch. He shared with me what happened to him over the years and how he rose from the depths of insanity. And I too told my story.

"A large man walked into the restaurant near the end of our lunch. I noticed him surveying the room when he entered and I assumed he was a policeman or, how do you say, a gangster. But, whatever he was it was no business of mine. He was there for fifteen minutes or so before I heard him yelling at the waiter for not announcing his presence to Roy. He was at the bar behind a small partition, so I couldn't actually see him clearly. But I heard a voice from my past that penetrated my eardrums with deafening ferocity.

"'Who is that man?' I asked Roy.

"'Oh, he's my agent, Mancel Marchant. I'll call him over after he's vented a few more minutes and introduce you.'

"'He's the one who told you that this Marie person never existed.'

"'Well, he didn't tell me that per se, but he did present me with a copy of the farmer's obituary and though it mentioned a son, there was no mention of the farmer having a daughter named

Marie. It all sure seemed real to me, but between years of therapy and medication, I have arrived at a better place. I spent much of my life chasing an imaginary woman and so knowing I still cannot get her completely out of my head. I never felt comfortable telling you the whole story in letters because you know *they* read the mail. But the government won't let me leave the country anyway. They've been watching me one way or the other for the last thirty years.'

"'What did you say the man's name was again?'

"'Marchant...Mancel Marchant. He's Corsican.'

"'You know, Roy, I have to run so I'll have to meet him another time. I forgot that I was on standby to Argentina and I have to get to JFK early. It has been wonderful seeing you after all these years, my friend.'

"It was all I could do to leave the restaurant without peering over the partition to get a good look at this man, Mancel Marchant. Hearing his voice alone sent me into a barely subdued rage. If I saw the face that matched that voice as I remembered it, then I would have killed him on the spot. But this was America, and Tel Aviv strictly forbade bird watching in America.

"I exercised patience and thoroughness. I investigated Mancel Marchant over the next several months and matched that voice over the partition with the face and history of a monster.

"This man latched himself to Roy with the tenacity of a leach and sucked the essence of life out of him. He filled your uncle's head with lies and conspiracies covered over with layer upon layer of genuine psychosis. At the time, I thought this was only my fight, though, and not your uncle's. I resolved to leave Roy out of it until he wrote me with a request.

"'Dear Daniel, I hope this brief note finds you and your family well. I am doing as well as can be expected. I very much enjoyed your visit and I hope you call on me again the next time you are in the States. I'm writing also to ask you a favor. As you know, I've had the obituary of my dear friend the farmer for several years now. Even though I can't fully trust my memories from that time in my life, I still treasured that article. I lost it recently. Through my own carelessness, I allowed it to fly into the fireplace and burn. Would you be so kind as to get me another copy? It was printed on 17 October 1962 in the *Giverny Times* on page 4. It was continued on another page for which I don't have the number. There is no great rush, my friend, just whenever you have the time and the opportunity. Your friend, Roy.'

"Of course, I went to the *Giverny Times* right away and searched their microfiche for the obituary. I found it on the date Roy indicated in his letter. Sure enough, the page 4 columns chronicled the farmer's life and that his son was predeceased. But the column continued on page 8 and also mentioned the farmer's daughter, Marie, and her service to the Résistance during the war. It also mentioned the American pilot they rescued and harbored in the latter days of the war. Coincidently, the farmer and Marie bore the same last name as the given name of the man your uncle knew as Mancel Marchant. Marchant kept the complete article from Roy. He lifted the second half of the article originally given Roy from another obituary in the same edition of the paper.

"Marchant harbored a pathological attraction to your uncle. It started with the cheese. But in time, I think he came to realize that Roy, even with a confused mind, was everything he was not. Most of all, Roy replaced Marchant in his father's and, certainly, Marie's heart.

"I realized that your uncle was the bait I needed to lure Marchant out of his sanctuary in America. I just needed something irresistibly compelling to lure your uncle to France first. He spent so many years believing that Marie was a figment of his imagination that I wasn't sure the article alone was enough. That's where you came in."

"Me?"

"Yes."

"But I didn't have anything to do with this."

"You don't know what you don't know."

"I guess not," I said.

"I am the creator, sole sponsor, and sole employee of The International French Essay Competition that brought you to France. Only one school in America received an invitation and submitted entries. Only one essay from that school ever had a chance of winning. I knew from your uncle's letters that the one person he loved more than any other in America was his nephew. You, Chris. I knew that he would go to the ends of the earth and back for you. You just needed a reason to go too."

"Oh my God, this was all some kind of scam."

"Yes and no. You *are* boarding at one of the best schools in

France. Are you not? Have not you learned to speak French eloquently?"

"But you used *me*, and you used Uncle Roy. What if Marchant killed us! What if you weren't there? You had no right to risk our lives for your personal vendetta."

"You were never in danger. I rented the flat across the street from yours. I selected it and your flat for the unobstructed views. I knew you and your uncle's comings and goings better than you knew them yourselves. I also knew that Marchant would strike there. He couldn't risk being seen in and about Paris...the danger was too great. So I waited too."

"But you had no right to use us that way."

"Ask Roy whether he would rather be cramped up in your parent's basement flat or here with Marie. I gave him his life back, in exchange for the life of someone who fouled the air with every breath he exhaled."

"You could have told Uncle Roy the truth. He would have taken care of Marchant back home."

"You are right of course. If I told your uncle the truth when I first knew it, then he would have made it right. He would have gotten on that train and rode to New York steeped in rage. The rage would have grown stronger the closer he got to Manhattan. Then, wherever he found Marchant, he would have closed his hands around Marchant's abundant neck and squeezed until blood ran from his pores. Then, my friend, your uncle would have been thrown into the hellhole of an American prison and left there to die. Is that what you wanted?"

"Why did you hate Marchant so?"

Mr. Cristol took a deep breath and sat back in his seat. He turned to face me. Sadness swept over him.

"I have no family."

"Of course you do. Have you forgotten that I met your wife?"

"I have no parents, uncles, aunts, nieces, nephews, or cousins anymore. I have a wife and children, that's all. I was thirteen when I moved to France with my parents from Germany in 1933. My father taught chemistry at university, and we only planned to stay here for five years. But life for Jews in Germany became increasingly difficult under the Nazis. So my parents left me at the boarding school you are now attending and returned to Berlin. My father thought that he could make things better. He would appeal, he said, to the government and the great German intellect. He and his friends were determined to help the Nazi party to understand that the Jews were good Germans.

"They stopped answering my calls after six months there. My letters were returned unopened. First my parents were gone, then my grandparents, uncles, aunts, cousins, nieces and nephews. Soon I was all alone.

"I heard that many were hauled by train to the ghettos in Austria and Poland. I believed that they would survive in such places no matter how difficult it became and I would meet them again after the war ended. Then came the rumors of gas chambers, mass graves and the harsh reality of the Final Solution. How could I be expected to believe such stories? Who could believe such stories? Surely, no human beings were capable of committing such cruel acts against innocent people...against their countrymen.

"I took up arms in defense of France and my people. We fought the Nazi invaders in the shadows of day and the starlight of night. We were in small bands, highly mobile and lethal. We didn't know names, ages or backgrounds. We were simply bound together by a common cause.

"But some Frenchmen collaborated with the invaders and even betrayed their own countrymen for money, privilege and power. Marchant was such a man. Behind his words and down the sight of his pointing finger, the Nazis pounded my eye from its socket and promised to take my life. I promised Marchant that one day by my hand his blood would run cold through the sewers of Paris.

"I lost everyone in the war. I was alone. I don't know why I lived. My children have no grandparents to visit in the summer, big-bosomed aunts to hug, crabby uncles to avoid or competitive cousins to challenge. What I didn't know of my family's history died during the war. I am done; there are no voices speaking in the background.

"Don't ask me for reason, my American friend. Maybe reason prevails in your young country, but not in Europe. Thousand year old blood feuds simmer just below the surface of modernity and feed an irresistible compulsion to annihilate that which cannot be subdued by reason alone," he said.

"Couldn't you have just had him arrested when he stepped off the plane?" I asked.

"I couldn't take that risk," Mr. Cristol responded, touching the patch covering his dead eye.

"That was riskier than what you put us through?" I asked.

After a pensive pause, he responded, "I don't know...I just could not risk that a court, an underpaid bureaucrat, or overpaid defense attorney would set him free. I tried Marchant over and over again in the court of my imagination. I sent his case up to the bench for a judgment, and ninety-nine times the judgment came down the same:

'These are matters of conscience. These are matters larger than you, Mr. Marchant, but, nonetheless, driven by the hearts and minds of common men such as yourself. Only in times of war can nations examine the courage and fortitude of its people and, at the end of such times, pass judgment on their worthiness. You, sir, are not worthy. You are not worthy of this republic; you are not worthy of this culture. You are a cancer on the liberty, fraternity, and equality we hold dear. We find you guilty of the most despicable crime one man can commit against a nation: treason. We declare that you shall be hanged, sir...hanged from the highest tower in Paris by your neck...hanged until you are surely dead.'

"It was the one-hundredth time when he was found not guilty that I could not risk."

The train stopped, and Mr. Cristol got up to leave. I remember him saying goodbye, but I don't recall if I said the same. My mind was occupied with questions I was reluctant to ask: How does it feel to put the final period at the end of another man's life story? What is it like to be the direct and deliberate cause of a human consciousness slipping out of existence? Had Mr. Marchant perpetrated such evil in the first thirty years of his life that the sum of all the good he may have done in his last thirty couldn't offset it?

But such questions were evidence of my internal deliberations on the rightness of Mr. Cristol's actions. My deliberations to Mr. Cristol would be evidence of my doubt about the moral certitude of his actions. I surmised that I could not display such doubt at that time.

It seemed to me that if there was ever a justification for revenge, then he certainly had one. I had one question I could ask, though. So I got up and ran to the door of the passenger car before it began to close and the train pulled away.

"Mr. Cristol."

"Yes, my boy."

"Was it worth it?" I asked while the train began to pull away.

"Excuse me?"

"Is it as good to have revenge as it is to want revenge?" I asked.

He stared at me with his hands down to his side and a look of deep contemplation on his face. He did not answer before the train pulled away. I watched him standing on the platform for half a mile, and he didn't move from that spot.

Chapter Twenty-Eight

Uncle Roy's Diary

"I know of an old wood burning stove that hasn't been lighted for nearly forty years. Its grated, rusty doors hang loose and its heat escapes through joints weakened by the passage of time. But it can still warm a little cottage in the cold snow-covered woods. It simmers even now, after all these years, desiring to bring warmth to a willing home nestled in the deep forest," I told Marie.

Marie answered, "I know a little cottage that has stood through storm and hazard, war and pestilence. It is indeed cold and its snow-covered woods have been long dark and desolate. Its windows hang loose and its creaky doors sag on rusted hinges. No tenants ever lay their heads there to rest, though it has wanted tenants it could love and cherish to make it feel complete. The time for tenants, however, has long passed. It longed through the years for warmth again--to feel heat radiating through its rafters, caressing its walls and blanketing its floors. It desires a reason to mend its broken windows and bind the hanging doors. It desires warmth even now."

I held out my hand and Marie placed hers in mine. There have been times in my life when this physical body could not contain the passion I have for her inside; times when souls touch in realms neither seen nor understood; times when you know that there is less to the world than you can see and far more to what you cannot see. Marie's hand meeting mine was one of those times. I brought Marie to me, and my hand nested the small of her back. She pulled herself against me and locked her arms across my shoulder blades. Until that moment, I could not recall having reached out to touch another human being in nearly thirty years.

Marie's touch made the wait worth every agonizing moment. If ever I doubted it, then I knew for certain that my entire life, all that I was, my every possession and thought were worth sacrificing for that moment. We fell to our knees, and our lips met on the edge of eternity. Being together again was more wonderful than either of us imagined it could be. We never made it to the bedroom.

Chapter Twenty-Nine

Fewer Letters

I noticed that there were fewer letters the longer Uncle Roy and Marie were back together. Here's one five years into their new life:

Just a quick note, Sis, to tell you we're headed out for the weekend. The past few years together have been absolutely perfect. We've been mixing with 20-somethings and 'clubbing' all over Europe. The answer to what you're thinking is yes. Yes, we're trying to make up for lost time.

Can you believe it? These old bones are running with twenty-year-old kids! Yes, they are begging for some rest. No way for now, 'cause I'm dating again...I'm living again!

On another topic, we were walking along the street in Paris last week and noticed the wonderful works of a young street painter. He was a whisper of a man, but his work beckoned us from the walkway. Even though they were landscapes, we asked him to paint a portrait of us. He refused at first and said portraits weren't his style. He agreed to do it only after we offered him half the money down. I don't think we will ever see him, a portrait or our money again, but Marie is confident we'll get the portrait. She said something about the Paris Street Painter's Creed.

The other day we found the very spot in the old man's garden where we married ourselves. It was a bit overgrown. We sneaked away from our tour guide to get there. We felt like kids playing hooky on a field trip. We stayed there for nearly two hours just laying in the grass and pointing out shapes in the clouds and the contours of branches.

We've decided to renew our vows there next week. The priest who would have married us the first time is still alive. He said he'd marry us if we'd promise there'd be no wild deer at the ceremony. You have to come!

The blind man is buried in another part of the garden. He died shortly after the war ended. Apparently he visited the garden regularly even when Monet was alive. The people of the village felt that the garden wouldn't be complete if he wasn't laid to rest there. The new owners protested at first, but were persuaded when a letter was found from Monet himself granting the Blind Man access to the garden forever.

The jasmine scented nights in Giverny are still spectacular. I still make cheese--I've enclosed some for the house. Tell Chris and his folks I said hello.

Chapter Thirty

The Painter

Dear Lil Sis, A young unsettled urbanite knocked on our door unexpectedly one brisk and damp morning. He looked tired and disheveled. I knew he wasn't from around here because he was too old for a rebellious teenager, yet too young for the countryside to tolerate his outward differences.

"I have your portraits," he said with assurance as if we were expecting him.

I didn't recognize him at first, so I hesitated before responding. "André?"

"Yes." He answered with a tone of disbelief at my uncertainty.

Nearly a year had passed since those few minutes on the streets of Paris when we commissioned a single portrait. Frankly, I never expected to see André, a portrait or our cash deposit again. Nevertheless, I accepted him at his word, since the bundles under his arms were sufficient evidence that he was who he claimed.

His exhausted appearance compelled me to look beyond him as he stood in the doorway. I half expected to see a bicycle pulling a two-wheeled cart leaning against the stone fence post. Instead, I saw a neat white paneled delivery truck parked just on the other side of the morning mist. The truck was so filled with what I suspect were paintings that its doors were propped open and blue tarps covered protruding works of art. The truck looked surreal in the pallor of the fog-distorted sunlight. It was a manmade machine certainly, with perfectly engineered straight lines and unnaturally round wheels, but it hinted at being something more; a chariot of the gods, perhaps.

André came with two-dozen or more paintings. He stood in our doorway with several tucked under both arms. Some were longer and wider than the walls of a small house, while others were no bigger than 8 x 10 photographs. He wrapped each in perfectly cut butcher paper and tied them cross-wise with packaging twine.

"Are all of these are for us?" I asked.

"They are yours if you want them and those in the truck also. You must choose," he responded.

Six or seven middle-aged men hovered around the truck. I assumed that they were his helpers, despite their snappy dress.

They drove their own cars I supposed because they couldn't fit in the overstuffed truck. They looked anxious, though, ready to go, jittery. They wanted to make the delivery and move onto whatever it was in their lives that they thought was more important, I guessed. A couple of them smoked slender filter cigarettes halfway down and stamped the remainder out under their feet in the street. They attacked the cigarettes similar to a starving man devouring his first meal, and then they discarded them halfway through the stem. Smoking was a passion in France nearly on par with a well timed and precisely aerated glass of fine wine, so discarding half of a cigarette seemed extravagant to me for working class deliverymen.

Each of the men staked out a position around the truck to guard it from would-be thieves, I supposed. I had an urge to yell out and tell them, "This place is safe; you can relax and come in for coffee, tea or hot chocolate." But I noticed that they seemed to watch each other more aggressively than they looked out for thieves. So I returned my attention to André, relieved him of the wrapped packages under his arms and invited him in.

"Your moving crew looks hungry," I said.

"Hungry? Perhaps, but they are not my moving crew," he answered.

I wrinkled my forehead, churned my hands in the air slightly, and looked with casual concern in his direction. That was my way of saying, without actually speaking the words, that his answer was not adequate. He understood and explained.

"Hungry indeed. They are two art dealers, four agents, three collectors, and one art-obsessed wine billionaire. They have been following me for days because they knew that I was finally coming here. I tried to lose them, but they are better followers than I am at not being followed. I am sorry. I do not think they will cause any trouble, not now anyway."

"What do they want?" Again, I looked at him dumbfounded with the kind of expression that demands an explanation. He understood again and elaborated.

"They want you and Marie," he responded in a matter-of-fact manner, not volunteering any more information.

I wanted to tell him that I hadn't seen him for nearly a year, that I did not know him when I saw him the first time, and that I don't really know him now. He, therefore, must give me more background information in this introductory stage of our relationship. But I didn't. Instead, I asked another question.

"They want *us*?" I asked incredulously.

"Well, they don't want *you* per se.... I mean not your bodies, your persons. They want you in these paintings, those in the truck and the hundreds of sketches and rejects littering my studio floor. They want to buy...buy is too subtle a word to describe their want. Let me say it this way; they will *buy* all of you and pay whatever price you demand. They've been circling for months like a pack of ravenous wolves--closing in, raised neck hairs, low growls and extended claws. I wasn't satisfied that I truly captured you, at least not the way I wanted. But I no longer have the energy or the time to paint and hold them off simultaneously. So, I'm here, they're here, my work is here and you must choose and end this."

"We asked for one portrait. What do you mean *end this*?"

"I did not intend to sound ominous. Since that day in Paris, when you first approached me, your images have haunted me. The truth is I never intended to paint your portrait. It offended me that you would even ask when that clearly was not my style. I took your money because I needed money at that moment. However, every time I'd set my easel up before an enchanting landscape, your images would intrude on the forefront of my mind. You were seared into my consciousness. There were times when I wanted to drill a hole in my skull and let you drain out on the floor. I could not paint a black landscape on a black horizon on black canvas... without first painting you. After seven weeks of rebellion, I gave in finally so that I could get on with the rest of my life. In my surrender I discovered that I could only drain you out through the end of a paintbrush.

"My brush has rarely left the canvas for more than a waking hour since that time. The result? I have you here, on the stoop and in that rather ordinary truck outside. I have you in impression, cubism, modernism, classical and realism. I have you regal, nude, common, reserved, carnal and angelic. I have you on 30 canvases and still your images reverberate in my head. Those men desire to possess one of you as badly as you have possessed me."

"I never expected to see you again either. If you did show up, I never expected more than one portrait. Funny, Marie and I were separated for thirty-plus years. Aren't you concerned those men might rush the truck?" I asked.

"No, not really. They don't know exactly what's under the butcher paper. There are no labels, names, and numbers. The risk is too great, and they've waited too long to risk offending me in that way."

"I suppose you know them."

I could not gauge whether André was happy, sad or indifferent about delivering the paintings. Was he relieved that he would soon be free of this burden? Was he proud of completing this massive undertaking? Was he hopeful we would exorcise whatever demons he believes we set loose upon him? Was he cautious about showing his feelings until we expressed ours? Was he a captive offering a last desperate appeal to his jailers for freedom? I did not know.

"They paid me too much for the junk I did before you just to keep me fed, sheltered and working uninterrupted. But what I have under my arms, on the stoop and in that rather ordinary truck belongs to you."

"Junk? Your work wasn't junk. We saw something insightful and compelling in your landscapes. That's why we asked you to do the portraits," I responded.

"They want these works. That's all they have ever wanted. They paid their money and carried my other pieces out of the studio to curry favor--no more, no less. My other works never made it into most of their cars. I was surprised one day, though I should not have been, when my building maintenance man asked if he could retrieve the paintings from the rubbish and keep them for himself. At least he wanted them. I don't...I don't...."

André's eyes suddenly rolled back in his head, his complexion took on a green tone, and he collapsed into my hands. I lifted him into my arms and realized that his body consisted of little more than flesh and bones. I could feel the knobs where his shoulder and arm bones connected that should have been cushioned by muscle. I could count each of his ribs pressing against my supporting arms. His skin was damp and slightly cold to the touch and his breathing short and quick. It's strange how situations escalate and evolve into the unexpected. I expected to reach into my wallet, pull out some petty cash and pay for a single portrait. Instead, I held a very weak man in my arms. I cradled him gently and wondered if he would die before I reached the sofa.

Not since the war had I seen life slip away from a man's body like I sensed in André's. I was reminded that death is not as dramatic as they portray it in the movies. Dying in the real world is a peaceful experience to those on the inside looking out. It's shedding dead skin and moving on; for the shedder it's barely noticed. Dying is not painful in and of itself, and the dying are glad to get rid of the extra corporeal baggage. The spark in their eyes flickers out, the struggle to heal a broken body ceases and the worth of an earthly existence simply vanishes. They seem to just walk through a one-way passage and on to a new life without the warm fleshy covering by which we define life.

The fear of the living is what makes dying horrifying. Fear is the true root of all evil. Life is good for most of us or at least it's bearable. We have an idea what's happening on this side of existence. It's not horrific or painful enough for most to give up in exchange for the uncertainty of some other unknown existence.

Death is an inevitable consequence of war, and I had long since hardened myself to its effects. Death and dying is the sole purpose of war. To think of war in any other context would be to romanticize it unnecessarily. I held my grief in abeyance for dead friends and enemies for a later time. A later time never came. So my guard was down when André went limp in my arms. I patted his face and called his name. "André, don't leave me, son. Come on. Wake up." Despair overflowed the dam I had erected more than forty years earlier. The sofa seemed much farther away than I remembered and harder to see. I doubted I'd make it there with André in my arms.

Marie sensed my distress and moved towards me with singular purpose. She placed one hand gently in the small of my back and guided me with the other to the sofa. She cupped my cheeks with both of her hands, stared into my eyes, and recognized the emerging fear and anguish I had kept long buried.

"We must help André, now," she said calmly and instructively. "There will be another time soon."

She gave me the strength I needed to regain my composure. I drove my personal demons back under lock and key and turned my attention back to André. I sent myself a mental telegram: "my demons Stop due clemency hearing Stop soon Stop." All demons need a fair hearing every now and then or we risk a personal Attica.

I carried André to the divan and laid him down gently. Marie

placed the back of her hand to his forehead to check his tempera-
ture and her ear to his face to monitor his now slowed breathing.
He faded back into consciousness and told us he'd be all right, he
just needed some rest. He spoke the words without opening his
eyes or in any other way acknowledging us. I wondered then what
disease ravaged André's body. I wondered if it had also laid waste
to his spirit. I didn't really know him; I had no points of reference
upon which to establish a norm. But I cared for him nevertheless,
because he was there before me and his needs were greater than
mine.

I started removing his shoes and socks to make him more
comfortable. He resisted at first, even in his weakened state, but
he simply couldn't afford to expend energy that way.

"What is it, son, you keep money in your sock?" When I pulled
the sock from his left foot, I noticed dozens of needle pricks on
his feet. Red pinprick sized blotches from heel to toe oozing pus
covered the bottoms of his feet.

"Heroin? That's his malady? How dare he come here high.
Who have we let into our house?"

I was repulsed and moved away from André and the sofa. My
compassion for him waned, turning to contempt and anger. "The
time for anger has passed, the time for anger has passed," I repeated to myself until calmer.

I noticed that André maintained his sense of artistry even
while shooting up. I brought his feet together and noticed the
track marks formed a Phoenix collapsing into fire, smoke and ash.
When his feet were apart, the track marks appeared scattered and
random. The phoenix was nearly finished. It descended into the
ashes tail first. One talon reached above the conflagration grasp-
ing at the air. Though it struggled mightily to break free, it sank
lower into the flames with each lunge. Only its beak remained undone. I hoped that it would never be done.

André asked us not to call the police or a doctor in a barely
audible whisper. His eyes remained closed, and he gestured with
his left hand. Though his voice was low, it was clear and his words
well chosen. We complied. I had always thought I would call the
police in these situations, but something in his voice restrained
me. Was it a dying man's last request?

Marie rolled up his shirt sleeves. His inner arms were beet
red, hard and pockmarked. Marie turned away and cried like the

mother of a stolen child. I held onto her, pulled her tight against my chest, and lied to her for the first time that I could remember. "He'll be all right," I said.

I suppose he *had* become our child in a way. We gave him something his biological parents apparently did not. We gave him a reason to live and a sign of better spirits. And he sought most of all to please us, to make us proud of him even to the exclusion of the rest of the world.

"I have been to painters' paradise," he slurred in his stupor. "It's a place the great ones visit. The lighting is perfect, the models never move and horizons go on forever. Color joyously celebrates the canvas. Brush strokes mimic the emotions of the heart. You can see every angle from anywhere you stand. The painters' paradise..." He drifted off again.

Forty-five minutes later, a shadow of André awoke, lifted himself from the divan and asked for wine, bread and cheese. We hadn't thought much about the paintings while he recuperated, but he returned to the subject almost immediately. He began the conversation exactly where he left off. He moved so easily back into fellowship with us that it was clear he had had many recent episodes of dropping in and out of life. He didn't waste energy on explanations or time collecting our sympathy. He demanded normalcy, and we complied, being less experienced than he was at this. His eyes were clear and his skin no longer damp. He pulled an array of colored pills from his pocket and ingested them systematically over the next half hour. Some he swallowed whole and chased with water, others he crushed and followed with milk, and still others he cut into bits and chewed slowly.

André warmed up like a rusted out old car. His engine idled roughly for a few minutes before he cruised at a good speed. Once moving, he chugged along reliably until the next time he stalled out. His running time was a little less after each restart.

"I hope that there is at least one that you will want. If not, then I will destroy them all and start again until I get it right. I have to get this right!"

He was very dramatic in his pronouncements. His pockmarked arms flailed and his eyes teared. His fatigue had fallen away. You know, maybe dramatic isn't the right word. It conveys a sense of pretense about him. He was not pretending or exaggerating his feelings. Passionate...he was *passionate*; that's a better word. I began to think he had painted in his own precious blood and was prepared to offer the little he had left to get it right.

I could see then how much thinner and ragged our little street painter had become since that day in Paris. He dressed in well-worn French knock-offs of American blue jeans, tattered deck shoes and a body-fitting black nylon shirt. He didn't look poor, just not bothered by outer appearances. His painfully pale white skin and naturally red lips set off by the black shirt made him look the part of a street mime's apprentice. His cheeks were sunken, and dark circles highlighted his brown eyes.

Part of me wanted to laugh at the bizarreness of it all. Marie and I had asked a street painter for a simple portrait, and now nearly a year later, we were nursing him back to health on our living room sofa. We learned that this virtual stranger had practically sacrificed his life at the end of a paintbrush for us. André, however, wouldn't see the humor in this or understand any laughter at his extraordinary effort. He was in such a state that my laughter would sound like rejection of his work. So I chose to display solemnity instead.

He directed us to the six neatly wrapped paintings now leaning against the wall just inside the cottage door. Marie and I, without further delay, tore the butcher paper from the paintings and took them in one at a time. What I saw forced me to sit just to compose myself. My heart pounded in my chest, and my spirit seemed to slip out of sync with my body. I saw Marie in André's work. She was so real to me that without thinking, I reached out to touch her. My finger bumped against the canvas. I was surprised for an instant that I couldn't caress her familiar cheek. There she was just as she was the first day she scaled that massive oak tree in the Giverny forest. She was beautiful, kind, radiant, and remarkable.

He took about thirty years and a few pounds off me, but that didn't matter since he got Marie right.

One painting depicted our nude bodies from the back. No faces showing, just the backs of heads, arms, legs, butts, and backs. It was us, even without the faces. I knew that I was looking at Marie, but I can't express in words how I knew. We were happy. We waded into a stream giddy with joy, free and filled with passion for one another. A cascading waterfall dominated the background scenery of a pine forest with trees reaching into the heavens. Ferns covered the forest floor. Moss clung to the exposed roots of the trees lining the other bank of the stream. The sun's rays shined through breaks in the branches and glistened on the mist.

The falls stirred up such a heavy mist that I could barely see the stone cottage nestled in the thick woods. A stoked fire kept the chimney smoking and a soft orange glow in the windows. The green lily pads, red geraniums, and yellow daisies were muted by the mist, but shown through deep and rich nonetheless. The painting evoked a dreamlike state whenever I looked at it. I felt a mild euphoria. It drew me into the stream, the waterfall, and the freedom of a stolen moment of utter joy.

Though our bodies were stripped bare, the lack of faces made our secret mischievous escape into the forest private, personal, and even sacred. Though we were close and our bodies seemingly intermingled, we were not touching. Why? I don't know. He left that question for us to ponder.

Then there were the children--three of them. There were two boys and a girl. The girl was the spitting image of Mama. She was beautiful. Her straight black hair flowed down her back, and her skin was the hue of cocoa butter. I could tell from the sparkle in her eyes that she was intelligent and filled with boundless love. And she looked at her mother with admiration and thankfulness. In other works, the girl wore a lab coat with a stethoscope around her neck and held a wet new born in her arms.

The boys resembled Marie's father, and I could tell they were strong and kind children. They were adventurers. The scars and scrapes on their legs and arms were evidence of that. They explored briar patches, chased trains on railroad tracks and wrestled tigers. The little one, Reggie, I think, flew planes for a living. The older one, Grady maybe, taught school in the mud huts of a Kenyan village.

They were our children, and they were alive somewhere in existence. Our love could not be without producing children. I hoped that I would meet them someday and hug them forever.

As we moved through more of the paintings, we realized that he had painted what our lives could have been in the time we were apart. But every event depicted seemed so real to me. They were less than definite memories certainly, but more than dreams. Our spirits, the eternal part of us, lived the life illustrated in those works. Our spirits went on with life despite the physical separation, despite Jim Crow, and despite the vastness of the Atlantic

Ocean, and they sustained us through all of those years apart.

André's paintings were the balm for our regrets. What could have been was there before us in time and space. Our conscious minds missed growing old together, but what our eyes did not witness, André presented to us in living color. I reached repeatedly for the canvas to caress Marie's face, hug the children, or straighten out the wrinkle in my slacks. It was all there--all the life lost and found again. All the emotion was there, too, and the immortality.

We were barely through the seven works in the house before André's art patron friends knocked at the door. I could hear them pushing and shoving on the porch. A bidding war ensued in three different languages when I opened the door. They smelled the exposed paint from the newly opened works and moved in for the kill. Barely imaginable sums of dollars, pounds, and francs swirled around in the still wet morning air. I closed the door without responding, turned, and walked to Marie.

They did not see in the works what we or André saw. I knew that when they asked to see my son, "the model and the girl model," they didn›t see me. They didn›t see Marie. I wondered if they were blind. I remembered the old man in Monet›s Garden; he was blind, but he'd be able to see Marie and me in André's work. Rather, I should say that the part of them that gives life real meaning was turned off.

You probably think I›m crazy. Paintings are merely paint and paper arranged in a way that makes sense to our eyes, no more. They have no life. Pictures aren›t alive; life isn›t in any picture. Life is people. Life is Marie, me, even what's left of André, or so I tried to convince my conscious mind anyway.

André insisted that we look at every painting before we made a selection. Some of his works made us laugh uncontrollably, while others made us somber. The other nude was as natural as Mother Nature intended, yet it drew Marie and me together in the passionate embrace of ancient gods thrust in immortal desire. I recognized every curve and contour of Marie's body. Her dark flowing hair and the full breasts were hers, truly hers. I looked at myself, and I saw the keloid scars from the Nazi shrapnel. *How could he know? Paintings aren't alive*, I kept reminding myself.

At the end of the day, piles of crumpled and torn butcher paper covered the entire living room floor. The truck was empty, and paintings rested against every wall, shelf, and piece of furniture in our downstairs. The room reminded me of moving day at the Louvre, but it felt like a good novel; each painting was an exquisitely written chapter. Marie and I fell back onto the paper cushion and surveyed André's works from our backs. (Our attempt at butcher paper snow angels was fruitless.) We saw bits and pieces more of each story he told on the canvas.

"Wouldn't it be wonderful to just walk into one of these paintings?" Marie said.

"Only if I go with you," I answered.

I'm pretty sure Marie threw the first butcher paper ball, and I retaliated in self-defense. Before either one of us thought about it, paper balls were flying from one side of the room to the other. She pelted me on the forehead, and I bopped her on the bridge of her nose.

"You're too old for this, woman!" I shouted. "Besides, you should never challenge a man who's played baseball to a paper ball fight."

She said something in French I did not understand, and then launched seven successive paper balls in my direction. I fell to the floor mortally wounded, and nurse Marie rescued me from the perils of paper cuts. André cheered our impromptu melodrama, jumped to his feet with joy, and yelled encore. We bowed in the Shakespearean fashion and waved off the encore. All in all it was a rather inelegant ending to a day well lived.

We rested for the night.

The next day we woke up early and ate a light breakfast on the patio. A tape of hauntingly beautiful Native American flute music played in the background.

"I need you to really want at least one of them," André said after arriving late to breakfast. The urgency in his voice was stronger than the night before.

"We like them all," Marie and I answered in unison in colloquial French I seldom heard her use in public.

"You don't understand. I need you to love them, to desire them with the passion with which you desire one another. I need you to commit to one and embrace it. If you cannot, then my work is not done," he said hauntingly.

"We do," Marie answered. "We love them all."

I concurred with a slight nod of my head and direct look in André's eyes. That direct look enabled me to see that André was not well. It was more than the dark circles under his eyes and his sunken cheeks. His sickness surpassed his heroin addiction. André's life was nearly used up. The fire was almost burned out. Whatever life-force he had left was ebbing quickly out of existence. He somehow bargained for much more time than the universe initially allotted him. The end of his grace period approached rapidly.

Marie gave André the heartfelt hug of a mother. She pulled his head to her shoulder, patted his back, and whispered in his ear, "You have done well, my son. We are very pleased with what you have done for us."

André cried the tears of a found child on her shoulder. His every manifestation of adulthood retreated to display the child inside of him. Marie sat him down on the divan, cradled his head, reassured him, and he fell fast asleep.

We spent the next several hours selecting five of his paintings. Our criterion was simple: we took only what could fit into our modest home and into our modest hearts. We showed André our selections, and the corners of his mouth turned up with joy. His eyes smiled at our selections. He was pleased. We offered to pay him the balance of what we owed and some additional for the other four works, but he refused it.

"You have to live," I said.

"I tell you what, let me sell the others to my friends camped outside. I›ll take a twenty-five percent commission, and the rest is yours," he said.

"Fifty percent commission, and it's a deal," I replied.

"It will be a long time before I paint again. I have given you all I have to give, but that which sustains me from day to day. It will take me some time to get my strength back. I have made you happy?"

"You have made us very happy. But listen, André, stay clean, man. Stay clean for us, for yourself. Stay clean or we'll track your narrow ass down and commission another portrait!"

"I will," he responded unconvincingly, and he ignored the humor completely.

The art collectors, agents, gallery owners, and billionaire assembled outside descended upon André when he left our cottage at dawn. The morning dew dripped from the thatched roof into the water barrel, dogs barked off in the distance and bluebirds chirped on the fence posts. André said something to the pressing throng, and they dispersed, jumped into their cars and sped off towards Paris. He climbed into his white panel truck, shifted it badly into first gear and sputtered away down the road towards Paris also. We never saw him again.

We read about his passing two months later in a Paris daily. "Brilliant Young Artist Succumbs to AIDS." The story reported that he rose from a simple street painter to recent prominence. The subjects of his most acclaimed works were two unknown lovers captured in several moments of their lives. Those works are now part of some of the finest art collections in the world. He grew up a penniless orphan in foster homes in and around Paris. He left a statement for reading upon his death: "I have done more than I can do. I have lived more than I can live. I have loved more than I can love." A brief service was held at Saint Paul's Cathedral.

Marie and I mourned for a son we knew for fewer than twenty-four hours. We turned off the electric lights, lit tea candles, and placed them under his paintings. We poured ourselves a glass of Chardonnay and saluted André's life and his magnificent work. We asked God for peace for his soul.

From that day forward, we never took another stranger or a chance encounter for granted. We knew that it did not take long for a good soul to enrich the moments of our lives. We, also, never missed an opportunity to enrich the life of a stranger.

I wondered if God visited André on his deathbed the way he did me during the war. I wondered when André finished God's work and how much of his life was finally his own.

Chapter Thirty-One

On Marie

I spent nearly two full days with Marie before Uncle Roy's funeral. She, surprisingly, let me do nearly all of the planning. It seems that neither she nor Uncle Roy gave much thought to dying and the ceremonies that surround it. I got to know a little something about her between the planning and the phone calls and the reporters, fans and curiosity seekers constantly demanding our attention. Up to that time, I only knew Marie through the eyes and words of Uncle Roy. He loved her without end. I'd say he loved her too much to make a credible source of information where it concerned her.

Marie gave me several bundles of letters. There were at least a hundred and fifty dating back to 1945. The United States Postal Service postmarked every one of them "return to sender." She wrote the letters to Roy through their long absence and continued to write and mail them after they were back together. She told me she had become so adept at expressing her feelings in writing that she just couldn't stop even after they were reunited. Already overwhelmed with Uncle Roy's letters, I tucked Marie's away for reading on my trip home.

In our brief time together, Marie shared with me some of the intangibles of their relationship. I have tried to express the essence of those "intangibles" here. But similar to so many aspects of their lives, words alone, especially written words, convey only a bare hint of the true nature of their relationship.

Marie spoke about their lives with a vibrant childlike fascination. She always spoke in the present, still living each moment of their lives together. She still willingly embraced the house they shared, its contents, smells, and lingering memories without sorrow or trepidation. She did not shun his well-worn slippers still warming by the fireplace. Her eyes never avoided the paintings of them hung throughout the house. She didn't flee from the spaces they shared. Rather, she seemed to absorb freely the remaining bits and pieces of Uncle Roy lingering about the centuries old cottage. Her behavior seemed more akin to that of a newlywed bride than a grieving widow. The scatterings of Uncle Roy in and about the cottage sustained her momentary happiness, even her giddy joy at their union.

Marie and I spoke at length for the first time shortly after she returned from the country. Her skin was slightly tanned, and the fatigue of the trip slowed her movements a bit. Her gray hair was pulled back and tied in a ponytail with a blue ribbon. Her small body sat perfectly erect in a high back chair, and she sipped homemade wine from a tinted glass. I consumed her words like a ravenous animal; she fed a hunger in me I didn't know I had. After the first day of our conversing, I cried myself to sleep over the pain and loneliness for their many years of separation. Her words to me were on a par with Holy Scripture demanding reverence, even worship. I began to understand what all of France seemed to already know about Uncle Roy and Marie. I understood clearly why the mourners stood vigil at their home. Their love was the kind that can affect human history: the time before Roy and Marie and the time after.

"How will you live with his passing?" I asked.

"You should never wonder, Chris, whether there is life after death. Life has no beginning and no end if there's love to sustain it. I cannot at this moment share an embrace with Roy, but there was far more unseen to our lives together than seen and subject to touch. I feel his presence even now. He prepares a place for me and awaits my arrival. Roy and I were joined before we were born. My only regret is that it took the rampage of a madman across Europe to bring us together. I have never been certain whether we were the cause of the war or the cure for the war. Nonetheless, I am certain that our love and the tragedy wrought in those days met at the intersection of life and death, and life prevailed," she said.

The less of a stranger Marie was to me, the more I listened to her. She moved up my scale of familiarity from Uncle Roy's foreign wife to Marie, to my beloved aunt Marie. Her gray hair, wrinkled complexion, and aged fragility faded in time to reveal a transcendent being free from the conventions of the mortal world and living off the strength of the moment. Though her words were simple and her inflection calm and consistent, I found myself compelled by her every thought and desperately wanting to share in what made her and my uncle special.

"God made Eve for Adam, we are told. He took a single rib from Adam's side, and from it, he formed his companion, Eve.

They represented all of humanity. Whatever feelings they shared for one another were the purest of all feelings two lovers would ever share. Rarely since have a man and a woman made of and for each other found one another on this vast planet, Earth. Time and space defy love, Chris. Roy and I defied time and space. It is difficult to say what I am about to without seeming arrogant at best and psychotic at worst, but what Roy and I share is on the order of Adam and Eve. Eve was all of woman to Adam, and he all of man to her. She was to him the most beautiful and perfect woman to ever live. Adam was to Eve the embodiment of her dreams, thoughts and passions. If there is any love between a man and a woman today, it is but a remnant of the love shared by Adam and Eve. So it was with Roy and me," she said.

Chapter Thirty-Two

The Cremation

I completed the arrangements the day before the funeral, and I had some time on my hands. It was the perfect opportunity to carry out Grandma's order to burn Uncle Roy's original letters. I retrieved a rusted mauve paint bucket from a mulch pile behind the gardening shed for that purpose. I wouldn't describe the bucket as elegant, but its rigid walls were solid enough to restrain the fire and deep enough to hold the ashes.

I placed the original letters one on top of the other in the bucket. I doused them generously with kerosene from a lamp I found in the kitchen and tossed in a lighted match from a Parisian bistro. I stepped back from the can, expecting a violent flame to explode inside and incinerate the letters instantly. No flames ensued. The match burned itself out from end to end and barely singed the kerosene soaked papers. I dropped in another lighted match with the same result.

I was convinced that the universe was conspiring to keep me from burning Uncle Roy's letters and I was content to let it. It would suffice to tell Grandma that I tried to carry out her wishes, but God intervened and stilled my hand. She'd dress me down, but she'd respect the will of God, I thought. I was deep in thought about how I'd break the news to Grandma when I heard footsteps approaching behind me. I turned in the direction of the steps and saw an exceptionally beautiful woman walking toward me. She occupied all my senses in the few seconds it took her to reach our greeting zone. She approached me with familiarity while I scrambled to recognize her and find the right words to make a lasting first impression.

"You silly Americans...you abscond boldly with the *pince à épiler* of a trusting stranger, yet you cannot light a fire without a knob to turn," the woman said sarcastically in Afro-French accented English.

She was the flight attendant from my transatlantic flight. I recognized her voice more than I did her face since I barely looked up during our first encounter. Her smooth, chocolate brown skin, slender, perfectly contoured body, and clear brown eyes took me back a step while I tried to take her all in. She was everything: woman,

225

Africa, France, and striking beauty all wrapped in a neat cosmopolitan package.

"I have come for what's mine," she said before I could find the right words.

"Don't they pay flight attendants well enough to give up a pair of tweezers?"

"I am a *pilot*. So, I cannot say that I know what flight attendants can afford to 'give up.' However, I know that there are some things worth retrieving."

"Oh, I'm sorry. Please accept my apologies. It's just that...."

"It is a common mistake that I have come to accept as a fact of life. Gracious apologies, however, are almost never a mistake. Your apology is accepted."

"Thank you."

"Are those the letters you brought with you on my plane?" she asked.

"Yes, they just won't burn. Either the letters were treated with fire retardant, or the kerosene is watered down," I answered.

"I think it is more likely that they refuse to burn. There is life in those pages. I could feel the passion in them on the flight. Here, give me the matches," she said while wrapping both of her hands around mine.

"I've tried a couple of times," I responded.

"Maybe it was neither the kerosene nor the paper. Maybe it was you...here by yourself, trying to do *this* thing...alone. Please, give me the *allumettes*," she said.

She struck the match with uncommon grace and handed it to me. She hummed a Wolof funeral dirge softly and joined her hands in prayer. The brittle paper and kerosene were just fuel for the fire to me. But to her, the papers were once alive and their cremation worthy of our respect and a dignified service. I forgot for a moment that I took a lighted match from her warm, soft hand. I was lost in her aura when the match reminded me that I held it in my hand. I tossed it carelessly into the bucket with no expectation that the letters would ignite. My expectations were wrong. The letters ignited and the ensuing flame reached briefly into the heavens.

"There are some matters that one must never handle alone, my American friend. *Et les questions du coeur sont principales sur la liste*," she said.

"I think you must teach me about all those matters. I'd be most obliged if you'd start at the top of the list. Christopher...by the way... my name is Chris," I replied finally finding the right words.

"*Je suis Iviose*," she responded.

Iviose and I took a slow elevator ride up the Eiffel Tower later that day. She stayed at my side every step along the way since our re-acquaintance. We stood on the second deck of the tower and surveyed the most beautiful city in the world spread out at our feet. This time, I planned an intricate ritual for spreading the ashes of Uncle Roy's letters. I stood on the observation deck of the Eiffel Tower intent on opening the urn, reaching in my right hand, pulling out a handful of ash and letting the wind draw it from between my fingers and spread it across the Parisian skyline.

I opened the urn, and the wind took the ashes without any prompting from me. It seemed to reach into the urn and scoop the ashes out quite well without my help. I conceded to forces greater than myself, gave up my attempt at ritual, and just held the urn above my head and let the wind reach in and carry away every flake. I watched the record of Uncle Roy's fifty-year passion spread across the Paris horizon and settle gently into forever.

"I have two bottles of Bourgueil and some Carré de Roucq I made myself back at the house. Would you share it with me?" I asked Iviosé.

"I would. I would like that very much," she responded.

"Then let us...let it be," I answered.

Chapter Thirty-Three

The End Of Times

I learned just how well-known Uncle Roy and Aunt Marie were in France at his funeral. A thousand or more mourners packed into the cavernous cathedral, and several thousands gathered outside lining the boulevard five or six deep. They weren't merely known, but they were legendary in France. Theirs was a modern fairytale unfolding in plain public view under the admiring gaze of the masses.

I recalled being afraid of the small group gathered outside of the cottage when I arrived in France just a week ago. But this time I let myself feel the warmth, love, and admiration this far larger crowd held for my deceased uncle. I felt their sense of loss and an undercurrent of thankfulness. They were genuinely thankful to Uncle Roy for allowing them to share in his love for Marie.

To my surprise, my cousin Lisa showed up unannounced at the funeral. I wasn't expecting her, and she did not let me know she was coming. I didn't really expect any of our family from the States at the funeral. Uncle Roy and I shared exclusively our love for all things French. No other member of the family ever made the trip or even expressed a passing desire to visit. *But Lisa would follow the ominous scent of money even if it led her to the gates of hell*, I thought. The 'I-couldn't-give-a-rat's-ass' side of the family scraped together just enough money to send her to the funeral and get her a descent hotel room for a few days.

I didn't know she was there until she tapped me on the shoulder in the foyer of the church. She asked if I would help her find a seat on the family side. There was something different about Lisa that I couldn't quite comprehend at first. A few years had passed since I'd last saw her, and she'd aged and gained some weight. I expected as much considering her lifestyle. But what was different about Lisa went beyond her physical appearance.

It was her demeanor that was different. She was decidedly timid, even emotionally fragile. *She is too far out of her element in France with the language and cultural differences,* I thought. My cousin Lisa *was* humbled for the first time in her life, but as it turns out, not for the reason I believed.

"Chris, can I ask you something?"

"Look, Lisa, now is not the time to ask about the will. So don't even go there; not there, not here, and not now. This is the time for friends and relatives to say goodbye to Uncle Roy, and that's all I'm interested in doing right now."

"It's not about money...at least it's not about money anymore. I'm not going to deny that that's why I came here. But I just gotta know...."

"Lisa, it's always been about money with you. Do I need to repeat your words?"

"Just listen, Chris! I know who and what I am. You don't have to remind me. I have never been ashamed or shy about letting the world known what Lisa Campbell is all about. So when I say it ain't about money, it ain't about money, Cou'in."

"Alright, alright, what? What do you want to ask?"

"Is this what love feels like?"

"Excuse me," I responded with a hint of confusion.

"Is this what love feels like? I mean look at these people. There are thousands of them, and they are crying and sobbing like their daddy's lying in that coffin. And look at her, the wife. She still adores him. I can almost feel it from here. Is this what true love feels like?"

Lisa's question took me aback. She asked sincerely, directly, and showed vulnerability I never saw in her before. She wasn't humbled after all, but she *was* in awe. I used to believe that I could answer all of her questions. But this one wasn't about the law, strained familial relations or money: it was about love. I certainly loved Uncle Roy, but I don't know that I would have if he were just a stranger or someone I knew only in rumor or legend. I didn't know enough about love to judge what it was beyond my own deeply personal experiences. I doubted that I could accurately answer Lisa's question.

I could see though that Lisa desperately needed an answer. Love eluded her in much the same way that it did me. But her dalliances produced heavy baggage, and she needed the hope of true love in order to carry that baggage through life. I decided that I must give her an answer even if it meant stepping outside of the order and reason that held my emotions captive.

"Yes. Yes, this is what love feels like. It demands nothing of you while giving all that it has. The same is waiting for you out there somewhere, Lisa," I answered with assurance.

"Thank you, Chris. I needed to know that love was real. It's been a long time since I've believed in love. Now I'll know how it feels when it comes my way," she said eloquently.

I felt a burden lift from my spirit. I realized that Lisa was my obligation to the universe, and I, in that moment, had fulfilled God's reason for my existence. My life was from that point forward was my own.

Marie was oddly content and even satisfied-looking the entire morning. It was as if she was savoring the best meal of her life and could hardly be bothered with death. I expected sadness, but she radiated contentment. I expected weeping, but she was almost giddy. I began to think that maybe the French think of death differently than Americans. Maybe death is a time to celebrate a life well lived rather than sadness that a life has ended. But I noticed that others were mourning in the traditional way around the sanctuary. Their tears and sobbing were normal to me, but apparently, not to Marie. She stood up in the middle of the service, quieted the priest with a direct glance and her index finger pressed lightly against her lips, and addressed those who were sobbing in the audience.

"Forgive me. Forgive me. Please excuse this interruption, but I must speak now. Roy and I have a love that will survive for eternity. We are one and our souls are at peace now. Please do not be sad... Please. We never wanted the sadness in the world. This is a time to be assured rather," she said and took her seat next to me. The sobs faded, and only the words of the priest were heard afterward.

Marie sat quietly through the rest of the service except when she leaned over to ask me for the time. I didn't know if she felt the service was taking too long or she had somewhere more important to go at that time. Nevertheless, I complied and gave her the time. I wasn't bothered by her question. I became accustomed to such odd behavior from Marie and Uncle Roy over the years. They inhabited a world entirely unto themselves, separate and apart from the world in which the rest of us live. They behaved according to the rules of their world.

Marie was the last family member to say goodbye to Uncle Roy at the end of the priest's liturgy. She bent over his coffin to hug and kiss him one last time. She laid her torso across his very gracefully, and she, too, slipped gently away into eternity to join her beloved Roy.

Silence swept through the ornate sanctuary, and all movement ceased when her legs gave way and she fell into my waiting arms. The silence should have lasted longer and been followed by more sobs, tears of sadness, and the renting of sackcloth. But there were neither sobs nor tears because we all knew in our hearts that this was the way it should be. The world would have been out of balance if one of them lived too long beyond the other. So we sat motionless and in a confirming kind of silence. The pallbearers were the first to move. They took her from my hands to carry her out of the church.

"No, leave her with him, she belongs with Roy. Let her be," Lisa's strong voice pleaded from across the sanctuary. Someone translated her word into French, and they spread throughout the sanctuary.

"Let her be. *Elle permettre d'*être," a chorus of mourners cried out.

Among them was the mayor's son from Marie's youth, who was now himself the mayor. The will of the people and the authority of the state spoke with one voice on this question of letting Aunt Marie remain at Uncle Roy's side. I looked up to the priest, and he gave the church›s blessing with a nod of his head and the extension of his open palms in my direction. I found Marie's adopted sons a few aisles over and noticed that they joined with the chorus chanting:

"Let her be. *Elle permettre d'*être."

The urge to give in to legalism and not my heart intervened in and delayed my decision-making process. *This is not the day for reason*, I finally concluded.

The soft rumble of "let her be, *elle permettre d'*être" spread through the church and on to the mourners outside until it became the duly expressed will of all of France.

The priest again looked to me for a decision. Iviose squeezed my hand in agreement. Finally, I nodded "yes" and added my voice to the chorus, "*Elle permettre d'*être." The pallbearers gently lifted Marie›s delicate body and placed it in the casket beside her beloved Roy. She was where she belonged. I could see it clearly now. They were together again exactly where they should be and always will be.

Jessie Norman sang *Wade in the Water* over a Baptist gospel choir. A cool breeze swept through the church that felt like fine silk caressing my face. The sanctuary smelled soft and sweet of the midsummer blooms of wild Oklahoma honeysuckle. Roy and his beloved Marie crossed over together into eternity, and I breathed again.

Author Bio

Our author was born in Okmulgee, Oklahoma (near Tulsa) and raised there by his illiterate and twice widowed grandmother. Three generations squeezed into a two bedroom shotgun shack. Nothing was guaranteed to them, but he says somehow his grandmother managed to feed (mostly beans), cloth (lots of hand-me-downs) and keep a roof over their heads. Her ambition for her children was that they finish high school and learn to read. He did both at her urging and went on to earn two degrees at Cornell University.

He now resides in Connecticut with his wife and three children and works as an attorney and insurance executive.

CPSIA information can be obtained at www.ICGtesting.com
Printed in the USA
BVOW05s1147150714

359235BV00002B/268/P